FOR LOVE & MERCY

A Novel

C. INGRID DERINGER

FriesenPress
One Printers Way
Altona, MB R0G 0B0
Canada

www.friesenpress.com

First Edition — 2022

Claire Mulligan, Editor

www.ingridderinger.com

ISBN
978-1-03-915495-7 (Hardcover)
978-1-03-915494-0 (Paperback)
978-1-03-915496-4 (eBook)

1. FICTION, SAGAS

Distributed to the trade by The Ingram Book Company

THANKS

Thanks to my editor Claire Mulligan, who's insight and wisdom is greatly appreciated.

Thanks to Suzannah Hahrt, my very talented best friend, who supports me in so many ways! She always goes the extra mile—from her creative input with the book cover design to storyline ideas and proofreading, as well as endless encouragement—I am forever grateful.

Thanks to my very talented daughter, Tania Elizabeth, who is an inspiration to me on so many levels. She's a naturally gifted editor, who took time out of her crazy busy life – as a touring musician, a singer songwriter with a new album coming out, and a mom to a toddler - to give her amazing input into this story.

In memory of my sister Mel

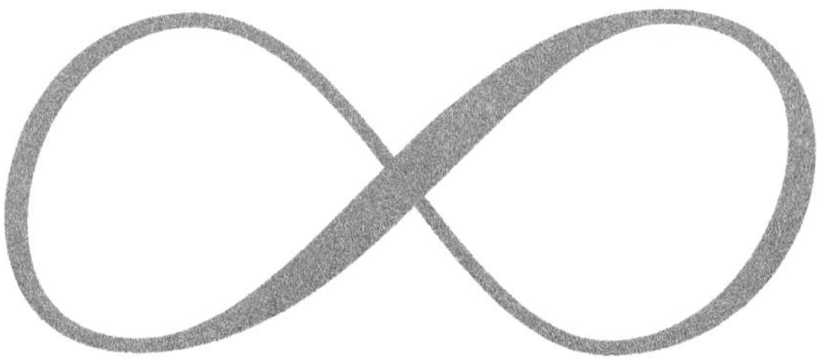

CHAPTER ONE
SUNNYDALE FORENSIC HOSPITAL

SEPTEMBER 19, 2022

"Storm, I liked your autobiographical story. I've given you a B."

I study Mrs. Brown's face and raise my eyebrows. "Glad you enjoyed it. But a B? I've never had a mark lower than an A in my life. Not in school except for Phys Ed, and not ever in university. And since when does one bother to grade a creative writing class that the student gets no credit for? And, by the way, it's Dr. Stormy Hera. I'm a music professor at the University of Victoria and a published author."

"Well, Doctor, whatever your credentials are, I have to grade you. It's my job, as well as part of your rehabilitation. Sunnydale Forensic Hospital has strict guidelines about reporting your progress. Do you mind me asking how much of your story is true?"

"What do you mean? It's the story as I know it—of my life."

"Yes, but the assignment is about the true story of your life until you entered this place. It's a writing exercise that's designed to help you understand what led you here. I gave you a B because I think your writing is exceptional. I like the way you narrate, the way you give voice to your characters, and the way you weave in and out. Your story is compelling. In fact, I'd even say you have a gift for storytelling. But let me ask you this: how much of it is made up?"

"I told you. Nothing."

"Stormy, I mean Dr. Hera, you're in a forensic hospital because you've been convicted of manslaughter. You killed your mother. From your story, though, it sounds like you had a pretty wonderful upbringing, and you were surrounded by a loving, supportive family. It really doesn't fit, considering where you sit right now. And your supposed near-death experience?" Mrs. Brown raises her eyes to the ceiling and then closes them, drawing in a deep breath as if to rally some unseen patience lingering in the stale institutional air. "Do you get what I'm saying? Personally, I don't believe in that sort of thing."

"Surprise, surprise," I say under my breath. I feel my jaw tensing up and a steady throb fills my ears.

Without acknowledging my comment, Mrs. Brown continues "Now, I'm not saying I didn't like your writing, but the purpose of this exercise that *you* chose to participate in as part of your rehabilitation, is to get to the truth of what brought you here."

"Excuse me, but didn't you say that facts are elusive and that our memories are often inaccurate? And that if you asked me what I said two hours ago word for word, I couldn't repeat it verbatim?"

"Yes, you're right. I did say that. We're constantly making up stories in our heads to try to make sense of the world. Accuracy is indeed an illusion. But there is a difference between interpreting your life as you look back on it and pure fiction, which is what this," she says as she points to my manuscript on the desk, "seems like it is to me." She taps her pink long acrylic fingernails on the desk and continues. "This is important for you to understand, if you are going to get anything out of this exercise." She hesitates for a moment. By this time, my heart is racing, and I am beginning to feel that I might lose my temper if she says anything more. "Are you writing pure fiction, Dr. Hera?"

I close my eyes. *Stay calm Stormy, stay calm.* I take in a deep breath and let it out slowly before I speak. "I tried to be as accurate as possible while giving a voice to the people involved in my story. I based my writing on what I've been told over the years. Now, whether or not you believe in near-death experiences is not my business. In fact, I'm well acquainted with skepticism, believe me. But my account of my NDE is by far the most accurate and true passage in this entire story. My memory of it is forever ingrained in my mind." I feel myself fidgeting. I want out. I'm not in any mood to try and convince her of anything. It just seems this is all a waste of time.

"Just remember, this is an exercise to help you. I can't help you if you don't help yourself." I can see she's losing her patience. Her tone sounds a little harsh.

"Okay. Anything else?" I roll my eyes and immediately feel ashamed for acting like an ungrateful teenager. But she's annoying as hell. As I listen to her spew words about what she's looking for in *my* story of *my* life, I wonder what a woman in her late sixties is doing teaching creative writing in a prison hospital with a bunch of crazy criminals. Look at her! Her ruby-red lips, her white hair cut into a perfect pixie with purple highlights, and dressed in expensive Eileen Fisher clothes and funky, Fluevog high heels. And the way she placed her Coach handbag in the middle of her desk as if she was somehow afraid it might get bumped onto the floor if it sits too close to the edge. God forbid, she hangs the bloody thing on the back corner of the chair where most women put their purses. It's all just too much of a contrast: her in her fancy attire and me in my pale-grey hospital prison uniform, runners on my feet, my nails in dire need of a manicure, no nail polish or makeup, and hair that's screaming for a cut and colour. I wonder what the hell her story is all about.

"I want you to re-examine what you wrote so far, and then continue your story up to the time you committed the crime." She doesn't look at me directly as she speaks; she's looking down at her desk while starting to gather up her things. I can see she's had about enough of me as I've had of her.

"Look," I say, "I get it. You want me to delve into what happened up until the incident." *I don't know if incident is the right word, but I don't know what else to call it. I don't want to call it a murder. It wasn't like that. I have memories up until a few hours before my mother's demise. And they are not memories I really care to revisit.* "But I don't really want to go there. It's too painful. And, of the actual crime and even days after, I still have no recollection."

"Dr. Hera, what do you think this course is for? Why do you think you are in this facility? You're lucky to even be here. Not that many years ago, you would have gone directly to jail for what you did. This is a state-of-the-art institution, very innovative in its programming and so far, showing great potential in rehabilitating criminals with mental health issues. This course is not for fun, nor is it some exercise to entertain you as you wait out your sentence. It's part of your rehabilitation. You are in a prison hospital for a reason. You killed your mother." She hesitates and takes a long deep breath. I see her expression change from annoyance to one of genuine concern and compassion. She stops gathering her things and looks me in the eyes. "Look, the bottom line is, if you want to get out of this place, you have to work the programs. From my experience over the last ten years of working with people like you, who have complex post-traumatic stress disorder, programs such as this one, are a very effective way to heal from trauma. We want you to get to the truth of why you're here. To heal."

As she rambles on, I can't help but be reminded of my husband Cody, the righteous all-knowing psychologist who has all the answers, all the time. "All right then. I'll get to work on it, ASAP. Not much else to do in this god-forsaken place." I say this in a bitchy, matter-of-fact voice. I'm pissed off at this whole exchange and can't bring myself to hide my anger, even though I know she's just trying to help me. As I turn to leave, I know deep down I'm just trying to save face at this point. I feel like a dog with its tail between its legs.

"See you next week then. I'm really looking forward to reading your additions."

As I close the door, I grit my teeth in silent fury. Since arriving at Sunnydale Forensic Hospital, my survival instincts have buried the pain and stress from the last few years that led me to end my poor mother's life. I've been trying to concentrate on the positive aspects of my life, be they minuscule. Dredging up all the hurt and pain is something I'm trying to avoid. The fact that Mrs. Brown doesn't believe in my NDE hardly lessens my anger at her request. I'm so damn tired of people and their close-mindedness. But I know I am not alone. I've talked to others who've had near-death experiences over the years. Not many people want to believe us, especially atheists like my husband and, oddly enough, devout Christians. Somehow, we are labeled as New Age crazies when we try to explain to people what we've experienced;

unfortunately, there's nothing we can do about it. Most people won't come out and actually say they don't believe you, like Mrs. Brown just did; they usually just change the subject, go silent, or excuse themselves.

"Fuck this, I quit," I say as loudly as I dare, walking down the hall. *I refuse to do it. What's the use anyway? Will it really allow me to get out earlier for good behaviour? Make me a better person? Bring back the memories that my subconscious is obviously hiding from me?*

My room is painted a soft blue and has plain furnishings, like a nice hospital room. There's a window with white rod iron decorative bars, secure but pleasant. It's on the third floor and looks down on to a small courtyard where people walk in circles and sit on wooden benches under the two old Arbutus trees. There's a serene painting hanging on my bedroom wall of a meadow with a stream and flowers. Nothing I would ever hang in my own house, but at least it is an original piece of art and not some Walmart mass produced piece of junk. When I first got sentenced, the image I had of where I would sleep and spend my days was nothing like the room I'm sitting in now. I have to give them credit, the place has more of an old folk's home/hospital feel than a prison. But of course, it is a prison—there are hundreds of rules and regulations. At night I am locked in my room, I can't leave the floor at any time, and there are curfews and such. From what I've been told, each floor is different. I gather I'm not in the ward with the mass murderers and severely mentally ill. I mean there are a lot of mentally unstable people, don't get me wrong, but I feel fairly safe and somewhat comfortable.

I slump down on the bed and look at the four photos I have pinned to the corkboard on the wall. One is an old photo of Dad, my stepmother Celeste, and me. Celeste and I are in matching aprons. We are in Celeste's restaurant, baking. We're laughing. Flour dust on our faces. A big mess on the counter. It was my eighth birthday, and I had asked Celeste if we could bake my birthday cake together in her restaurant. It's one of my favourite memories.

Next to that is a sweet photo that Brittany, my half-sister, gave me on her last visit. It's of her and her wife Sarah and their precious little girl; all three are holding up matching pom poms. "It's to remind you that we're here for you, cheering you on just like you did for me my whole life," was what Brittany said when she handed me the picture. She also gave me a book that she said I needed to read: *Loving What Is* by Byron Katie, which still sits untouched on the end table beside my small cot.

Then there is the photo of Valentino and Mom from when they were on the El Camino de Santiago pilgrimage in Spain. They had stopped at a hostel in Mansilla de Las Mulas. The picture freezes them in time, mid-toast with glasses of red wine, backpacks on the ground, hiking boots and socks tossed off, still in their dusty clothes but with their bare feet on top of one another's, radiating pure joy. I love that photo so much that I commissioned an artist friend to paint it, and then gave it to them on their first wedding anniversary in 2016, right before I had my near-death experience.

I smile and touch the photo gently, remembering how adorable the two of them were. How in love they were. There's comfort in knowing they're still together and always will be.

The last photo is a dog-eared one of Cody and my son Jonas sitting in our backyard, holding up a sign they had made together that says WE LOVE YOU. Jonas is so cute with his curly, light-red hair and bright, green eyes, and handsome Cody with his smile that seemed to always make everything okay. It's a photo I've kept in my wallet over the years that's kept me going in times of stress. They gave it to me when I was in my last round of chemotherapy.

Surely, Cody has cooled down by now, and he will bring Jonas to visit soon. I stare at Jonas's beautiful face. More than anything in the entire world, I want to see my son. I'll get back to writing as Mrs. Brown instructed; if there is even the slightest chance that it means I can get out of this place early and be with Jonas, it's worth it. I sit down on my chair and begin to reread my story. Back to the very beginning, when my beloved mother, Evangeline, was a child.

CHAPTER TWO
MÈMÈ LILLIAN

My grandmother, who I called Mémé, once confessed to me that she was one of those women who had always wanted to have a daughter. Resigned early on in life to the fact that she would be a farm wife and a mother, she nurtured her own inner vision of a little girl she could identify with; one she would share recipes with, go shopping with, one who would reciprocate all the love she had to offer. She wanted to have a relationship with her daughter that she dreamed about having with her own mother but never had.

Growing up, Mémé witnessed the connection other mothers and daughters had and knew that not everyone had the same issues she had. Her sisters and sisters-in-law seemed to have special bonds with their girls. As she raised her six boys—whom all loved trucks, rodeos, and sports—she couldn't help but feel pangs of jealousy. No matter how deeply she loved her sons, she longed for that closeness. Six years after John, her last boy, was born, she fell pregnant again. Something inside her told her this pregnancy was different, but she shoved the feelings of hope that it was a girl deep down, afraid of being disappointed. She had almost convinced herself of the inevitability of yet another son, so when she heard the words, "It's a girl," she almost didn't believe it was true. It wasn't until they placed little Evangeline in her arms and they locked eyes that she could truly allow her heart to open. But (and she would laugh in the telling, as one does after many years have passed and one gains perspective), her little girl was anything but her dream girl and was a hell of a lot harder to raise than all her sons put together.

"Slow down, Evangeline! How many times do I have to tell you? Watch for cars."

"I know, Mommy, cars don't have eyes."

"If you slow down, we can go to Kresge's and have anything you want after the dentist."

"Even a banana split or french fries with gravy?"

"Yes, even that. But you have to slow down and let me hold your hand. We're in the city and you have to be careful." Mémé grabbed her daughter's hand and yanked it.

"I'm too old to hold your hand, Mom. I'm almost eight years old." She wiggled to try to get free from her mother's grip.

"Slow down. Please. And how did you manage to get your new coat dirty already? We just got here! God, child, you wear me out. Don't know why I buy you anything new. Should just let you live in hand-me-downs from your cousins."

"Mommy, look, the Eaton's store has the Christmas display up in the windows. Look!"

"Beautiful, yes, beautiful. But we have to go so we're not late for our appointment."

"But look at the little village and the train. It's so cute! I want to go on a train."

Mémé yanked her hand even harder.

"Come on, we have to go. I promise we'll come back to the display windows after the dentist."

Evangeline had only a small cavity in the back of her mouth, which the dentist filled quickly. They left the office and as promised, went to admire the Eaton's Christmas window display. It was a highlight every winter to see the elaborate displays, and she always made sure to bring the children at least once to see it. Though the boys enjoyed it, they never showed the same enthusiasm as Evangeline did. It was as if she was imagining herself actually being in the scenes—in the little workshop making toys, with Santa at the North Pole, or on the trains going through the miniature towns and countryside. She would squeal with delight, pointing and laughing, pressing her nose against the glass windows trying to take in every last detail. She had to admit that it was enjoyable to watch Evangeline get so excited even though it would be a tug of war to get her to leave.

Later, they sat at the lunch counter at Kresge's department store and shared french fries with gravy. Mémé knew she shouldn't encourage my mother to eat so much sugar and fried food because she could see that her little girl was already a little too chubby for her age, but it was their outing, their time together without the boys, and she wanted it to be special.

"Let's look at some shoes for you. They have nice ones here."

"No, I want some boots. Not shoes. Boots with a buckle on it like Jeannine has."

"We can look. But Jeannine comes from a family with lots of money so they're probably out of our price range. Maybe we can find something like them but ones that are unique. Don't you want to be unique and not like everyone else?"

"My teacher says I'm already unique. She says everyone is unique. But I like Jeannine's boots. I really, really like them."

"We'll finish up and go shopping and see what we find." She leaned her forehead on her hand and as the waitress filled up her coffee cup and placed a banana split in front of Evangeline, she said "Six boys were so much easier to raise than this one girl."

"Yes. But isn't it so much more fun?" The middle-aged waitress asked with a smile.

"She's a whirlwind. She exhausts me, to be truthful. Do you have kids?"

"Yes, three girls, all grown up now. They all live nearby. Have a grandbaby on the way. Can't wait. All wonderful daughters. Just wait and see."

But Mémé wondered what the world held for my mom as she watched her enthusiastically devour her banana split. Her little Evangeline, with her insatiable appetite for food, adventure, reading, and writing, already did not seem the type to ever settle down, have children, or live nearby, as she had envisioned. At seven, she had already informed her of her plans to travel the world and be a famous writer. "Her favourite pastime was to read the encyclopedia set I bought from the travelling salesman when she was six," my grandmother told me. "Your grandfather and I had the biggest fight over me buying them. But your mother was so excited, and I swear those books were the best investment I ever made. That and the globe I gave her for her eighth birthday. She read those encyclopedias every day for hours on end. I knew in my heart of hearts that she was not going to be a farm wife like me."

On the way home from the city, Evangeline asked her mother if she wanted to hear a story she made up about the North Pole.

"Yes, tell me the story, Evangeline."

"Well, once upon a time . . ."

Lillian half listened to her daughter while she made a mental inventory of what she had on hand that could be whipped up quickly for supper. Might have to be canned beans and wieners that her husband hated but the boys loved. She was just too tired to start a big meal after a day in the city with Evangeline.

"Mom, what did you think of my story?"

"Very nice, Evangeline, very nice."

CHAPTER THREE
MÈMÈ LILLIAN

The farm where my mother was raised was two miles from the town of Paris; a town founded by French Catholics who immigrated from Paris, France in 1893 and whose French heritage was still deeply rooted in their everyday life. Most people in the area still spoke their mother tongue at home and kept their customs and traditions alive. A sign as you came into town, indicated that the town's population was 512.

My mémé was always telling me idyllic tales about when my mom was a little girl and how it was for her growing up on a farm with her six brothers. On a visit for a family reunion when I was a teenager and having a hard time relating to my parents, Mémé told me stories as usual, but this particular time they were different; they were more confessional and less rosy. We were in the garden, weeding, just the two of us. Growing up, we never had a garden like Mémé's. We had a little plot in our backyard for salad greens and a few tomato plants, but Mémé's garden was huge. There were rows upon rows of vegetables. She called it her haven. She would always say, "I'd rather be playing in my garden than stuck in the house." Come spring, her love of the outdoors was evident: dishes piled high on the counters, dirty floors, and a perpetually full laundry basket in the living room just waiting for someone, anyone, to fold and put away its contents. On rainy days or in the evenings, she was baking and cooking, freezing and canning her produce. Her harvest was massive, and it was nothing to sit for hours shelling peas in the summer kitchen or hauling barrels and barrels of potatoes all day long to the cellar. Growing up, I cherished my visits to the farm, but once I turned thirteen,

I decided all adults were lame and the less time I had to spend with any of them, the better my life would be. I fought hard to get out of going to Saskatchewan for the reunion with my mother. I wanted to stay at my dad's place in Victoria and hang out with my friends. But as usual, Dad sided with Mom and said I had to go. "It's a reunion, and it'll be fun. Your mémé would be devastated if you didn't show up."

I highly doubted the fun part. I stomped out of my dad's house. He and my mom had some kind of pact that they never undermined each other. Even though they were divorced, they were always on the same page. It pissed me off. I couldn't get away with anything, not like some of my other friends with divorced parents.

I really don't know what my mother said to Mémé that morning before we went out to the garden. I imagine it was something like "Can you talk to her because we can't seem to reach this child anymore?" Whatever it was, it was in the garden that day that Mémé told me stories that helped me understand my mother better and planted the seed of doubt about the direction I was taking.

"So, I hear you weren't too keen on coming to the farm. How come?" She handed me a pail to put the weeds in as we dug around the rows of tomatoes. It was a cool morning, there was still dew on the ground and the plants. It always smelled heavenly in her garden. Dill was growing wild everywhere and the scent mixed with carrot tops, raspberry bushes, orange calendula, and giant sunflowers made me feel like I was in another world.

"I dunno. My mom just bugs me, and she's always on my case. You know? I can't do anything right. Mom doesn't like the way I dress, my friends, my grades. I just thought I could stay at Dad's and get away from her."

"Hmm, I see. Well, I think your mother just wants you to be all you can be. Maybe she just thinks you are not living up to your potential."

"No kidding! I don't think I could ever live up to her expectations. Not in a million years."

"Well, let me tell you a little about this family, and maybe it will help you realize where she's coming from."

"I like your stories, but I doubt they are going to help, Mémé."

"Have I ever told you about your mother's high school graduation? It's not a time I am particularly proud of, but it might help you to understand your mother better."

"No, I don't remember that one."

"In those days, your pépé Louis wasn't the most supportive or loving parent in the world—at least to your mother—and he wasn't any better at being a husband."

She stopped weeding and sat back on her haunches and began to tell the story …

I was washing dishes in the kitchen when I overheard Louis talking on the phone. "Yeah, see you Saturday then."

I heard the clunk of the receiver, the rustle of *The Western Producer* newspaper, and the flick of the match lighting his cigarette.

I came around the corner. "Louis, Evangeline's graduation is on Saturday. I told you, you have to be there. Why did I just hear you telling Nick that you were going hunting on Saturday? It's your only daughter's graduation. Honest to God!"

"Stop worrying. I'll go hunting in the morning after chores. I'll be there. What time does it start?" He said without even looking up from his newspaper.

"For the umpteenth time, awards are at four, supper is six, and then the dance. You are going to the entire thing. How many more times do I have to tell you?" I wiped my hands on the tea towel and stood in front of him; my hands on my hips.

"Don't worry. Plenty of time. And if I miss the awards, what's the big deal?" he said, obviously disinterested.

"What's the big deal?" The pitch in my voice rose an octave. "She's probably going to walk away with some of the awards. Don't you want to be there when it happens?"

"What kind of awards? First time I heard of this." He said, still looking down at his newspaper.

"I don't know which ones! She's bound to get something though. She's got straight A's on her report card, and she's already been offered a scholarship, which I'm sure they'll mention at the very least. Do you even care at all?"

He finally looked up at me "I've been to six of these graduations over the years. They're boring. The boys never got any awards, and they've done just fine," he said as he flicked his cigarette in the ashtray and looked out the window.

"Boring? Shame on you." I shook my finger at him as I said it. I hated when I did that. It was something my own mother always did which I despised, but sometimes, when I was at a loss for words and frustrated, my mother's gestures and words would appear. "And please, do not compare her to the boys. She's not anything like the boys, and you know that. They weren't interested in school that much. But Evangeline has loved school since kindergarten. Your daughter, if you haven't noticed, is really smart. Where her intelligence comes from, I've got no idea. Not from you or me that's for sure." I could hear my voice start to crackle. I didn't want to cry.

"She's not that smart. Maybe book smart but as for practical smarts, what you need to live in the real world? Ha! She hasn't got a clue, Lil."

He put up his hand as if to dismiss me. I hated it when he did that. I usually backed off, trying to avoid another fight, but not this time. I was determined to get it through his thick skull that he was going and that there was no way in hell he could get out of it. I wanted our daughter to have the perfect day, and be damned if he was going to ruin it by not even showing up.

"Do you even know your daughter at all?"

"What she needs is a husband, preferably rich, to take her to all those places she wants to go and do all the shit she wants to do. She's a goddamn dreamer. You should've been stricter with her. Taught her to be more practical. No awards are going to help her raise kids or get supper on the table on time if she's sitting and reading all day or gallivanting around the country. What man is going to put up with that nonsense?"

"What do you know about dreaming? Mon dieu! Imbécile! Your big dream is farming, hunting, playing hockey, and watching sports on TV! Dream? You know what? I have a dream that our daughter sees her parents in the audience." I pointed to the bedroom, my face red with anger. I could feel my chest tighten. "Go! Go and pick out what you're going to wear so I can clean the stains out of it before you put it on tomorrow. God forbid, you buy something new to wear to your only daughter's graduation!" I turned my face away from him and dismissed him with a flick of my wrist. I couldn't look at him anymore.

He looked down at his newspaper. "Why do you always have to blow everything out of proportion? Make a big deal out of nothing? Honestly, Lil. Get a hold of yourself. I said I would go."

I stomped out of the kitchen and went outside to my garden, muttering under my breath. "How can I be married to such a man? Why do I stay and put up with him? I should just leave, leave with Evangeline to British Columbia. Secousse égoïste." I stayed in my garden for over an hour as I tried to gain control of my emotions, tears rolling down my face as I filled my wheelbarrow full of ripe tomatoes, onions, and carrots.

"I was so mad at him, Stormy; I just knew he wouldn't show up for the awards. The gym was packed with parents, relatives, and town folks. It was a big deal to celebrate graduation every year in Paris. The town news reporter was there taking photos. The stores and credit union were closed during the ceremony. People were dressed in their Sunday best. A portable wooden stage was set up at the front and the twenty-three graduates sat in their caps and gowns, facing the audience."

"It's the biggest class since 1961!" Principal Douglas said, as if it was some kind of achievement. " . . . and the AP Scholar Award goes to . . . Evangeline Boisseau." The principal began to clap his hands as Evangeline stood up and went to the podium. "You might as well stay right here because you are also the recipient of the Governor General Award for Academic Achievement. This award is given to those who have achieved the highest-grade point average in a Canadian high school." He waited until the applause died down, then continued. "Evangeline has also won a scholarship to attend the University of Victoria from the Department of English," Principal Douglas said, his chest puffing out with pride. As he shook her hand and handed her the awards, he leaned into the microphone again and said, "Congratulations,

Evangeline. You have a bright future ahead of you, and I know you'll make us all very proud."

"Stormy, your mother glowed in a way that I had never seen before. I knew my Evangeline was bright, but I was shocked by her confidence and composure as she walked up to the microphone to thank her teachers in both English and French. I've regretted not taking photos—but I was enraptured. She looked so radiant up there, her blue eyes sparkling like diamonds. That camera was sitting on my lap ready to go, but I was so surprised at hearing her name called out again and again that I didn't even think of picking it up. All I have is the front-page newspaper clipping of her standing at the podium."

"I've seen that! She looked so young. I didn't know she won all those awards though."

"Well, it wasn't just the awards. There were even more as the ceremony went on. I was grateful that your uncle John and aunt Donna were there, at least sitting on the other side of me. I don't know how I would have gotten through it all alone. I felt all eyes in the gym staring at me, watching my reaction when Evangeline's name was announced again for being the editor for the school newspaper and the yearbook, and then for being on the honour roll. I could hear people whispering. "Evangeline again?" "Couldn't they at least make the awards more spread out?" "I never knew she was so bright, did you?" The clapping that was so enthusiastic at the first announcement dwindled as her name was called over and over, and the whispers and comments felt like a heavy black cloak. Don't get me wrong, I was proud of my daughter's achievements, I truly was. But afterwards, as other parents and teachers came up and congratulated me, I could feel the weight of your pépé Louis's words: *She is not smart in the ways of the world.* My mind was jumping back and forth, seeing Evangeline as a little girl, so full of desire to learn, and then envisioning a future Evangeline, full of disappointment once she realized how unkind the world is to women with ambition. There was this nagging sensation in the pit of my stomach telling me that I had made the wrong decisions for her."

Mémé stopped pulling weeds and looked me in the eyes. "Stormy, the one thing I tried so hard to avoid was having your mother turn out like me. It was as simple as that."

"What do you mean, Mémé?"

"Well, I too had dreams and ambitions as a young girl and well . . . let's just say I prayed that life's lessons wouldn't be as cruel to Evangeline as they had been to me."

"What kind of ambitions and dreams?" I asked.

"We'll get back to that in a minute. Follow me." She stood up and grabbed the pail, and I followed her to the rows of beans that seemed a mile long. We got down on our knees and began weeding again.

"Did Pépé Louis ever show up?"

"Yes, he finally showed up for the dinner. He sat down with us. He ate his meal, and as soon as the tables were pushed to the side, he got up and went to the back of the hall. Whenever there was a function and the dancing started, he'd do that. He would rather talk about farming and sports and smoke with the other men in the back than dance with me. I didn't like it, but I was used to it. Evangeline and her date Guy and John and Donna got up to dance, and I sat alone at the table. I wasn't in the mood to join the other women to talk about their gardens and kids. I had too much on my mind. I was still embarrassed about Louis's failure to show up at the ceremony, and I was feeling like people were still whispering about all the awards Evangeline received. It made me feel uncomfortable. I'm not one to brag about my kids, unlike a lot of women. I've always preferred to stay out of the limelight. Boasting about my children or even grandchildren is just not my way."

"I get it. Mom is like that too. She always says she has no use for braggarts."

"She gets that from me, that's for sure. Maybe my mother too, come to think about it."

The night of my mother's graduation, my mémé sat at the table in the hall. Alone. The dishes were removed from the tables, the lights were lowered, and the music was blaring. She was content to just watch Evangeline dancing with her classmates to Three Dog Night's "Joy to the World."

"Your mother looked radiant. Her long, straight hair was swinging as she danced in her flowing purple dress that we had designed and sewn together. It had a white, daisy-patterned neckline and a matching wrist corsage that

Guy bought her. You should have seen her with her arms flinging around like some crazy happy bird as she danced to that rock and roll. Guy was such a nice boy. I even foolishly imagined that he would be a potential husband for your mother."

"You mean Guy, as in the neighbour down the road?"

She laughed, "Yes, that's the one."

"Oh, that's so funny, he doesn't seem like Mom's type at all. Not that I would know, I don't even know if she's dated anyone since her divorce from Dad."

She smiled. "Well, he probably wasn't her type, but I couldn't let go of the dream of having your mother live near me. Guy was quite a catch in those days though. Really. He was a real hard worker, even had his own herd of cattle before he graduated high school. He was so polite, and he adored your mother, you could see it in his eyes. Like a little puppy dog. Your mother liked him, but I knew in my heart that she saw him only as a friend. She had plans and living in a small prairie community and being a housewife was not part of them."

"Yeah, Mom loves British Columbia, I couldn't see her living anywhere else really."

"It was hard because I wanted her to stay, but at the same time I wanted her to leave and follow her dreams. I didn't want her to end up like me." Mémé stopped weeding and looked at me with a frown.

"I don't get it, what's wrong with your life?"

She inhaled deeply and let out a sigh. "Well, this is the part where it gets embarrassing. But I want to tell you. I think it is important to know the history of the women in your life."

I lifted my head and looked at her. I noticed her eyes were starting to water.

"I never graduated high school. I was pregnant at fifteen and married a week after my sixteenth birthday."

"Really?" I could feel my eyebrows rise and my eyes grow big. I tried to censor my facial expression but unfortunately, Mémé registered it.

She looked down at her hands, and I could tell she was embarrassed. I felt bad for her and mad at myself for my reaction.

"And," she said, taking a deep breath and looking at me, "I had twins at seventeen."

The sadness in her face made me realize that she still felt regret after all these years. My heart sank, realizing the heavy burdens she had carried most of her life.

"I never had time to make or keep many friends. I was busy doing laundry, changing diapers, running after toddlers while my classmates were having fun, being teenagers. My best friend Carmen came to visit and help me out, but she left after graduation and became a principal of a high school in the city and never married. We stay in touch, but it's hard. We lead such different lives. I was a failure. In my own eyes, my family's eyes, the town, and even Mrs. Schmidt, my grade ten teacher. Her words still feel like daggers in my heart, even though they were spoken so long ago. *You were the brightest in the class, Lillian. So much potential. Despite being a girl, Lillian, you could have been a science teacher or maybe even a scientist, but you made a bad choice and have unfortunately lost out on your chance at becoming someone who could have made a contribution to this world.* And they were all right. I blew it. My future was determined by a one second decision. I let Pépé talk me into having sex. He said everybody was doing it and that I wouldn't get pregnant. I had only dated him for a few months and didn't really understand what he meant. In those days there was no such thing as sex education, and we never talked about it at home that's for sure." She sighed and frowned.

"I am so sorry, Mémé. That is terrible. Mom never told me."

"I know. It's not something I talk about much either. I mean, I have wonderful children and well, we can't go back and redo our lives now, can we? But we can learn from our mistakes and help others to be wiser. Right?"

"I guess so. Mom says the same thing all the time. Were you smart like her too?"

"Well, I loved the sciences. I was obsessed with biology, and I read anything I could get my hands on, which wasn't too much in those days. Guess that is why I like my garden so much now. I had such big plans though, so I guess in that way, I was like her." She looked past me across the field, I could see she was imagining what her life could have been.

She returned to gaze at me, "It was different back then. If you got pregnant before marriage, you got married to save face. There was no question about it, well, according to our parents anyways. I should say, I *thought* I had no choice. We were so young and immature. So, we did what our parents told us to do. The thing is, people don't ever forget in a small community; every mistake you ever make is brought up over and over throughout the years. There's somehow a belief that people can't change and grow. Like poor Sarah Jones. She got caught shoplifting at the grocery store when she was eleven and even to this day—she's in her sixties—town-folk still say, *'You gotta watch Sarah. She's a thief, not to be trusted.'*"

"That's terrible. I'm so sorry you had to go through all that!"

"There is no way to be free from your past nor to have one's mistakes forgiven. In Paris, I will forever be seen as the bright girl who could have had a successful career, but who got pregnant and never amounted to anything except being a farm wife with a brood of children. You know, Stormy, the only good thing after that graduation was that I became known as the mother of Evangeline, the smartest kid in town."

"But didn't your parents realize that you didn't love each other? I mean you hardly knew anything about each other."

"There's a little more to the story. After we had sex, we broke up. I hated it and didn't want to do it ever again. We grew up together but you're right, we didn't really know each other. His sister, your great aunt Simone, was a close friend since grade one, and we hung out a lot. It was how I ended up with Louis. Anyway by the time I realized I was pregnant; I was already six months along. I did know before that deep down, but I was in denial. My mother figured it out and took me to the doctor. She shook her finger at me one day and looked at my bump and never said a word. Her silence was punishment enough. In those days and in a small town, there was no question that we would marry. Our parents made it clear they were not about to be embarrassed by having a grandchild out of wedlock. Choices? No, we didn't have many, not like you kids have today."

More than anything, Mémé said, she didn't want her daughter to end up like she did. Watching Guy on the dance floor that night was enough to convince her that the poor boy, as sweet as he was, was way out of her daughter's league. He was a nice boy from a good family, but the poor thing seemed awkward in his own skin, whereas my mother was dancing like no one was watching. "Evangeline," she said "was in her own world, as usual, and she was stunningly confident and the best dancer on the floor by a mile. Yes, your mother was destined for something more interesting than what rural Saskatchewan had to offer. She stuck out like a diamond in the rough in our little town that day, on stage as she gave her acceptance speech, and even on the dance floor. I prayed that along the way she could find someone to look after her or someone who would keep her grounded in reality but, more importantly, someone who really loved her for who she was and would not bring her down from the clouds too much."

It was obvious that Mémé didn't want her daughter to have the kind of husband she had. Pépé seemed to be fine as a provider and as a father to his sons from what she told me, but it was plain as day when I went to visit them at the farm that he didn't love my grandmother. Well, not like she wanted to be loved anyways. I never witnessed him show her any affection, and he was always cutting her down: *the soup was too salty, she was too fat, she was too easy on the kids* . . . And, as I learned from the stories over the years, he took no interest in his only daughter from day one. In fact, after Pépé died, Mémé confessed that her husband didn't have much use for women in general. "He was a misogynist. It was a sad but true fact," she said in a matter-of-fact way. Which explained a lot of his behaviour toward me when I visited. I always had this urge when I was there to ask if he even knew my name. It was like I didn't exist.

My mother left immediately after graduation, and Mémé said it was bittersweet. Evangeline leaving brought up her own past, which made her afraid but happy for her at the same time. Mémé had achieved what she had set out to do as a mother: to make sure Evangeline was not going to suffocate in a small town and in a loveless marriage like she had. Her unhappy life was her fate. But she was adamant that her little girl was going to have a better life than she had. Evangeline was leaving the nest and, although it worried her to no end that she couldn't protect her or teach her anything anymore, she knew it was the right thing for her daughter. Still, she wasn't quite ready to let her go. She knew she would worry more about Evangeline than all her sons put together. She recalled the day my mother left home. . .

"Mom, quit crying! Why are you crying anyway? Aren't you happy I'm finally leaving home? You always say I drive you crazy. You'll finally have peace," Evangeline laughed.

"Oh, ma petite fille! I don't want peace. I want to be driven crazy," Lillian sobbed as she blew her nose.

"Oh, Mom, I'll be fine. I'm so excited. And I promise I'll call every week. I promise."

"Not just every week. I want to know the minute your train arrives in Vancouver and the minute the bus gets to Victoria and the minute you step foot in your dorm room. Hear me? Call me collect. I don't care how much it costs. Once a week is not good enough yet. I need to know you're okay. I need to know where you are at all times. Understood?"

"Okay, I promise but, Mom, I'm eighteen years old. I'm not a baby."

"I should have gone with you to get you settled in at your new place or at least sent one of your brothers to go with you."

"Mom, I'm going to be okay. Stop worrying."

The train arrived at the station. Mémé Lillian watched as her baby girl stepped onto the railcar. She stood in the same spot, crying till the train was out of sight.

"That girl, she'll be the death of me from worry. She has no idea of life outside of our little bubble," she said aloud to no one. Mémé wasn't the most religious person. She went to church because that's what was expected in her community, but that day as she stood on the train platform, she made the sign of the cross and looked up into the sky. "Please watch over her, dear Lord, if you are out there."

CHAPTER FOUR

EVANGELINE

1977

On the west side of Salt Spring Island in the southern Gulf Islands off the east coast of Vancouver Island, is the summit of Mount Maxwell. It is one of the highest points of land on the small gulf island. As you meander up the mountain you will meet Douglas-fir forests, Garry oak meadows, moss-covered rocky outcrops, and spectacular bluffs. Chances are good that you will see Bald Eagles and Red-Tailed Hawks soaring above your head. On a clear day the view will take your breath away. Fulford Valley, Burgoyne Bay, and the Sansum Narrows that separate the Southern Gulf Island from Vancouver Island in British Columbia, can all be seen from the top.

My mother was editing a guide book on Salt Spring Island while she was finishing her Master's Degree in English at the University of Victoria. That particular passage stuck in her mind, and she knew she had to hike up Mount Maxwell one day.

Salt Spring was one of the Gulf Islands that sat protected from the harsh elements between the mainland and Vancouver Island. It had a rich history. It was part of the traditional territory of the Saanich, Cowichan, and Chemainus First Nations, and aboriginal use of the island dated back at least 5,000 years. In the 1800s, Black immigrants fleeing the United States came; Japanese, Hawaiians, and Europeans also came to fish and mine, search for gold, and farm. In the sixties, draft dodgers arrived, followed close by hippies, artists, and musicians. As Evangeline read more about Salt Spring Island, she felt something inside herself awakened by the stories of carefree communities on the Gulf Islands; the idea of island life, of living so close to the sea, the mild weather, and the small-town communities intrigued her.

When she finished the last of her classes and had only her Master's thesis to defend, she finally decided to take a break from writing on the weekend and go. She grabbed her roommate's tent and camping supplies and drove to Swartz Bay terminal just a few minutes north of the little town of Sydney.

The ferry was small, less than a hundred cars could fit on. She grabbed a coffee at the little cafeteria, then stood outside on the deck, gazing over the rail as the ferry glided across the deep blue water. She watched seagulls flying in the clear sky and searched for whales in the distance. The smell of the salt air mixed with seaweed filled her nostrils while the mild ocean breeze tousled her hair. And in that moment, a sense of peace came over her.

Being from the prairies, she had always felt a certain comfort when she could see far into the distance. As she stood there, it reminded her of the first ferry ride she had ever taken from the mainland to Swartz Bay and the realization that she had back then as she looked across the vast sea. It was that same comfort she felt at home on the farm when she gazed across the fields. She knew she could never live in the mountains. The ocean had cast its spell on her. And she knew then that island life was where she needed to be.

When she landed at Fulford Harbour, she felt excited, as if she were about to discover something new. She was even more excited than six years earlier when she had first arrived in Victoria. It had been a while since she had a new adventure. She had been so focused on her studies and part-time jobs that she hadn't really taken the time to make many friends or create much of a social life.

She drove off the ferry and followed the signs to Ruckle Provincial Park. She kept the windows down and felt the breeze on her face, smelling the fresh lush green fir and cypress mixed with salt air as she meandered along the narrow-paved road. She pitched her tent on the grassy meadow that faced the Swanson Channel. From there she could watch the parade of boats and ferries and hopefully spot sea lions and killer whales. She wandered along the rocky headlands and explored the tidal pools that were full of pink and orange starfish and purple mussels clinging to rocks. She had decided before she left that she would eat her breakfast at the campsite and treat herself to restaurant food for the rest of her meals. She really wanted to get a feel for the island and the people as much as she could.

It was an incredible weekend spent hiking and shopping at the little stores, eating in restaurants, and going to the art galleries that dotted the island. She bought homemade bread, eggs, vegetables, as well as jam and garlic from the farmer's vegetable stands along the road, leaving money in their jars. The sense of community, of trusting your neighbours, was so evident no matter where she turned. People were always waving at her as they passed in their vehicles or said hello when they passed her on the street. By the second day, she realized she was falling in love with the island.

On her first night there, she went to the local coffee house in the village where there was an open mic with locals getting up to sing and read poetry. As people walked into the cafe, she observed how they greeted each other, as well as how they smiled at her and engaged her in conversation. She asked questions about what life was like living on the island and what they did for entertainment besides poetry readings. One of the things they mentioned was dances, and they told her she was in luck because there was a dance the next evening at Fulford Hall with a local band.

On Saturday night, she drove to Fulford Hall. It was a rustic older building with lots of windows, nestled in the trees off the main road. The hall was filled with people chatting, some sitting at the tables that lined the sides of the hall, others just standing.

"Welcome. Are you new in town or visiting?" the gal at the entrance asked as she took Evangeline's dollar.

"Just visiting, but I'm in love with the island already. Have you lived here long?"

"Just over six years. Best move I ever made. I'm from Edmonton. I came for a holiday and never left," she said as she reached out her hand. "Darlene's my name."

My mother shook her hand. It was a strong handshake for such a petite woman, she thought.

"Nice to meet you. I'm Evangeline. Quite a handshake you have," she said, laughing.

"I know. Everyone comments on it. I'm a potter. I work with clay all day. I guess that's where I get my muscles. Also, my father taught me that a handshake says a lot about a person. Firm, not too long, like you really are glad to meet someone. You have a good handshake yourself, Evangeline."

"Milking cows growing up," she said with a chuckle.

"Another stubble jumper?"

"Ha! Haven't heard that one before. But yes, I guess so. From rural Saskatchewan. But I live in Victoria now."

"Well, welcome to our little island!"

Evangeline got a glass of wine, sat down at a table, and looked around at all the people. She didn't sit but ten minutes when Darlene came and sat across from her. She was a tiny woman, her long thick curly brown hair in braids that accentuated her brown eyes and dark freckles. She looked like an artist, Evangeline thought. Her clothes were an assortment of bright colours, and she wore many accessories, including leather necklaces, peace signs, pottery medallions, and some kind of horns hanging from leather. It was the type of look she admired and tried to pull off but never seemed to manage it. She would have to ask Darlene where she shopped, she thought. They chatted like old friends and a few minutes before the band started, she said, "Come on, I want you to meet some people." She introduced her to most of the people in the small hall that night. It was strange, but it seemed that everyone was genuinely glad to meet her: asking her about her writing, her interests, her passions. The conversations were interesting and had nothing to do with the local gossip. She danced almost every dance and before the night was through, she felt she had somehow found her tribe amongst this motley group of hippies, artists, writers, and musicians.

Reading my mother's journal about her first trip to Salt Spring brought tears to my eyes. I could picture my mother, for perhaps the first time in her life, feeling a sense of belonging in a place that fit her. Sunday afternoon before she had to head back to Victoria, she climbed up Mount Maxwell. She wanted to save the hike for last. She left her camping gear in the car, drove to the base of the mountain, and wandered up, taking in the sights and smells. When she reached the summit and looked at the view, her eyes teared up. It was even more spectacular than she had imagined from the passage in the guide book. The blue sky, glistening water, and panoramic view made her gasp. She had never felt so happy in her life as she did that day.

As she boarded the ferry back to Vancouver Island and watched Salt Spring Island grow farther and farther away, she had the feeling that she was leaving her community. She loved Victoria, but there was something about Salt Spring that just felt different. It was like she was destined to live there. Before the ferry landed, her mind was made up. She would move to Salt Spring the minute she graduated. She had no idea how she would make a living, but she didn't care. She touched the napkin in her pocket that Darlene had handed her at the dance with her address and phone number. Her words were still fresh in Evangeline's memory: "Don't hesitate to call or come over any time. I have an extra bedroom, and you're welcome to it. Stay as long as you like."

As I read her journal, my heart broke to know that, years later, she would give up her home and wonderful life in Salt Spring to move to Victoria, for me.

CHAPTER FIVE
EVANGELINE

FEBRUARY 1980

As the train left Athens and began the journey to the Peloponnese Peninsula, a sense of calm washed over my mother, and she took a deep breath in. Though she loved Athens, the constant noise and the snoring roommates at the hostels and the haggling merchants in the Plaka had worn her out. She opened the window to let in some fresh air. There were only a few people in the railcar: an elderly woman with a small boy at the front, and a middle-aged businessman in the back. She was happy to be alone and take in the scenery and relieved to not have to struggle with speaking Greek, if for only a few hours. The hard bench didn't bother her; she had her feet resting on the seat across from her; glad they were close enough for her short legs to reach. She watched the rows of giant pencil pines from the window give way to olive groves, and a heavenly perfume filled the train. She found it warm, even though it was the end of February. She wore handmade leather sandals she had bought while strolling along the labyrinthine streets of the old historical Plaka neighbourhood in Athens. She wore her volunteer T-shirt from the previous year's 1979 Salt Spring Fall Fair for editing work on their promotional materials and her one pair of jeans that she had brought for the trip. She wished she had worn her long skirt instead; the jeans felt tight, and she knew why. It wasn't the first time she had gained weight on a work trip.

Besides being an editor, my mother had written for travel magazines and Fodor's Travel guides since graduating from university. She always said that sampling food was both the worst and the best part of her travel writing assignments. In Greece, with its wonderful, tasty souvlakis, salads, baklava, gyros, spanakopita, hummus, and everything swimming in olive oil, going to work meant putting on weight, which she would struggle to lose once she got home. In England, it was another story. Though she generally loved to eat, the food in the United Kingdom did nothing for her palate. Flavourless steak and kidney pie, soggy french fries, shepherd's pie, and toad-in-the-hole meant she only ate a bite or two so she could write her review, which meant going home a few pounds lighter.

Before she left for Greece, she had read an article that said that the Mediterranean diet was one of the healthiest in the world. In Athens, convinced by the article that she would not gain weight this time, she ate her way through her ten-day stay.

As she sat in the train, feeling the waist of her jeans digging into her skin, she realized that clearly, she had a problem. She had an insatiable appetite. Feeling "full" was not something she often experienced. She wished she did. When she was younger, she found she could eat as much as her brothers who were twice her size. Not only that, she ate faster than most of them too. She just loved good food and loved to eat and never felt full, and she ate fast. In fact, she did everything fast. There was always a feeling of urgency to experience life, to accomplish things, to eat, to feel. It was like she didn't want to miss out on anything.

It wasn't a big deal. She knew how to lose weight when she went overboard, and she went overboard often; in France, Greece, Italy, Germany, and especially Louisiana, where she couldn't resist buckets of crawfish dipped in butter. My mother's philosophy in life was to experience life to the fullest. That included eating good food, and always taking the scenic route. It was not something she had been taught; she really didn't know where it came from. Certainly not her family. Her mother's voice, which was the voice she most often heard in her head, was always telling her to slow down—when she ate, when she walked, on her dreams. She hated the fact that she spent so much energy on consciously ignoring that voice, not just when she was eating but pretty much any time her mother's voice of reason, as she called it, entered her head. But she told herself, if she hadn't ignored it, she would still be living in rural Saskatchewan, married to Guy instead of traveling on a train in Greece and getting paid for it. Evangeline just couldn't see herself ever milking cows and shoveling snow again. Not that raising cattle and shoveling snow were bad, they were just not for her. Her brothers seemed happy enough. All of them had stayed back and were into farming in one way or another. John, the youngest, was a dairy farmer, some raised cattle and grew grain; and one brother was a mechanic who fixed farm machinery. They all got married right out of high school and had loads of children. Evangeline loved them dearly, but she felt like an outsider in her own family and in her own home town a lot of the time. That is why the minute she graduated she hopped on a train and headed to the west coast.

The squealing brakes from the train brought her mind back into the moment.

When the train stopped and more people got on, Evangeline noticed the local people wearing jackets and scarfs and hats. It made her sweat just looking at them. It was so sunny, and she guessed at least sixty-five degrees out, which for February was plenty warm for her, but obviously cold for them. She kept the window open so she could feel the breeze on her face and that was probably why everyone who boarded the train on the many stops along the way, kept far away from her. She rested her chin on the heel of her hand with her elbow on the window ledge. When they passed through towns, the pungent smell of the multi-coloured oleanders filled her nostrils. She was so glad that she had decided at the last minute to jump on the first train out of Athens.

The train stopped in a little town and, as usual, the merchants were selling coffee and snacks through the open windows to the passengers. She was sipping sugary espresso out of a little plastic cup when she heard a voice say: "G'day. M-m-mind if I sit here?"

She could tell he was an Aussie the second he opened his mouth. He was a nice-looking man. Had a pleasant smile.

"No, not at all, have a seat," she said as she moved her feet off the bench.

He wore a brown wide-brimmed weather worn leather hat, and his chin was slightly dark. She had always liked a five o'clock shadow on a man, it gave them that little rough around the edge's kind of look. She was never attracted to clean shaven men in fancy suits. She could tell by his shoes that he came from money. Pay attention to shoes. That was the only good advice Evangeline's father had ever given her. He said you could always tell how well-off people were by their shoes. She'd tested his theory many times over the years and, so far, the theory had seemed spot on. The Aussie's shoes were a little dusty and worn, but she was pretty sure from the stitching that they were expensive, Italian hand-made ones. He had an angular face, light-red hair, and kindly bright green eyes that turned up. He was thin and tall, maybe over six feet. He placed his backpack in the rack above his seat and sat down.

CHAPTER SIX
VALENTINO

FEBRUARY 1980

Valentino shook hands with the Maestro. "Magnificent show. Thanks again for a great run," he said in Italian.

"Where are you headed next?"

"Off to Greece. Just for a week and a half before heading home."

"Sounds wonderful. See you again soon. It has been a pleasure, as usual."

"Yes, a pleasure. Arrivederci."

He walked down the dark hallway to the back door of the theatre where a taxi was waiting to take him to his hotel suite. He sorted his clothes—a suitcase to be shipped back to Melbourne with all his work clothes and a backpack filled with jeans and T-shirts. He didn't sleep all that well despite the magnificent four post bed with the French linen sheets and soft pillows that he loved. He was always that way before he flew the next day on an early flight. He was awake long before the hotel did his wake-up call. At six in the morning, he called the concierge of the Hotel Artemide and asked them to ship his suitcase home and to get his bill ready.

The taxi went straight to the Fiumicino airport, passing the Capitoline museums. Valentino had been to them several times during his time in Rome. He gazed at the top floor at the Caffé Capitolino, his mouth watering from the thought of the Cacio e Pepe pasta dish grated with his favourite Pecorino Romano cheese that he knew he would miss. The traffic was flowing nicely, even on the bridge going over the Tiber River and past the entrance to the Vatican. He arrived right on time. He boarded the plane, expecting to be in Athens in less than two hours. All his worrying was for not, as usual, he thought.

He was in first class. He found it funny that whenever he was in street clothes in first class, he was treated differently than when he was dressed in a suit and on the company account. Fame was a funny thing. It often felt as if he were two different people. He was thankful that he was rarely recognized; he would just as soon blend in than stand out anyway. As people were boarding, Valentino was careful not to make eye contact, just in case. He took out his book, *History of the Peloponnesian War*, which his father had given to him from his own vast library and insisted he read. Now, Valentino opened the leather-bound cover and tried to concentrate on the first lines, but his mind kept wandering off with thoughts about his plan.

He had a couple of places he wanted to explore in the Peloponnese. One was Voidokilia Bay and the other was Olympia, where he intended to spend a week. His father had told him about the exceptional beauty of Voidokilia Bay with its magnificent beaches that stretched beneath the Old Frankish Castle and the Cave of King Nestor. "On these beaches you'll find the lightest, finest sand on earth," he told him. After that, he planned to hike around the famous Gialova Lagoon, then meander into the hills nearby that were covered with olive groves. Or perhaps he'd hire a moped. He wasn't sure. It was a tour his father had taken over twenty years before and highly recommended. Valentino almost felt obliged to do the trip just out of respect for him.

After that, he planned to hop a train and head to the ancient town of Olympia to celebrate his birthday. Just the thought of going back to Olympia made him smile to himself. He was in love with the little village for a reason he couldn't really pinpoint. He hadn't stopped thinking about it since he had spent a few days there two years ago. He thought it was because it was still undiscovered by tourists, which seemed strange to him. There were no tour buses or line ups like at many of the ancient ruins in Greece. Perhaps that was because it was February and not the high season for visitors. But still, it was the site of the first Olympics; he had expected some tourists. But happily, two years ago anyways, there was this very sweet village that just happened to be near one of the most amazing ancient ruins in history. He had seen it happen over the years, and he and his father would often talk about it. The tourists discovered a great place and, before you knew it, the feeling of being transported into another time and place was ruined by endless stores and peddlers trying to sell made-in-China souvenirs. He hoped the quaint village was still as he remembered it.

As he thought more about Olympia, he realized it wasn't just the lack of tourists; he felt a connection to both the ancient site and to the village. Both places seemed to be in a time warp in their own way. When he stepped into the entrance of the ruins, he could immediately sense a historical membrane that held the souls and thoughts, the myths and dreams of the people throughout the ages. It was as if the past was just within reach, as if through a veil. When he walked along the streets of the village, he imagined he was transported to the late 1800s, back to when life was simple. Some of the old whitewashed buildings with colourful doors were still occupied, even after hundreds of years. The fragrant flowers donning the balconies, the twisted old trees, the herds of goats and donkeys packed with supplies, and the hundred-year-old olive groves seemed to hold the secrets of existence. It was a magical place.

"May I ask you a personal question, sir?" the stewardess asked him, interrupting his thoughts.

"Yes, of course."

"Are you Valentino Lombardo? I was working on a flight you were on last year."

"Ahh, yes, I am the one."

"I thought so. I saw your performance last night, and it was fabulous. You look different without all the makeup, but I recognize your face from the playbill."

"Yes, thank you, and I'm glad you enjoyed it." He smiled.

"Well, it's an honour to have you on our flight today. If there's anything you need, please don't hesitate to ask."

"Thank you kindly. I'm fine," he said as he looked down at his book.

It was a difficult situation. He regretted not being more friendly, but it was hard for him. Valentino knew he was an oxymoron. He could perform in front of thousands of people yet a one-on-one conversation was painful. It would be much easier if they just saw him as a regular twenty-eight-year-old guy backpacking through Greece who just happened to be in first class.

He was looking for a relaxing holiday exploring the Peloponnese Peninsula. He thought of how his university classmates had teased him and nicknamed him "Dag" for his geekiness. He didn't mind the term. He knew he was a geek and a bit of a nerd. A history geek, and a music geek. He was eccentric, peculiar, and socially awkward, and he was okay with all of that, for the most part. He was an only child to parents who had him in their forties, and who confessed to him early on that he was an unplanned but welcome surprise. They were a pair of intellectuals. His mother was a linguistics professor who was overly social and could charm the pants off anyone anytime. His father was a famous mathematical genius who made Valentino's own geekiness look trivial.

Valentino wasn't like his father. Well, no one was like him. Professor Lombardo had difficulty looking people in the eye, that was, unless they were talking about math. He literally could not boil water for a cup of tea, and he was known to get lost crossing a street. But he was a good, solid man and did his best at parenting. They, of course, didn't play catch in the backyard or go fishing like many regular boys did with their fathers, but he did teach him to play chess, bocce ball, math games, and how to solve difficult puzzles. As he got older, their shared love of history was what really created the bond they now shared and that they never had when he was young. Now it was nothing for the two of them to sit in the library in the evenings discussing history, art, music, and a little bit of politics for hours on end.

Valentino often wondered how his parents ever got together. He was pretty sure it was all his mom's doing. All kinds of people gravitated to his mother. She had a special affinity for strange people, people who had trouble fitting in, people from every walk of life—homeless people, dignitaries, immigrants who couldn't speak English. She always had an entourage. Once he got older, he began to appreciate his mother much more. He realized she had a real gift for accepting people for who they were. Warts and all. She used to tell him, "Everyone has some goodness in them, you just have to discover it." There was an ironic side to her though: as friendly and warm as she was, she was not demonstrative in her affections. She rarely gave him a hug or a kiss, even when he was a small boy. He didn't know this was strange until he started school and saw his classmates getting hugs when they were dropped off or picked up. Even with her husband she was undemonstrative. Indeed, there were very few times in Valentino's life when he even saw his parents hold hands, let alone hug or kiss.

Valentino wanted to believe there was goodness in everyone, like she said, but it was difficult. He had been teased at school for so many reasons: his stuttering, his geekiness, and even for his name. Valentine's Day was the hardest, and he always tried to stay home. When he finally asked his mother when he was around seven or eight, why they had named him Valentino, she said it was her maiden name and that he should be proud of it, as it meant strength. "And," she added, "Valentine's Day is a celebration of love and affection." The explanation helped a little, but again he found it ironic that she alluded to affection. He could see his parents were in love, but the physical demonstration of their feelings, as far as he was concerned, was sadly missing in their home. It was for this reason that he vowed to be more affectionate should he ever have a wife or children.

Having a painfully shy, stuttering son who was constantly bullied, didn't seem to weigh on his mother. Her answer to his stutter was simply to avoid using words with the sounds that caused it, and to teach him to sing and to learn a few other techniques. Mostly she urged him to be patient, because as he got older, she assured him, the stuttering would diminish. As for the teasing, she just kept repeating: "Find the goodness, Valentino, find the goodness." It was her answer to every complaint he made.

It was good advice and had, to a point, served him well over the years. Overall, Valentino was happy with his life. His career was amazing and allowed him to travel; he was healthy; he loved living in his own house, even though it was a guest house on his parents' property. The only thing that really bothered him was that he felt lonely at times. His shyness and his stutter meant that he did not have many friends and was uncomfortable and just plain awkward with women. He tried, but his shyness engulfed him like a dark cloud so that speaking to people, one on one, was excruciatingly painful, especially with women. His heart would race. His hands would sweat. And he could feel his face flushing—every time.

Valentino boarded the train for Olympia after the amazing tour that his father had suggested. He was looking forward to getting out the postcard of Voidokilia Bay and writing his father a note about how much he had enjoyed it. There were not many seats left on the train. An elderly woman in her eighties with a blue scarf tied under her chin had a space beside her. A man in a business suit who was reading a book had a space, but his leather briefcase sat open on the empty seat. Then he spied a young woman sitting alone. A pencil stuck out of her blonde hair that was swept up in a messy, delightful bun. On the rack above her head was a giant backpack with a small Canadian flag sewn on the flap.

The window was open. Valentino decided the seat beside her was the best choice. He hoped she didn't want to chat too much. The benches were small and quite close to the facing seats. Considering the close proximity, it would be awkward, rude even, if he didn't talk to her, just a little.

Valentino sat across from my mother. She sipped her espresso and when she smiled at him, he was reminded of a painting of a cupid that hung in his parent's house that he loved. It was the cutest smile he had ever seen. He introduced himself.

CHAPTER SEVEN
EVANGELINE

FEBRUARY 1980

My mother smiled at Valentino as he sat down. "From Canada I reckon?" he asked as he pointed to another Canadian flag that she had embroidered on her canvas purse.

"Yes, I guess my Canada flag tipped you off?" She laughed a little. "And I gather you're an Aussie?"

"Yup. T-t-true b-blue. Melbourne to be exact. H-h-hard to h-h-hide the accent."

She was surprised to hear his stutter.

"Headed t-t-to Olympia?"

"Yes, I am, and you?"

"Yes."

"First t-t-time to Olympia?"

"Yes, I just finished an assignment in Athens. I do freelance work when I can, so I can travel, which I love, and at the same time write off my holidays. I finished earlier than I planned, and I decided to spend a week or so outside of the city. I went to the train station and took the first one departing. I've never been to Olympia so I thought, why not?"

"It's my second t-t-trip. I'm a Greek m-mythology geek. Valentino's m-my name."

"I'm Evangeline. But everyone calls me Angie." She smiled at him, noticing that he was nervously rubbing his middle finger against his thumb. "Well, sounds like you're the kind of person to hang out with while I'm here. I haven't researched this area at all and know very little about mythology, I'm afraid."

"What kind of freelance work were you doing in Athens?"

"I'm a travel writer for fun, but I make my living mostly as an editor for a small publishing company in Canada. I was doing a piece called "Athens on Five Dollars a Day." Not too glamorous, I'm afraid, but it was entertaining enough."

"I love Athens. But I can't say I've ever only spent five dollars a day there. That would be hard for me," he said without stuttering. She could see he was more relaxed because he stopped rubbing his finger.

He rummaged in his backpack, taking out a bag of pistachios and holding the bag open toward her. "Would you like some? Grown here in Greece. Fresh as can be. I'm addicted, I'm afraid."

"Sure. Oh, they are delicious, eh?" she said as she chewed the nuts.

They chatted and within a short time, she noticed his stuttering of T's and M's lessened until it was barely noticeable. The conversation came easy to both of them. He was a walking encyclopedia when it came to the history of Olympia and, she gathered, of Greece in general. And she, with her insatiable quest for knowledge, kept the questions coming.

"What is the best wine in the Peloponnese Peninsula? How many people live in Olympia? How long does it take the Pencil Pines to grow that tall, do you think?"

"Wow, you sure ask a lot of questions," he said, laughing.

"I know, and if it gets too much just let me know. People tell me all the time to slow down with the inquisition. It won't hurt my feelings. But when I'm with someone who actually knows things, I get so excited. My mother called me the queen of questions. She would tell me over and over . . ." Evangeline cleared her throat, and then began again in a high-pitched voice. "When you were three years old, you started asking questions, and you never stopped."

"Does your mother actually talk like that?" Valentino smiled, which made his eyebrows raise up and his forehead wrinkle.

"Yes, well, maybe not that high, but I'm trying to give you a feel of what her voice sounds like in my head."

They both laughed.

"And you should know I like to be right," she continued. "It's my worst trait after asking too many questions. I can't help it though. I do know a lot about things and if I don't know, I like to find out. It's an endless cycle really."

"Well, I like it. I love challenges, and I have a wealth of knowledge. In fact, I feel like my brain is going to burst sometimes because I know so much. So, we should be okay together." He started to belly laugh, and she joined him, and soon they were both almost in tears.

There was not a pause in the conversation after that moment.

Valentino pointed out the valley formed by the Alfeios River. The hills were lush green. Kronos Hill came into view and at its base was the small town of Olympia. As they neared Olympia Station they were greeted by hot-pink and purple oleanders juxtaposed against white-washed buildings. They grabbed their backpacks. As they stepped onto the platform, there was a moment of awkwardness. They had arrived at their destination, but what now?

Valentino turned and stood directly in front of my mother, and he looked her in the eyes. Then, with just a hint of hesitation in his voice, he said, "I don't want t-to be t-too forward, Evangeline, but I know a great little pension I stayed at last t-t-time I was here. It's close to the Olympic ruins, very clean, and not t-t-too expensive. Or do you have a place already reserved?"

My mother could tell that he was nervous, as he was stuttering again. He hadn't stuttered for the last hour and a half.

"No reservations. I didn't make any because it was a last-minute decision to come. So, I'm happy to follow you."

She saw his shoulders relax and a look of relief which was slowly replaced by a smile that lit up his whole face. She was enamoured with him.

Valentino was a fast walker and that pleased her. She easily kept up to him even with his long legs. She couldn't stand walking with people who dawdled along. She took in the sights and smells of Olympia. The contrast from busy Athens was welcoming. Being in Athens always felt like stepping back in time: the old architecture, and the ruins, the small mom-and-pop stores, the restaurants where waiters beckoned you inside, the streets filled with haggling merchants trying to entice you with their wares. As exciting as it was, after a time the business, dusty streets, and never-ending honking of vehicles wore on her nerves. It was such a contrast to living on Salt Spring Island. But after walking in this village for just a few minutes, she already felt relaxed and calm. Olympia seemed to be further back in time than Athens did and, despite being so close to the famous site of the first Olympics, it wasn't the tourist town she had pictured in her mind. There was no one trying to sell souvenirs; no one was trying to entice her into their shop or restaurant; and there wasn't a tourist in sight. It just looked like a small village with people going about their daily business. The streets were mostly light brown dirt, with only a few that were cobblestone. As they turned one corner, they nearly ran into a man leading a donkey that had sacks hanging off its sides. On the corner, an elderly woman in a long dress with a flowered apron, pink sweater, and purple scarf was sweeping her front steps. A man passed by, his long walking stick thumping the cobblestones as he tipped his hat and gave them the sweetest smile. She was enchanted with Olympia. It was peaceful, quaint, and exactly what she was craving after being in Athens, she decided.

Valentino pointed out the pension—a three-storey, white, concrete building with black wrought-iron balconies with pink bougainvillea flowers spilling off the sides. They entered through the aqua blue wooden door. The floors looked to be white marble. Valentino was right, she could tell right away, the pension was as clean as a whistle.

An elderly woman with a big grin greeted them at the front desk and, as my mother was digging in her pocket for her Greek/English dictionary, Valentino, in what sounded like perfect Greek, started to converse with her. "She said she has two rooms available. One has t-t-two beds, and one has a single bed. The one with t-t-two beds has its own bathroom with a shower and a t-tub. The single shares a bath with other guests on the floor. Which would you prefer?"

"I would kill for a bathroom with a tub, I haven't had a bathtub to soak in for weeks. But I'm sure you would too."

"No worries."

"How about I take the one with the bathroom and if you want to use the shower or tub, you can just come on over instead of sharing with God knows who?" The minute the words came out of her mouth, she wondered what in the world she was doing inviting a man she just met to use her shower. But his answer was immediate, and she couldn't back out of it.

"Perfect!"

It was after three by the time they got settled into their rooms. A few minutes later, Valentino knocked on her door. She opened it, and she found him standing there, grinning, his wavy light red/blonde hair slicked straight back, his tanned skin making him look polished and sexy. He had his jacket folded over his arm, and he was wearing a brown scarf. She felt the guilt rise up at the thoughts swirling in her head.

"How about a coldie, I mean a beer? I know a great little t-t-avern down the street."

"A coldie sounds great."

"Bring something a little warmer, it does get cool in the evenings."

She grabbed her purse and sweater and a scarf, and followed him down the stairs to the street.

It was only a couple of blocks to the small pub. It was an old building, like most in the town, with the typical whitewashed walls and colourful old wooden pink and blue shutters and doors. It was like stepping back in time. Above the door they entered was a worn-out sign with the paint half peeled off, but it was still clear enough to read. She asked Valentino what the sign said. He explained that there were two entrances, pointing to another entrance steps away.

"This was the women's entrance and that over there was the men's entrance. Years ago they were not allowed to sit together. Obviously, they don't enforce that anymore." But it made her wonder for a second, how things had changed even in this little village that seemed still so behind the times. She wondered what it was like for women here even twenty years ago. She doubted that she would be sitting in a pub at a table with a man like she was now.

The beer tasted delicious. She always found it funny that at home she never drank beer, but the minute she entered another country she craved it. They were on their third glass, and she was beginning to feel the tension from the last week-and-a-half drain from her body. In fact, she felt slightly drunk. The conversation was easy, and non-stop. She couldn't believe how comfortable she felt with him. The beer was taking its effect, the guilt that was eating away at her earlier, was dwindling.

"I'm starving. I was just thinking of octopus ceviche with fresh bread and Greek salad smothered in olive oil. Mmm," she said, drawing out the M's.

"I know just the place. A sweet little cafe down the street that's not fancy, but the ceviche is out of this world."

It was still light out as they walked along the cobblestone street, and the air was fresh and crisp. She donned her sweater and wrapped the scarf around her neck. The little cafe was nothing more than what looked like a deli with a few tables inside and a few outside. He was right that it was nothing special. They ordered inside, then went outside to sit on the tiny deck. The owner came and placed their food in front of them a few minutes later.

"May I offer you some ouzo?" he asked in Greek.

They both said "yes" at the same time, then laughed.

Evangeline moaned with her eyes closed with every mouthful. Valentino couldn't help but smile. He'd never witnessed anyone enjoy food to the extent that she was in that moment.

"It's the olive oil. It's the best in the world, and it comes from this region," he informed her.

"Oh, my God! You're so right. It the olive oil. Incroyable!"

"I know. And when I was here last, the owner told me the secret to making a Greek salad. Want to hear it?"

"Yes, of course I do," she said giggling.

"The trick is to squeeze fresh lemon on the vegetables first and let them marinade in the lemon juice for at least an hour. Then add the olive oil, basil or oregano, and feta. I do it all the time now. I'm lucky though, I have at least ten lemon trees in my backyard."

"You live in Melbourne and you have lemon trees in your backyard? Nice!"

"Well, most people have lemon trees in their backyard. It's not that uncommon in Australia. But Melbourne, yes, I'm lucky to live there. I love it. Most people don't know it, but Melbourne has the second largest population of Greeks outside of Greece. Actually, it's a true multicultural city. Lots of immigrants besides the loads of Greeks, settled in Melbourne: Turks. Lebanese. Italians. And the nice thing is they each have their own little communities within the city. To say we have the best authentic restaurants in the world is an understatement."

"I didn't know that. I'm intrigued. The only time I was in Australia was when I did a travel piece on the Great Barrier Reef but, unfortunately, I didn't have the time to tour around the rest of the country. I flew to Brisbane and did a whirl-wind trip. Snorkeled my face off and ate enough seafood that I grew gills and had to get them removed when I got back to Canada."

Valentino laughed, holding his mouth. "You nearly made me choke. Gills. You are funny."

"But seriously, the Great Barrier Reef was one of the most favourite adventures of my life. So far anyways. I'm only twenty-six. Going back to Australia is definitely on my bucket list, although I have to admit Melbourne wasn't a city I intended to check out. It sounds like I'll have to add it to my list now."

He chewed on the ceviche, nodding and smiling as she went on and on about the Great Barrier Reef.

Evangeline finally took a breath and asked him, "So what do you do back home?"

Without saying a word, Valentino held his hand to his heart. Then he leaned forward, looked right into her eyes, and in the softest most beautiful tender tenor voice she had ever heard, he began to sing in what she recognized as Italian. When he finished, she sat in silence, a tear rolling down her cheek.

"I have no idea what you just sang to me, but you somehow touched my soul."

"Yes, that's what opera does. It's why I love it so much"

She looked at him, stunned. "That was divinely captivating, Valentino. You're an opera singer? For real? You actually sing opera for a living?"

"Yes, that's what I do." He chuckled. "I know it's not a typical profession. And to be truthful, I don't tell many people."

"I'm honoured that you felt comfortable enough to tell me and even more honoured that you sang to me," she said as she gently touched the back of his hand.

Valentino blushed.

Interesting, Evangeline thought as she watched his face turn pink. He just confessed to being a professional opera singer, which meant that he sang in front of hundreds if not thousands of people all the time. It was in that moment that she sensed a shyness beneath his persona that somehow, she wanted to protect. Why? She didn't quite know. She could see Valentino was not quite sure what to say next, and she herself was still somewhat in shock from his performance. "What's the translation of the song? I recognize some words, since I speak French and the languages are close, but not enough to get the full meaning."

He let out a long breath that he must have been holding on to. "Well, it's from the Italian opera L'elisir d'amore, which translates as The Elixir of Love.

He straightened up in his chair and closed his eyes for a moment as he conjured up the English translation.

"Softly a furtive teardrop fell,
shadowed her sparkling eyes;
Seeing the others follow me
has caused her jealous sighs.

What is there more to prize?
What more than this could I prize?
Sighing, she loves me,
I saw that she loves me.

Could I but feel her heart on mine,
breathing that tender sigh?
Could my own sighing comfort her?
and whisper in sweet reply?
Her heart on mine, as heart to heart we sigh.
So tenderly we'd share a sweet reply!

Heaven, I then could die;
no more I'd ask you, I'd ask you,
ah! heaven, I, then, I then could die;
no more I'd ask you, I'd ask you.
I then could die; I then could die of love.

Evangeline was awestruck as she watched his face light up while he recited the poetic words. She remained silent, transfixed by him. She wondered for a second if her mouth had been hanging open the whole time he was talking.

Finally, after a few seconds of silence, she said "That was so beautiful." She was instantly mad at herself for saying *beautiful*, such a mundane word to describe what she just heard and felt.

"I was in Italy for a small part in an opera and when we finished our run, I came to Greece. It is one of my favourite places, Greece that is. I come whenever I can."

"Well, I'm so glad we met." Evangeline raised her glass of ouzo. "A toast to Greece and to opera!"

"And to our meeting!" he added.

They clinked glasses and their eyes met in a way that made Evangeline feel she could see into Valentino's soul. Somehow a bond had developed, a connection that was so deep it scared her. How in the world could that happen so fast? How could she have let it happen? *Get a hold of yourself. You're heading in a direction that won't be easy to retreat from. Change the subject*! "Tell me all about the opera that the song came from. Who wrote it? What's the story?" she blurted out.

Still a little flushed, Valentino let out a long breath, as if he had been holding on to it for dear life. She could sense his shyness. Was it that he was beginning to have feelings for her like she was for him?

"Well, it was written by Donizetti, an Italian composer, in 1832. It's an aria about heartbreak but with a twist of comedy. Nemorino is in love with Adina who is rich, but she is not interested in him at first because he is poor. He buys a love potion with all the money he has, but the love potion is really just a cheap red wine sold to him by a traveling, quack doctor. She drinks the wine. Nemorino sees Adina weeping and is convinced she has fallen in love with him and that the potion worked, which, of course, it didn't. Many years later, Adina realizes that she really does love Nemorino and is willing to give up everything for him. They eventually marry and she gives up her wealth and privileged lifestyle. But it is short lived, because her parents die and she inherits a fortune and so, by golly, they end up not just rich but also bound by true love." Valentino put his hand over his heart and bowed his head.

"A classic love story. Well, I'm glad it worked out for them in the end!" Evangeline giggled, and then continued. "You know, I've never been to an opera? In fact, I've never even thought of going to an opera."

He smiled at her. "Well, one day I hope I can take you to one."

"I hope so too." And she meant it, although in her heart of hearts she knew it would never happen. My mother wrote in her journal that night:

> *Life back home feels like a world apart from where I am sitting, and I keep having these moments where I am engulfed in a profound sense of sadness. I know once I get home and back to my life that this time with Valentino will just be a wonderful, extraordinary memory that I will relive for years and years.*

The next morning as they walked to the ancient ruins, my mother marveled at the sea of pink, white, and purple flowers in the streets and the lush, green terraced hills covered in olive groves that framed the tiny town of Olympia. She told Valentino of the side trip she took in Crete on a moped up into the hills to watch the farmers harvest the olives. There had been a group of them from the hostel who rented mopeds and decided to meander up into the country hills. The scenery was breathtaking. In the distance they saw the olive groves in terraces that encapsulated the entirety of the hills. The musty smell of goats hit her nostrils before she turned the corner on the switchback and saw hundreds of them. A toothless goat shepherd waved them down. He had the sweetest smile. She asked in sign language if she could take his picture and he indicated, yes, but only if she gave him a cigarette. Luckily, one of the gals in the group had a cigarette. (It was one of my mother's favourite photos—her and the toothless shepherd, both grinning ear to ear, standing in front of a herd of goats with olive groves in the background.)

"I can see the picture in my mind. I also took a trip on a moped up to the olive grove terraces last week, but I never met a toothless shepherd." Valentino smiled. "Maybe we could fit that in this week? A trip up through the groves? Maybe bring a picnic? And we should pick up some cigarettes to bring along, just in case."

"I would love that." Evangeline smiled at him, thinking he was the most interesting, romantic man she had ever spoken to in her entire life.

As they walked to the ruins, they noticed there were a few tourists heading the same way. Among them was a French couple with their little son, who looked maybe five or six. The man was reading aloud from a guide book as they walked. His wife, who didn't seem to be listening, was looking up toward the hills, grinning to beat the band.

Then there was a pair of middle-aged men. With their golf hats, white socks, starch-white runners and Bermuda shorts, and with their cameras hanging from their necks, they looked like they had just got off a tour bus. Their wives walked three steps behind them and were dressed in matching purple-and-pink velour jogging suits and chattering in English with an accent my mother guessed was from southern USA.

"Now, how do you know they're from the south?" Valentino asked.

"Because I heard one gal say, 'he looked lac a wet dawg.' And nobody says 'lac a wet dawg,' except people in the southern USA."

Valentino smiled as she imitated their southern drawl. "Never been to the USA, but it sounds like they have their own way of talking, just like Australians. In some parts of Australia, you need a translation book just to figure out what in the world people are talking about."

"Yes, I remember that. But you don't seem to use so many slang words like *bloody, fair dinkum, and randy,* although I do hear a hint of another accent on top of your Aussie one. Is it Italian?"

Valentino laughed and slapped his leg. "Randy? Who was saying that to you? No, don't tell me. I'm sure you figured out what that one meant."

"Yes, I did! I'll save that story though, for another time over a beer."

"I'll remind you!"

"So back to my observation . . . Your accent. It's not Greek, although when you speak Greek, it sounds perfect to me. Italian then? Anyway, I don't have to try and figure out what in the world you are saying."

"Well, that's because my mother is a linguistics professor and speaks over sixteen languages fluently. I wasn't allowed to use slang. Only proper English or Italian was allowed in our house. Even my father, who was from Italy and had a doctorate in mathematics from one of the most prestigious universities in Europe, is continuously corrected by my mother. She is brutally proper when it comes to language. And the Italian accent probably comes from my father. He spoke only Italian to me from the moment I was born. And I learned Greek because I am in love with Greece."

"Do you sing opera in any other language than Italian?

"Yes, Greek, French, and German, but my conversational German is terrible and my French, I can get by. Much to my mother's dismay, I don't have her gift for picking up languages easily."

Valentino stopped at the entrance of the temple dedicated to Hera. My mother noted the look of reverence in his eyes. Pointing at a statue at the right of the column's entrance, he said, "This sculpture is of Hermes, the son of Zeus and Maia. The infant he's holding is his half-brother. The statue was created by the renowned master sculptor Praxiteles in 340 BC."

"Why is he holding his half-brother?" Evangeline asked.

"That's Dionysus. He was the son of Zeus and a mortal woman named Semele. Hera, whose temple we now stand in, was Zeus's wife and she was jealous of his affair. So, when Semele was pregnant, Zeus implanted the fetus into his thigh, and Dionysus was actually born of Zeus's thigh. When he was born, he called on his son Hermes to take his infant brother and hide him from Hera. The story goes that he took the child to a kind couple to raise. They raised him as a girl to try and trick Hera from finding him."

"Interesting. So, Hermes was the son of Zeus?" She peered at the marble statue, marveling at the expression in Hermes' eyes as he gazed at his half-brother.

"Yes. He was one of the cleverest and most mischievous of the Olympian gods. He was the patron of shepherds, and protector of travelers, thieves, and merchants. He was called upon as a messenger because he was a very fast runner."

"You said we were entering the temple of Hera? Tell me more about her."

"I've always had a soft spot for Hera. She was the true wife of Zeus, and she was the goddess of women, marriage, family, and childbirth. Due to her status, she was highly revered by women, who saw her as their patron and protector. She possessed the powers of the Olympian gods, which include super-human strength, immortality, eternal youth, and the ability to bless and curse. Zeus was not the most loyal of husbands. He slept around, and he even liked to turn himself into a mortal and fornicate with them. Hence, fathering many children—Dionysus being one of them. She had to put up with a lot being married to Zeus. She would do anything to protect her family. She had good intentions, even though she didn't always act in the best way."

"I read a book on archetypes," Evangeline said. "I thought I read Hera was a queen—Queen of Heaven, is that right?"

"Yes, she was, and also the Queen of the Olympians. So, the queen archetype signifies the power of women who rule over anything from the office to the home environment. But she is also the companion archetype too."

"Companion to Zeus. Ahhhh. The wife. Of course. She is loyal, tenacious, and unselfish to her husband. The typical wife role of providing emotional and practical support so her partner can concentrate on his mission in life. That is, despite his disloyalty," Evangeline said, nodding her head.

Valentino walked slowly around the large Doric columns of the entrance to the temple ruins, and she followed him.

He continued talking, "Yes, and of course the negative part of the whole arrangement is that she has a loss of identity and suppresses her own needs."

"So, she has these enormous powers but is still bound by this loyalty to family and marriage. It overrides it," my mother said.

"Exactly, so she sometimes uses her powers in an indirect way to get back at Zeus. I think in psychology they would call it passive-aggressive behaviour."

"This is fascinating. As a travel writer, I miss a lot of this stuff. I'm hired to write about the cost and basic descriptions of accommodations, food, and tours. Seldom in an article can I get into the real history or depth of a place. Short, sweet, and to the point. So, thank you Valentino, this is a real treat."

"I'm glad. I hope I don't sound too much like a teacher. I just eat all this up. I love history and Greek mythology in particular."

"Are you kidding? I'm loving every minute. Teach away." She couldn't help but notice how his face lit up as he talked. He held her gaze as he explained how the eastern side of the temple at the altar of Hera was where the Olympic flame had been lit since 1936, using a parabolic mirror to concentrate the rays of the sun. She was not one to be interested much in sports, but she was beginning to see the importance of how sport, since ancient times, brought people together.

As they walked amongst the ruins, Valentino continued telling her stories of ancient Greece, the lives of the gods and goddesses, and the rise and fall of the Olympic Games.

"In 776 BC, in honour of Zeus, athletes were massaged with olive oil so the power and strength of Athena would be bestowed upon them. The winners were awarded olive leaf crowns and olive oil. But it wasn't just athletes who benefited. It was also believed that if you polished a statue of Zeus with olive oil, Zeus would be so honoured that he would grant you a long and happy life. The olive wreath, also known as kotinos, was the actual prize for the winner at the Olympic Games."

"I see. So, in ancient times a simple crown of olive branches was the prize?"

"Yes, the branches were from the sacred wild-olive tree near the temple of Zeus and were cut with a pair of golden scissors. They were assembled on a gold-ivory table at the temple of Hera. The judges made the wreaths, then crowned the winners of the games."

My mother wrote in her journal that after a while she found it hard to concentrate on what he was saying because she became mesmerized by his eyes. It was a strange feeling, not one she had ever experienced before.

It was like there was an invisible cord connecting us at a soul level.

Later, heading back to their pension, my mom felt an unexpected and profound sense of optimism. She stopped and put her hand on Valentino's arm.

"The Olympics is probably the only event when people from every corner of the world, with different views and beliefs, come together peacefully."

"I agree. In peace and war, the Olympics have assembled people together to celebrate. It is amazing that for a tiny fraction of time, human beings can be bound together with no ethnicity or borders and in peace. It is quite astonishing. If only we could figure out how to do it, not just every four years, but forever."

"Exactly, if it is possible for days why not longer? Maybe one day. Although I doubt it will ever happen."

"Well, perhaps on a smaller scale we can try and have peace within our own lives, our families, and maybe even within our communities. For starters anyway."

"It reminds me of a saying from Gandhi: You must be the change you wish to see in the world. So don't preach peace, do peace. Or something like that." She laughed.

"Yes, do peace, I like that!"

They reached their pension near sundown. The hum of cicadas had finally ceased, and the gentle sound of the wind took their place.

"What's on the agenda for tea, I mean dinner, right? That is what you call it?" Valentino asked.

"Yes, dinner or supper. Let's see . . . Tonight, I want roast chicken, Greek salad again, roasted potatoes with rosemary, and maybe some dolmades."

"Oh, all my favourites! I know the perfect place."

"I thought you might!" she said as they walked up the marble stairs to the third floor where their rooms were, their footsteps echoing in the stairwell. "Want to use the shower before changing for dinner?"

"That would be great. I'll grab my things and be over in ten minutes. Give you a chance to have yours first."

She showered and dried her hair, then twisted her long locks using her signature pencil, putting it up in a messy bun. She put on a flowery long skirt and a blue tank top and changed her earrings to the new silver and turquoise ones she'd bought in Athens. She only ever used mascara and eyeliner if she was going out, and when she was on holidays, she seldom wore even that, but this particular evening she decided to put some on. She wondered why she was doing it. She was not trying to impress him, she told herself out loud as she looked in the mirror. But she knew she really was. *God, what are you getting yourself into?*

As Valentino showered, Mom sat at the little desk in her room and wrote in her daily journal, sipping a glass of Peloponnese Moschofilero that they had picked up earlier. Valentino said it was the best wine in the region. She delighted in its spicy, bold flavour as she listened to Valentino singing softly in his delicate tenor voice. Inspired, she wrote:

> *It was like he had an intimate relationship with the gods and goddesses and had lived in ancient times. I was mesmerized and couldn't help soaking in every word that sprang from his lips.*

She looked over to the bathroom door. She wanted to pinch herself. Was there really a handsome opera singer/geek historian in her shower right now? Her body tingled. She poured another glass of wine and continued to write in her journal.

I can't believe I just wrote that. I am lying to myself. I'm afraid to admit that I am hypnotized by him, not just his words but his essence. I am feeling something I have never felt with anyone before. I feel like I have no control. My body is on fire just thinking about him standing in the shower. The slightest touch from him sends electricity to every cell in my body.

By the time they got to the packed restaurant at the edge of town, they had finished the bottle of wine and were feeling a little giddy. The food was delicious. There was a live band made up of local musicians playing traditional Greek music. As soon as the music started, the locals were up dancing, arms over each other's shoulders, laughing as they shuffled and dragged the traditional Sirtos dance. The entire place was like a big party—people laughing and visiting, dancing, toasting each other with glasses of Retsina. It was infectious. They watched for a while, then Valentino stood up and held out his hand.

"When in Greece, do as the Greeks do?"

She stood up immediately, taking his hand, staring into his green eyes.

They joined the chain of dancers. Before the night was through, they'd been invited to go fishing and even attend a wedding. As they walked back to their pension, they couldn't stop laughing as they reminisced about the evening.

"I had so much fun tonight. I don't know how to thank you," she said as they stood in the hall near the door to her room.

"Thank me? No, I have to thank you. I've been coming to Greece for years, and I have had more fun with you in these last few days than I've had in all the years put together. And it happens that today was my birthday." He leaned against the wall and looked at her with a look of contentment. "And I must say that it was by far the best birthday I've ever had in all my twenty-nine years."

She punched him lightly in the arm. "Your birthday! Why didn't you say something? We could have gotten some free cake I bet."

"Free cake?"

"Yeah."

"It always comes back to food with you, doesn't it?" He laughed.

My mother noticed his eyes when he laughed. His eyebrows raised up and his eyes, which were normally narrow and turned up, grew more round. They were, she decided, the most beautiful, laughing eyes she had ever seen.

"Yes, the food. Always the food . . ." She shuffled, unsure what to do next. She wanted to kiss him in the worst possible way, but she knew she must resist the urge.

Finally, he broke the silence and asked her, "Do you mind that I call you Evangeline and not Angie?"

"I don't mind at all." The fact was, she loved it. When he pronounced Evangeline with his Aussie/Italian accent her heart melted. He somehow made it sound exotic.

"In the Greek language, Evangeline means bearer of good news. And well, since I met you, I feel like a new person. It's like some higher power sent you to me. Oh, God, too deep, too soon?"

Evangeline looked at him. They were headed to a place she was sure she shouldn't go. She grabbed the door handle. "Yes, you are deep. But in a good way. Sleep well, birthday boy."

When she closed the door behind her, her head was spinning, and her legs were weak. She leaned against the door to steady herself: *Calm down, girl, calm down*. As she brushed her teeth, she saw his T-shirt, reflecting in the bathroom mirror. It was slung over the back of the chair. He had left it there when he came to shower. She crawled into bed, clutched the T-shirt, and buried her face in it. His scent was intoxicating, the earthy scent of cedar and lemon. She curled up on her side, his T-shirt under her cheek, and breathing in his scent, she fell asleep.

She woke to a knock on the door.

"You up yet? I've got fresh cappuccino and bougatsa."

"Coming."

She opened the door to find Valentino smiling mischievously. She liked that he hadn't shaved yet. He wore a brown T-shirt under a light brown corduroy jacket, and he was wearing his fancy, Italian shoes that he had cleaned up. *God, he looks good.*

"I couldn't sleep. My window was open, so I could smell the bakery across the street, and all I could think about was getting a fresh bougatsa. The custard inside is to die for. Or is it too early for breakfast?"

"Oh, it is early but, oh, my God, that smells so good. You are forgiven. Come in."

Valentino set the coffee and pastry down on the balcony's wrought-iron bistro table. The morning was hot and very humid, and so he took off his jacket. He turned and looked at Evangeline as she put on a light sweater over her pajamas. She caught his eye and saw that he was looking at the bed. His T-shirt was still crumpled up on her pillow. Her heart stopped. The expression on his face was like a theatre into his soul. He knew.

When she sat down, their eyes met. He leaned forward. "May I kiss you?"

My mother described in her journal that the moment their lips touched she knew there was no turning back. She closed her eyes and felt his breath and let his lips touch hers so gently that if an outsider would have seen it, they would have mistaken it as an inconsequential kiss, but for my mother it was anything but. Electricity coursed through every inch of her body.

"God, you smell good" she said, astonished that she had actually said it aloud.

They ate breakfast in silence and just stared at each other. When the last sip of coffee was finished, he got up and gently took her hand in his. She stood up, her eyes locked into his. He placed his hands on either side of her face. Her legs felt limp.

Oh, God, this can't be happening. This shouldn't be happening. But it was, and there was nothing she could do to stop it. There was a magnetic force pulling them together.

As they began to make love, without warning the sky turned dark, and it started to pour. The winds came with such force that it blew their cups and saucers and plates off the table, crashing them into pieces on the floor of the balcony. They could hear the thunder and feel the rain and wind whipping through the balcony doors, dampening the sheets and their bodies, but there was no way to stop their lovemaking. Only hours later when they saw puddles of water on the floor amongst the broken dishes and noticed the power was out, did they realize the ferociousness of the storm that had swept through the town.

They spent the rest of the day and next morning in their hotel room.

"We need to eat so we can keep up our energy," she said as she looked at him with dreamy eyes. Their naked bodies were intertwined, his scent blended with hers was comforting.

"I have an idea. How about we get out of here and spend at least one day touring the coastline of the Cote d'Azur of the Peloponnese?"

"Great idea. You get up first."

"No, you. I am too comfy." They both laughed as they tousled in bed.

They bundled up in their warmest clothes and hired a private water taxi to take them along the coastline. They sat in the boat, snuggled up together under a blanket, sipping on the hot chocolate the driver gave them. The sun was bright, the air was cool, and there was not a cloud in the sky. The coastline was spectacular. There were quaint villages dotting the shoreline, small coves with pine trees, their reflection dancing on the shimmering water. They were hypnotized by the beauty, their cheeks sore from the permanent smiles on their faces. That evening, my mother wrote that she was deliriously happy and in love and no matter how hard she tried to deny it, she knew in her heart that it was much more than just a fling.

They never went to the wedding, the fishing trip, or to the hills on mopeds. They stocked up on all their favourite food and the last day together they stayed in the hotel room, eating, drinking wine, making love, and talking. Before the night was through there was almost nothing, they didn't know about each other: favourite foods, places they'd seen, and their hopes and dreams. He told her about how his stutter was both a gift and a curse. A gift because it led him to sing opera, which he loved, and a curse because it contributed to his shyness. She told him about being an outsider in her own family and in her little farming community. How she thought she was accidently incarnated into the wrong family, and definitely into the wrong place. They learned every inch of each other's bodies and confessed to the fear that comes with the pure madness that being in love brings.

There was only one thing that my mother kept from him. She just couldn't bring herself to go there and ruin the blissfulness. She had never felt such a connection to a human being in her life and she knew deep down, she would never experience it ever again.

The last morning together, they lay spooned in bed, a gentle breeze caressing their skin as the morning sun shone through the window and highlighted the curves of their hips and shoulders. They could hear the roosters crowing. They could smell the bakery across the street. Valentino had to leave. Their time together was over, and the serenity my mother felt in the moment was clouded by a sadness so profound it made her heart ache.

"Evangeline, I want to ask you something."

She knew what he was going to ask, and she knew she wanted the same thing.

"I don't want this to end. I've thought about it all night. I want to go to Athens and change my ticket, and then come back. It'll take a day. You have another week left. I can get the time off. I . . . I think . . . No, I know for sure, I have fallen in love for the first time in my life. But I'm not stupid. There is falling in love, which is this madness that we are experiencing right now, and then there is true love that comes from the aftermath. The love that is left over after the madness has subsided. I want to know if what we have is true love."

She hesitated. The pause was thick. Her heart pounded.

Without looking at him, she said, "I know that I've fallen in love with you too. I have never in my entire life felt more connected to someone. It feels like we were destined to be together. But a part of me says it's a romantic fling, the madness, as you call it, but of the most incredible kind. But I don't know for sure."

"One more week together. That's all I am asking. To see if it's the real thing."

Evangeline turned in bed, meeting his eyes, and then slid her leg over his body. How perfectly their bodies fit together! And he had the most beautiful, clear, loving, kind eyes. She searched for any indication at all that what they were feeling was mere infatuation. But the only thing she saw was a pure loving being looking into her soul. She felt, in that moment, that somehow, she must let go of the life she had planned and embrace the one that the universe had orchestrated for her.

"Yes, I will wait for you. One more week."

CHAPTER EIGHT
VALENTINO

1980

Valentino's recounting of the event that led to the greatest disappointment in his life was not told to me by Valentino himself. I found the passages in one of his journals after his death. I believe that his writing down of the conversation, word for word, was a way to convince himself of exactly what transpired so he could make sense of it all.

"Mother, can you hear me?" Valentino said into the telephone.

"Yes, dear, is everything all right? How was your birthday?"

"Yes, everything is fine. Had the best birthday ever. I met a woman."

"You met a woman? Oh, my Questo é Magnifico! Valentino!"

"I'm staying another week. I just wanted to let you know I changed my ticket, same flight, only a week later. Thankfully, I still had some traveller's cheques, so I should be okay with cash."

"See, I told you to always carry extra. You never know, Valentino."

"I have lots more, but they're from the company for work, and this is definitely not work," he said, almost giggling.

"You sound so happy. What's her name?"

"Evangeline. She's from Canada."

"Beautiful name. Well, I hope you and Evangeline from Canada have a wonderful week together."

"I will. Say 'Hi' to Papa for me, and tell him my trip to his favourite places was wonderful."

"I will tell him. Arrivederci amore mio."

Valentino cashed his traveller's cheques and was about to go back to the train station when he decided it would be faster to get a limousine to take him back to Olympia. It cost way more money and was not in his budget, but he wanted so badly to get back as quickly as possible—back to Evangeline. The limo driver drove fast, and Valentino was pleased; that is, until they narrowly missed getting into an accident on one of the harrowing turns through the mountains. Valentino finally politely told the limo driver to slow down. He wanted to get there quickly but in one piece.

On the journey, Valentino convinced himself that it was definitely the real thing. How could two people be so perfectly compatible in every single way possible?

He got out his notebook and began to write down all the reasons why he knew he and Evangeline were truly in love, underlining key words.

1: For the first time in my life, I feel comfortable with who I am. When I first met her, it was as if all the different aspects of myself suddenly and miraculously were unified. Carl Jung calls it 'living an authentic life.' Yes, <u>authentic,</u> *that is the word.*

2: Mentally, we are perfectly <u>compatible</u>. *We are both intellectuals. We both have insatiable appetites for knowledge. I see a clear picture of the two of us being really old, sitting in our easy-boy chairs, drinking tea, holding hands, and chatting away about our travels, history, art, literature.*

3: She loves to walk, and we walk at the same pace. Even when we hold hands we are <u>in sync</u>.

4: She smells right. *I could smell her all day long. I read just recently that none of the other senses have a more direct and intimate connection to the area of the brain that processes emotion than the sense of smell.*

5: On a soul level, I feel a deep connection. When we look into each other's eyes, I feel like I transcend time and space. There is a knowing that we have about each other that is not in this physical realm—we are soul-mates.

He wrote down 6: and then stopped. Valentino didn't need another reason, nor even a week to see if his love for her was real. He shut his notebook and looked up and sighed, a big grin on his face. He knew he was completely and utterly in love with Evangeline and that she was the one he had been waiting for his whole life—there was no one else who could ever come close to being the perfect mate for him.

By the time Valentino reached Olympia and his feet hit the dusty ground, he knew deep within his soul that he loved Evangeline and that he needed to be with her for the rest of his life. He wondered how he could propose. Where could he buy the perfect ring?

It was late afternoon when Valentino arrived at the pension. He ran up the stairs, taking two steps at a time. He entered the room they had shared the last few days they were together. His heart was racing with excitement as he opened the door.

Evangeline was not there. He glanced around the room. Her things were gone. Valentino picked up the note that lay on the bed, his hands trembling as he began to read. He fell onto the bed and rolled into a ball, clutching the note to his heart, and he began to sob.

CHAPTER NINE
SUNNYDALE FORENSIC HOSPITAL

My half-sister Brittany picked up my mother and Valentino's diaries from their empty house and brought them to Sunnydale for me to read. I knew they had both kept journals. My mother had heaps of them in her closet full of detailed descriptions of her feelings, hopes, and dreams. She was a good writer and even at a young age, her vocabulary was exceptional. In her early years, she always started with Dear Diary. It was the sweetest thing. Later on, she would have a date and place, and then furiously write what was on her mind. She never wavered from her writing, only missing an occasional day. Valentino had only a handful of journals. His earlier entries were more about describing places he had been and not much on what he was feeling. But once he met my mom, it all changed, and his entries were all about what he was feeling.

I have to commend my mother for writing so religiously since she was a small girl. Through reading them, I discovered that it was Mémé who encouraged her to keep a diary. Mémé started writing in scribblers when she was a teenager. "My diary," she told me, "Was my outlet. It helped me get through the rough times." It was through my mother's journals that I discovered so much about who she was and why she made the choices she did in her life.

Ironically, as I read *my* mother's journals, I came across a passage about *my* mother reading *her* mother's diary.

My mother wrote:

May, 12, 1970

Today, I found a large stack of my mother's scribblers in the attic. Thinking they were just full of school notes, I didn't pick them up right away. They were tied neatly with a purple ribbon, and I thought it was odd that she would have a ribbon tied around school notes. I unwrapped the ribbon and discovered they were diaries. They were in chronological order starting when she was fifteen. I feel bad now for reading some of them. I was looking for old photos for a school project on family history. Mom was in town getting groceries, and I was alone in the house. I knew there was a trunk up in the attic with old photos because John and I would look for treasures up there sometimes. It was easy to get to, just a set of stairs my father built in the back storage room upstairs that led easily to the attic. I found lots of old photos in the trunk and was putting them in a bag when I eyed a pack of scribblers. I wasn't trying to snoop; it was simply out of curiosity that I opened them. I recognized my mother's handwriting. I was up there in the attic for over two hours, till I heard her drive up. I didn't want to stop reading. I learned that she had planned to go to university and become a teacher, but one night of sex with my dad, who she had dated for only a month, changed her life forever. I cried my eyes out as I read what she wrote. "He told me everyone was doing it and he just had to pull out in time, and I would never get pregnant. I hated myself for agreeing. I hated it and never wanted to do it again." Later, she wrote how she broke up with him right after they had sex, only to find out six months later she was pregnant. It breaks my heart to realize that my parents were forced to get married to save face.

I feel a little guilty for reading it, but really, I am glad that I did. It made so much sense. My parents don't seem to be that happy together, and I now understand why mom is always on my case about not dating till I'm eighteen, about getting good grades, and always telling me to stand up for myself.

The revelation that day helped my mother cement the notion that she did not want to end up like her mother. She wanted an education and a career and maybe one child down the road. Out of respect, though, mom wrote that she never let on to her mother that she had read her diaries.

It makes me wonder what my mother would think of me right now if she were alive, reading about her innermost thoughts. I picture her smiling down on me. I like to think she would be pleased.

I keep the journals in a small box under the cot in my room and read them most every night. The one thing I've realized as I read them, is that no one ever really knows anyone. We make up stories in our head about who people are, their motives, what they like or dislike, what they think, why they do the things they do. We judge the shit out of people based on a bunch of made-up stories that often have no basis in reality. If you think about it, we can't really know someone unless we are in their head. I see the journals as a small window into getting to know the real Evangeline and Valentino. I feel privileged and at the same time, I feel I am learning about myself too. I'm questioning my beliefs, values, and morals, as well as asking myself about the stories I've made up about myself over the years. I'm changing as I read their journals and as I write. I'm becoming a better person, more kind and accepting, and the anger that consumed me when I first came to Sunnydale has diminished significantly. I'm beginning to see what Mrs. Brown was alluding to and how she was right about how effective this writing exercise is for my healing.

CHAPTER TEN

EVANGELINE - SALT SPRING ISLAND

1984

There was always a sadness that seemed to hang over my mother. Like a cloud; it would come and go. I never understood it when I was young, and it made me angry. I was always wondering what I did or what Dad did to make her so unhappy. Not knowing, of course, that we had nothing to do with it.

In 1984, my mother described in her journal how the previous four years had been the hardest years of her life. How Mount Maxwell became her refuge. It was her go-to place when she needed to quiet her mind from the guilt and sadness that consumed her. She had tried over the years to forgive herself. She had tried professional counseling, meditation, and numerous workshops. She had read every book on forgiveness, but if there was ever any relief, it was short-lived.

When she was feeling the after-glow of a workshop or a counseling session she would list all the things she was grateful for, just as she had been instructed to do. And it helped for a while.

- I am a mom to the sweetest little girl in the entire world

- I love both my jobs: my part-time job as a travel writer allows me to crisscross the globe, which I love. My editing job is rewarding, and it pays well and gives me so much flexibility.

- I live in one of the most beautiful and interesting places in the world. A place where celebrities, musicians, artists, farmers, hippies, and monks live in harmony, and sheep still outnumber the people.

- I have an abundance of good friends.

- My parents, well, my mom and my brothers, have been supportive of me my whole life, even though my lifestyle is so far removed from what they deem as normal.

- I have a beautiful home that I own.

- I am healthy.

But being grateful was never enough. There was nothing that would erase the guilt she felt deep inside. It lingered there like a wound that could never heal.

Mount Maxwell was the only place where she felt a real sense of peace, even if it was temporary. It was a place where nature overrode her anguish, where the cloak of sadness fell off and disappeared. Normally, it was a hike she did alone or with her daughter, but it was Karl's turn to pick the Sunday 'family day activity,' and he chose Mount Maxwell, which she found strange. She knew he preferred other hikes and activities over Mount Maxwell. He usually chose the coastline, swimming or fishing in the summer, or crawling along rocky shores and finding treasures in the tidal pools. He always said the coastline was his love; it was in his bones.

As they walked up the mountain, she watched his muscular legs climbing effortlessly, even with a four-year-old on his back. Her mind drifted off to when she first met Karl. It was on a ferry boat. He was island hopping, and she was going to work on Pender Island at the publishing house for a few weeks while her bosses were away on holiday. With his thick Danish accent, baby-blue eyes, blonde hair, and muscular body, he looked like a Greek god in jeans. He was traveling alone, so she offered to show him around Pender Island, then Salt Spring Island. Before the month was through, she had shown him all the Gulf Islands. They slept on beaches, camped on the water's edge, hiked the bluffs of Hornby Island, and swam in the ocean. They hung out at bookstores, art galleries, and coffee shops, went dancing at Fulford Hall, and hit every folk music venue they could find. They were inseparable. A few days before his visa expired three months from when they first met, they married in her backyard on Salt Spring Island.

Evangeline's favourite brother John, six years older than she, accompanied their mother Lillian on the trip to the west coast for the wedding. Lillian had never been on a plane before but she was determined to come and meet Karl and check him out—and if need be—talk some sense into her daughter's rushed marriage. When she met Karl, she interrogated him, much to the dismay of my mother. She then took her daughter aside and told her that she was making a huge mistake.

"Evangeline, what are you doing? You need to slow down. Please don't marry Karl. You hardly know each other." The disappointment showed through the deep creases in her mother's frown.

"Look Mom, I think I'm old enough to make a decision on who I should marry and when I should marry. I love him."

"But why not just live together, try it out? Nowadays people do it all the time."

"I want to marry him. Can't you just be happy for me? You're here to celebrate with us. I didn't invite you so you can give me permission to marry. I don't want to have this conversation, Mom. Let's just let it go and agree to disagree. You'll see that you're wrong about him and his motives."

But Mémé couldn't let it go. It was hardly the celebration my mother was hoping for: having her mother crying through the entire ceremony—and not tears of joy. By the time Mémé left, they were barely speaking.

Karl's intrigue for island life was what led him to end up on the ferry boat where he met Evangeline. He had grown up on a tiny island in Denmark, which he described as beautiful but way too small for him to live on, so he left, determined to explore islands all over Europe until he found the right one to live on. One day, he met a Canadian couple on a ferry boat in Denmark. He told them about his quest.

"Well, if you ever come to Canada, you must check out the Gulf Islands that lay between the mainland of British Columbia and Vancouver Island.

They are like a taste of the Mediterranean but with a unique Canadian flavour." The woman said.

"But cold and snow, I'm not interested in." He laughed.

"Oh no, the winters are mild, rarely is there ever snow.

They went on to describe the five islands as stunningly beautiful and full of independent thinking residents. My dad told me the story growing up, about how he was fascinated by the stories the travelers told him and how as soon as he got his journeyman carpenter papers, he took his savings and headed to Canada to check them out. He loved Denmark, but he was looking for more free thinking, less conservative people to live amongst than the Danes, who were, in his eyes, set in their ways with rules upon rules. Life on the Gulf Islands sounded like it fit with the type of lifestyle he was searching for to settle-down in and raise a family.

Karl fell in love with Evangeline the moment he met her—at least that is what he always told Evangeline. But as she walked up the mountain, she began to wonder if it was true. He loved Canada and all the islands on the West Coast. He loved exploring and discovering new places, hidden ones that the tourists never went to but now she found herself questioning if he was ever in love with her. Did he marry her just to stay in Canada? Evangeline's family and friends alluded to it when they first got engaged, but she never wanted to believe it. Lately though, the thought crossed her mind more often than not. As she meandered up Mount Maxwell, she thought back to a conversation she had with her friend Darlene when she told her she was engaged.

"Evangeline, why not wait? Karl is your first real serious boyfriend. As long as I have known you, you've had no desire to even date. I have tried to set you up, but you always refuse. You say that a boyfriend, let alone a husband or children, will squash your plans and ruin your career. Now, you tell me you are getting married to a guy you only just met?"

"I know, I know, it sounds like a giant leap but I really do love him, and we have a lot of fun. And he knows my lifestyle and is okay with it. I have a good steady job as an editor for a small but growing publishing company. I have over twenty travel writing assignments a year for newspapers and magazines across Western Canada, the southern USA, and even some in Europe and Australia. I own a sweet, little cottage in one of the most beautiful places on earth. I have loads of friends and an amazing social life with like-minded people. I've been living my dream life. I'm ready for romance, marriage, and maybe even a family. I guess I didn't realize it till I met Karl."

"It sounds like you rehearsed this speech." She laughed a little. "Been having to explain yourself lately? Your mother perhaps?"

"Hit the nail on the head. You know me well."

"Angie, you're a big girl. I apologize for not thinking that you thought this through. It isn't that I don't like Karl, I really do, and I think he is a good, kind man. It is just that, well it's fast, is all."

"I know it's fast. But his visa is going to run out, and we don't want a long-distance romance."

Darlene gave her a hug. "I'm sure it'll all work out. I'm sorry I said anything."

When she told her mother she was engaged, she hoped she would be happy for her. But it wasn't to be. Her mother's words echoed in her head right up until she recited her vows. "You are rushing as usual. Slow down! Live together first. It's not like when I was young. It was frowned upon to live with a man before marriage. But your generation does it all the time, and I think in this case, it would be wise."

Karl wasn't able to get an extension on his visa, an antidote she never revealed to her mother, knowing that the information would be fuel for her argument.

As time went on, there were some nagging questions in the back of my mother's mind: Was he really the one for her? Did he really love her? Or did she really love him? But once they were married for a few months, she wrote in her journal that those questions faded away. They got along, and Karl was supportive of her career right from the get go. The only question that still lingered—having heard the stories of his idyllic childhood in Denmark—was why on earth he had decided to put his roots down in Canada? Could it be that he was running away from something? But even that was put to rest after they went to visit his folks.

As Evangeline walked up Mount Maxwell, following Karl, she reminisced about her trip to meet his parents. They arrived via an electric ferry from mainland Denmark to Aero Island. It was one of the quaintest, most picturesque places she had ever seen, with its brightly-coloured houses and narrow, cobbled streets and beautiful bike trails that meandered along the coast. She fell instantly in love with it and felt an immediate urge to pitch an article to her editor at the travel magazine. She could see the tagline in her mind: *The island where at midnight at low tides, you can almost hear crabs playing checkers*, or something to that effect.

His adoptive parents lived in an eighteenth-century house and were friendly, lovely people who welcomed her with open arms. They never came to their wedding in Canada even though they were invited because, they explained, they didn't think flying in an airplane was good for a person or the environment. And she got it. They were the real deal. True environmentalists who walked the talk, and she respected that about them. But, by the end of the week, she could see the pain in Karl's face every time they opened their mouths to speak.

Karl and Evangeline rode bicycles all over the small island. After one week they had pretty much done everything and seen everything there was to see, according to Karl. The visit with his parents was "killing him," he said.

"The most exciting things my parents talk about are: the latest books they read, what to eat for supper, the mayor who got drunk at the bar yet again, and their favourite subject—their annoyance at the council for promoting their island as a wedding destination, which they are convinced will completely ruin its charm. I can't take it anymore, Angie. They drive me crazy," he whispered to her in their bedroom.

So, she wasn't at all surprised when he woke her up on the morning of the eighth day and handed her an Aero Island T-Shirt and said, "Got the T-shirt to prove you've been here. Let's go. I must have been crazy thinking I could stay here for two weeks."

She understood that he had outgrown the tiny island—and his parents. She knew the feeling well. The last time she had gone to Saskatchewan for a family reunion, it had nearly killed her too. As much as she loved her brothers and all her nieces and nephews, as well as getting to spend time with her mother, in a short amount of time, the small-town gossip nearly did her in. It seemed that all the conversations started with: "Did you hear the latest about . . ." or "Did you hear what so and so did?" Gossip was something she could never get used to and wondered each time she went home, if whatever she said or did or didn't do, would be used for the latest rumour thread. She did love lots of things about going home though, and she often felt homesick when she would arrive back in Salt Spring. But as soon as she was in Paris, she felt out of place; like she didn't belong or fit in, even with her family she felt like the black sheep. Salt Spring Island, although small, had a different vibe. There were so many implants from other places, lots of artists and musicians and writers and poets, that she only ever felt inspired and delighted by the conversations she had with people. So, when Karl said he was ready to leave Aero Island, even though she was dying to try out some of the restaurants, she said she understood completely. She discovered in that moment that disappointment always comes from having expectations.

I was asleep in the child carrier, strapped to my dad's back, as they approached Mount Maxwell summit. Suddenly, Dad stopped and turned around and looked at my mother.

"Angie, we've been hiking for over an hour, and you've not spoken a word. I've tried to start conversations, and I get no response. Nothing. I'm done. I can't take it anymore."

My mother looked at him, stunned. "What? What did you say? Sorry, I was daydreaming I guess."

"We need to talk. I can't do this anymore. I've had enough. I want a divorce."

She could see he was angry; his face had red blotches, and he was clutching his fists as he spoke. "Divorce? What on God's green earth are you talking about?"

"You are too hard to love. I can't do it anymore. I have tried, God only knows. But I'm done." The bitterness in his voice was not lost to her.

"You're done? What are you talking about? What did I do that's so wrong that you want a divorce?" Her heart pounded and her hands grew sweaty as she struggled to make sense of what he just said.

"You're not the same woman I married. I mean, you're depressed or something. You don't talk to me. You're not present when you're with me. And I can't reach you. I haven't been able to reach you since you got pregnant over four years ago. It's like your mind is always somewhere else. You've built some kind of wall around you, and I can't get through it. You're a great mom, I give you that, but you're a crappy wife, Angie. I don't know how else to put it. I can't do it anymore." He drew in a deep breath. "I found a place in Victoria. I'm moving out next week. I got offered a job with a construction company in Victoria, and I accepted it."

"You accepted it? Victoria? You're moving to Victoria? You're leaving Salt Spring?" She noticed her voice rising. "But what about our daughter? You can't just up and leave her too!"

"I loved Salt Spring when I first moved here, but now I feel so damn alone and stifled, like back home on Aero Island. I need the city. I need a life. I want to go to the movies whenever I want, go to pubs and listen to music, go to festivals, golf, not take ferries and stay at hotels every time I want to do something fun. There is just so much more to do there. And besides, everyone on this island is so . . . klikkende, what's the word in English, cliquey? It's too much like home. I can't stand it. And I'm sick of begging for construction work. I'm a journeyman carpenter, and I'm good, but all they want to give me are grunt jobs. If you're not 'from here,' they don't want to hire you. The local tradespeople are a different breed than your artsy fartsy crowd. They've lived here all their lives on the island, and they see me as a foreigner. I'll never be able to make a good living here. I'm just done on so many levels," he said as he raised both arms in the air. His eyes had softened, replaced by a look of sadness.

She watched dumbfounded as he rattled on about how unhappy he was with his whole life. "Karl, honey, I get it, you don't like it here, and the jobs have sucked. But divorce? That's a pretty drastic move. Shouldn't we discuss it? Maybe all of us can move to Victoria?"

"Discuss? Now you want to discuss? You don't discuss anything. You don't talk to me. You're in your own little, sad world. Don't you get it? Look, we haven't been good for so many years. I'm just so sick of trying to love you. I'm so fucking tired. I have stayed because of our daughter, but I feel like I'm dying inside. I feel unloved and unwanted. It is like you, you . . . Oh, forget it. What's the use? You'll never change. I've come to that realization. You can't change. You don't know how to love."

There was a dense silence as they both turned and looked over the summit. Then, without a word, Karl turned around and began to walk down the path, me sleeping in the carrier oblivious to the discussion that would change my life forever.

My mother wrote in her journal that evening that as she stood on the top of Mount Maxwell, she looked at the blue sky and saw an eagle dip its wing toward her and circle above her head several times. *"It was as if the eagle was giving me a sign that everything was going to work out."* She breathed the salt air deep into her lungs, and then let out a long breath. *You don't know how to love*—his words stung. She felt the tears welling up, but they refused to fall. She looked up at the eagle. She was surprised at what she felt. It was a feeling of overwhelming relief. *I don't need to pretend anymore.*

CHAPTER ELEVEN
SUNNYDALE FORENSIC HOSPITAL

Movement within Sunnydale Forensic Hospital is restricted depending on a patient's risk profile. Some are in assisted living accommodation with access to kitchens and cutlery. Some can hold down jobs outside the perimeter walls. Others can't go much further than the next room. There's a good reason for the precautions. Most of the people here have either killed someone or seriously harmed them. The majority suffer from serious disorders like schizophrenia, manic depression, and post-traumatic stress disorder. Then there are those with the label of sociopath. They are the hardest to gage because they can be charming as hell and suck you into thinking they are your buddy, then bam, they are trying to kick the shit out of you because you took too long in the shower. Overall, though, the really dangerous inmates, on my floor anyway, are pretty drugged up and quite harmless from what I can surmise.

I guess I'm in the middle. I'm in the secure part still, no access to cutlery for me! But at least I can move about the entire floor and go to my activities freely. I'm in lockdown at night and of course can't leave the perimeter walls yet, but I'm hopeful that'll change soon. Meanwhile, I try to keep to my own business as much as possible, and yet still try to look like I am participating. I've come to see that most people who are sentenced to time in this place are seen as deserving treatment rather than punishment, which is reassuring.

The thing I've learned most since being here, is that the way out quickly is to first and foremost go to all the therapy groups. I don't have a choice about going to my one-on-one therapy even though I don't think it does anything for me. But for the group programs, I get some choices. Mrs. Brown explained to me when I first arrived, my chance of *recovery* and being released back into society, are deeply correlated with how much I participate in the group programs which I think are a joke, but I go anyways. The only one I really like is yoga. But the group *therapy* stuff is a joke – for me anyways. And don't get me started on the stupid team building bullshit. But, the trick, I've discovered, is to *look* motivated and seem interested, even if you aren't. Their motto, in layman's terms, seems to be *get up off your ass, get to those therapeutic groups, and do the work.* So that's what I do. If it gets me out of this place sooner, I'll play their little game. Whatever it takes to be able to see my son and hold him in my arms.

There has been one really positive aspect of being incarcerated; it has allowed me to get back to being creative again. The last few years, I was so consumed with trying to get through all the chaos of life that I didn't have time to do what I love, which is play music just for fun. Music has always been one of my greatest pleasures in life and thankfully, after much pleading when I first came into this place, they allowed me the *privilege* of being able to play music in the music room alone, at scheduled times of course. I think the music has been one of the things that is helping me keep my sanity in a place where there is a fine line between sane and insane. That, and yes, the writing. Writing *is* helping me discover more about myself.

Anyway, back to the story . . .

CHAPTER TWELVE
VICTORIA, BC

JANUARY 2015

Victoria, British Columbia, known as the Florida of Canada, has the mildest winters in all of Canada but in January especially, it can get quite dreary. There's still green grass, and lots of evergreens and red arbutus trees that don't lose leaves, but it's green because it rains all the bloody time. The damp and cold penetrate inside your bones and no matter how many layers you put on; it lingers there till mid-February. It was late January, and I was feeling down and out and looking like a drowned rat, when I walked into my house. I carried a bag of groceries in my left hand, my right hand was on my ten-year-old son Jonas's shoulder, trying to hold him still.

"Come on, honey, take off your muddy shoes."

"Dad! Look what I made at school!" Jonas shouted.

"Jonas, take off your coat now, and please hang it up on the hook."

But he was gone, running into the kitchen, dragging the mud across the floor.

"Dad! Look, I got an A in my art class."

Cody bent down and kissed our son's forehead and patted his head.

“Let’s see. That’s amazing. I love it! How about I give you some tape and you go hang it up in your room? After you take off your shoes. You should be really proud,” Cody said as he handed him some scotch tape.

Jonas threw his shoes in the corner of the hallway and ran upstairs while Cody gave me a quick kiss on the cheek. “Stormy, let me take those groceries. How was your day?”

“Alright, I guess. I’m so damn cold though, and I hate going to work in the dark and coming home in the dark. It’s depressing. And the weather is turning nasty out there. The wind is crazy strong and the rain is pouring, but not down, it's actually raining sideways, I swear. I hope we’re not in for another rainstorm. I’m so tired of the rain and of never seeing the sun and of being frozen. I can’t wait for spring.” I said as I towel dried my hair.

“I just listened to the weather, and they said this system is going to move through Victoria quickly. Not to worry. Spring will be here soon. Only a month till the Victoria flower count. Keep that in mind. I’ve got a roast in the oven. I made a nice fire, so go sit by it and warm up, meanwhile I'll get you a nice warm Gluehwein. I’ve had it simmering for a half hour. I had a feeling you might like something warm when you got home.”

“Oh honey, thank you. I can smell the cinnamon and cloves, it smells divine.” My mother introduced us to Gluehwein after her last travel assignment in Germany in December. It was the end of a long day, she said, and she was cold from walking around Heidelberg all day. She went into a pub and told the bartender to make her something to warm her insides. He set a large glass mug of warm red wine, with cloves and a cinnamon stick and a little orange peel floating on the surface, in front of her–*Gluehwein*–he announced. We’d been making it ever since. It was the perfect drink for a west coast winter.

Cody handed me the mug and said, “Your doctor’s office called a half hour ago. They said to call them back as soon as you got home. They’re there till 5:30.”

“I wonder if Linda got the test results back. I’d better call right away.”

I rested my feet on the ottoman and covered myself up with my favourite purple, crocheted throw blanket that Mémé had made for me when Jonas was born. The fire was crackling, and Cody had Chet Baker playing jazz softly in the background. The enticing aroma from the kitchen made my mouth water. I took a sip and felt the tension begin to melt away. I reached for the phone and dialed the doctor's office.

"Hi June, Stormy Hera here. Linda said she wanted to talk to me about my results? Is this a good time?"

"Yes, can you just wait a few minutes? She's almost done with her last patient."

"Sure, I'll hold on."

I took another sip of the warm wine, thinking it was probably good news. I felt better, no more nose bleeds, which was good. I just felt a little more tired than usual.

"Stormy, sorry to keep you waiting. Are you there with Cody?"

"Yes, he's just making dinner. Why?"

"Storm, I got your results back, and I want you to come in tomorrow first thing. And bring Cody with you." I could hear the alarm in her voice.

"Why? Linda, you're scaring me. Look, we've been best friends for ten years. What is it? You can tell me." I sat up and looked over at Cody to see if he was listening, and he wasn't. My heart began to race.

"I would rather tell you in person."

"Linda, tell me, please. I promise I'll still come in tomorrow." I sat up straight, threw off the blanket, and waved my hand at Cody to get his attention.

She hesitated. "It's acute myeloid leukemia (AML). Cancer. You have cancer." Linda's voice cracked as she said the word 'cancer.'

"Linda, are you sure? Cancer? How can that be? I had a nose bleed. Sure, I'm tired, but cancer?" I could feel my jaw tighten. I looked over at Cody. He was looking at me, his skin taking on a pale hue.

"Yes. Look, we need to treat it right away. Please come in tomorrow and bring Cody. I am so sorry." She paused, and I could hear her blow her nose. "I have an appointment set up for you with the oncologist, the best in the city. After you see me, you'll go straight to the hospital and meet him there in the emergency ward. It's the quickest way I could get you to see him. His name is Dr. Lafontaine. He's the best. I would trust him with my own daughter." She paused to blow her nose again. Her voice breaking, she said, "I'm so sorry, Stormy."

"I guess I'll be there. I'm sure this is all a mistake though."

"We'll do more tests to make sure. I promise. See you tomorrow. Make sure and bring Cody or your mom. I don't want you to be alone."

I hung up the phone. Cody stood there staring at me.

"Cancer? Did I hear right?" he asked as he knelt down beside me and grabbed my hand.

"Yes, AML, whatever the hell that is. I just don't get it. It just seems so unreal. I felt a little tired, and I got a nosebleed that wouldn't stop. Those are symptoms of cancer?" My chest felt like an elephant was sitting on it. I could feel the anxiety rising in my throat.

Cody put his head in my lap. "Oh, honey, I'm so sorry. I'm so sorry. We'll beat this. I know we will. Don't worry," he said as he squeezed my hand.

I tried to sleep. Cody had given me one of his pot brownies that he kept in the freezer for special occasions when we were alone or on our date nights. He thought it would help me to sleep. But it just made me high and even more anxious than I already was. I felt my heart would burst from my chest. After tossing and turning in bed for an hour, I went downstairs to the computer and googled everything about AML.

When I did finally crawl into bed around three in the morning, I was physically exhausted, and sleep came quickly.

As we sat at the breakfast table, I read what I had found on the internet to Cody.

"Listen to this. Adult acute myeloid leukemia (AML) is a cancer of the blood and bone marrow. This type of cancer usually gets worse quickly if it is not treated. It is the most common type of acute leukemia in adults. Survival rate is 25 percent for those over the age of twenty. BMT, also known as a bone marrow transplant or blood stem-cell transplant, can treat patients who have AML, including older patients. It replaces the unhealthy blood-forming cells (stem cells) with healthy ones. For some people, transplant can cure their disease."

I turned away from the computer and looked at Cody. "The success rate is much better if the donor is a relative. I have to call Mom and Dad and Brittany." There was an urgency in my voice that I didn't recognize.

"Honey, you're jumping the gun. You may not even need a transplant. Isn't that a last resort?"

"I'm just trying to be proactive. After everything I read last night, it seems I do have all the symptoms, like I'm in the late stages."

Cody raised the palm of his hand up. "Whoa, slow down, honey, let's back up. You're doing the Evangeline thing again—jumping into something with two feet before knowing all the facts. Let's slow this down and take one step at a time, get the facts from the experts before you diagnose what stage you're in. I don't think the internet is the best source of information. Let's see what the doctors have to say first. Okay?"

We didn't have to sit in the waiting room, as Linda called us into her office immediately.

"Linda, you look awful!" I said as I looked at my friend. And she did. Reddened eyes, no makeup, and her hair in a ponytail. She only ever wore a ponytail when we were walking in the park or at yoga classes.

"Now that's not the nicest thing you ever said to me, Storm." She gave a weak attempt at a smile. "I didn't sleep, and I'm sure you didn't either." She hesitated. "My good friend . . . Oh, shit." Her eyes misted with tears again. "I'm sorry. I am trying to be all professional but, Storm, we've been best friends since ninth grade. I love you. But I think it's only right that I hand you over to one of my colleagues. I just don't feel I can be objective through all this. I thought a lot about this last night."

I walked over to Linda and gave her a hug. I looked her right in the eyes, holding her shoulders firmly. "You're my doctor. You've been my doctor since you first set up your practice. You know me inside and out. You delivered Jonas. You can't back out on me now. I trust you 100 percent. We'll get through this."

"I can't believe my patient is consoling me. Shit, this is not right. Are you sure?" She was wringing her hands.

I grabbed both her hands in mine. "It's alright. And yes, it is as shitty as it gets, but I need you as my doctor and my friend. Please, Linda, don't abandon me, not now."

Cody stood up. "Okay, you two. Enough, or you'll have me crying, and I rarely cry. Let's just all sit down and figure this out." He put his arm around me and walked me back to the chair across from Linda.

Through the tears, Linda, Cody, and I got the information and talked about the probable course of action. June, the receptionist, knocked lightly at the door, then popped her head into the office. "He's ready for Ms. Hera in fifteen minutes."

"Thanks, June. Okay, now go to the hospital. Dr. Lafontaine, the oncologist, will meet you in fifteen minutes."

"I'm ready to fight this, Linda."

"I know. I know," Linda said softly.

Dr. Lafontaine walked into the examination room. He was a short man with wavy grey hair, bushy eyebrows, and round, wire-rimmed glasses. He spoke with a slight French accent. "Stormy Hera?"

"Yes, and this is my husband, Cody."

"Thank you for seeing us Dr. Lafontaine," Cody said, shaking hands with the doctor.

"Well, I know, Doctor Bahr, and she is an excellent doctor. So, when she called, I knew it was important to get on this as soon as possible. I've looked at your blood work she sent over, but before we go any further, we need to do a bone marrow test. I'm going to take a biopsy." I could see he wasn't a man who beat around the bush. He motioned me onto the examining table.

"Please lay on your side. I will take it from your hip bone. This is an important test, as it will confirm our suspicions and give us a really good idea of what course of treatment we're going to take."

"Will it hurt?"

"Unfortunately, yes, but it'll be over soon."

I laid on my side. I felt the intense pressure like my back was going to break in two. I squeezed Cody's hand and breathed deeply as the doctor instructed.

"Good. It's over, Mrs. Hera, and you did very well."

"Please, Doctor, call me Stormy. Mrs. makes me feel old." I said as I sat up, still feeling pain in my back from the procedure.

"Fine, Stormy, it is. Now I should have the results by tomorrow morning. My receptionist will call you as soon as we get them. Now go home and relax. Try and get some rest. Rest is very important. Would you like me to give you a prescription for something to help you sleep?"

"No, I'd rather not. To be truthful, I never slept last night, and I'm so exhausted right now that I could probably sleep standing up. I'm fine. Really." I made sure to make eye contact with him so he was convinced that I was strong and could handle whatever came my way. In hindsight, perhaps I was trying to convince myself more than the doctor. It also didn't help that my people pleasing personality was in high gear. I wanted to be the best patient. It was a real head game that to this day, I don't wish on anyone.

We picked up Jonas from Mom's house. We'd been at the hospital and the doctor's office half the day. Cody and I had decided that morning that we didn't want to tell anyone yet about the AML until we knew for sure that's what it was. Cody went to the door while I stayed in the car. I was afraid if I saw my mother, I'd break down, and I didn't want to worry her until I knew for sure what we were dealing with.

Later, that evening, Cody told me about the encounter he had with mom when he picked up Jonas.

"Where's Stormy? Why not come in for supper. I have a nice Greek salad and some ribs. We can have a little wine. It should be ready in an hour. You know I like to eat early," Mom said as she put a container of the peanut butter cookies she and Jonas had just made into Jonas's backpack.

"Thanks, Angie," Cody said, "but we're beat. It's been a long day. We've been running errands all day."

"Maybe come over this weekend?" She was wiping her hands on her tie-dyed apron, one that Jonas made her for Christmas the year before. She was aging, at sixty-one, her hair was pure white, her hands were filled with liver spots, and purple veins popped up like rivers through her thin skin.

"Sure, I'll talk to Stormy and let you know tomorrow."

"Come on, little man. Your mom is waiting in the car." She put his knapsack on his back and rubbed the top of his head, then kissed it.

"Thanks again, Grandma Angie. I really had a great time."

"Believe me, it is my absolute pleasure. We did have a great day, didn't we, Jonas?"

"Yup, it was awesome." Jonas hugged her, and Cody noticed he patted her on the back a little. It was adorable, the way he was with Angie, he thought. He sometimes did things like that, as if he was the parent and you were the kid. It was the cutest thing.

"I can keep him anytime, if you're too exhausted," she said, looking at Cody with concern. "I don't leave for my trip for another couple of weeks."

"I know. You really are the best. And we may take you up on it. Thanks again," Cody said with a forced smile as he closed the door.

The call from the doctor's office came before we finished breakfast. We dropped Jonas off at school and continued to Dr. Lafontaine's office. He motioned for us to have a seat. He looked directly into my eyes with grave concern. "I'm afraid the bone marrow confirmed AML. Doctor Bahr's diagnosis was correct."

"Oh," I said looking down at my hands instead of at the doctor's face. "I guess I still had hope that it's all been a mistake."

"Let's hear what the doc has to say," Cody said as he grabbed my hand and gave it a little squeeze.

"I am truly sorry. Let's talk about the best course of action. First, we will do what is called remission induction therapy," Dr. Lafontaine said matter-of-factly, looking down at his notes in the file.

"Remission? I like that word," I said, as I looked at Cody hopefully.

"Yes, well, we will use chemotherapy to kill the leukemia cells in your blood and in your bone marrow. You do need to stay in the hospital for this. I've arranged a bed for you. You'll start therapy in two days."

"So fast?"

"Yes, unfortunately, with this type of cancer and given the stage you're in, we need to work quickly."

"What happens after that?" asked Cody.

"Well, once she is in remission, then we try different drugs to destroy any remaining leukemia cells. We may do a bone marrow transplant at that time. But let's see how this chemo goes first." He switched his gaze to me. "There are also drug trials that I'll look into to see if you qualify for any of those."

"Should we be asking our relatives to get tested for being a donor?" I asked.

"I see you've been on the internet?" Dr. Lafontaine said with a smile.

"Yes, I've googled everything on AML."

"Well, first, let's stay off the internet for now. What you're reading is general information and now that we have your test results, we are tailoring a treatment plan based on your age, symptoms, subtype, etc. Now saying that, it wouldn't hurt to alert them. We can do testing on them after you're finished your chemotherapy. We may or may not take that route."

The next day, I walked a few blocks to where Brittany, my half-sister, lived. I knocked on her door and walked straight in. She lived in an old quaint, red brick walk-up apartment a few houses down from the Rosewood Inn where she used to work part-time while going to university. The apartment was somewhat run-down but it was handy to downtown, Beacon Hill Park, the ocean, walking distance to the grocery store, and more importantly, only a few blocks from Dad and Celeste, Cody and I, and even to Mom's little house.

Brittany was sitting on her green velvet couch and curled up in a white throw blanket with super long tassels. Her style always made me smile, she was such a jock, never dressed up, wore mostly jogging attire except on the most special occasions when she would wear a simple cotton dress with short boots. But she had this thing for outlandish coloured furniture and art. Her favourite place to shop for her apartment was from Shabby to Chic Designs or Chintz and Company. Her newest piece was a bench that looked like a peacock, which I couldn't help but tease her about. It just always seemed like an oxymoron seeing her in her sweat pants sitting on crazy hip furniture.

Her eyes were red. A pile of used tissues was on the black and white checkered coffee table. Her long blonde hair was a mess of tangles instead of the usual tight, perfect ponytail. She was still in her grey pajama bottoms and UVIC grey T-shirt.

"Hi Brit." I said softly as I sat down beside her and put my arm around her. Brittany rested her head on my shoulder.

"I've no more tears left. I feel completely drained," she said.

I realized the minute I saw her that she knew about the cancer. But who told her?

"How about a little walk, or go for a coffee?"

"I don't know."

"I think it would do us both some good to get some fresh air."

Brittany smiled. "Okay. I could use some fresh air."

"Come on, let's get you dressed."

As we walked, I noticed she was walking much slower than normal. Was she slowing down for me? Despite the fresh salt air and gentle breeze, the air felt heavy around us, as if we were walking in a cloud of grief. We were at the crosswalk heading to Beacon Hill Park when I finally said something.

"Okay, spill it out little sister. Who told you, Cody or Linda? I doubt it was Linda. I wanted to tell you in person," I said.

"Cody. He needed to talk to someone. He was crying so hard. I think he was hiding in the garage when he called me last night. How are you doing? Oh, forget it, that was a stupid question."

"It's okay, sis." I put my arm over her shoulder and gave her a little hug. She felt like a rag doll as her body leaned into mine. "Chemo starts right away. I can't believe this is happening. That I'm even saying the word chemo. I mean, I had a nosebleed a week and a half ago. Now I have cancer that I'll not recover from. It's all just so unreal. I'm probably going to die," I said quietly.

"No, don't go there. You're a fighter. You're going to be in the percentage that is cured. I just know it. Nobody is as disciplined and health conscious as you. You've got so much going for you."

"I'm sorry, I don't mean to bring you down with all my negativity. But the truth is I feel embarrassed. And I'm embarrassed that I feel embarrassed. It's crazy. I'm embarrassed that I have cancer. I'm a health nut, and I preach about health and wellness to my friends and my family. I'm so ashamed of myself."

"Omy!" she cried, using her childhood name for me. "Oh, my God, you can't be ashamed. It's not your fault. I researched AML. It could be a genetic thing. It's not because you did anything wrong. But I think because you live such a healthy lifestyle it'll help you with your recovery."

"Well, if you researched it, you know the survival rate is not that great. A whopping 25 percent."

"Don't say that, Omy, please don't give up before you've even started fighting."

"I know. I know. I'm not giving up really, it's like there are two parts of me. The optimistic part that says I will beat this, and the pessimistic part that says I'm going to die soon. Unfortunately, the pessimist in me seems to be in the forefront. It's strange, but I feel I have to be realistic, for Jonas mostly. I have to plan this out, organize a way to make sure Jonas is okay, looked after, you know? I don't want to be one of those people who are in denial till the day they die; leaving a mess of unfinished business for people to deal with. I want to plan it all out. I don't know how long I have, so I want to get prepared. Do it right. Die properly with all my ducks in order, you know?"

She grabbed my hand, and we walked in silence through the park.

That night as I lay in bed, my thoughts went back to when I was six years old and was at my dad's house for the weekend. His house was an older home that he had completely renovated. I could still recall the smell of the new furniture—a mixture of plastic wrap and chemicals mixed with the paint smell from the white walls. Everything was blue and white: blue and white sofa, blue chair, white coffee table, white rug. Even the pictures on the wall were scenes with blue and white in them. It looked sterile but pretty at the same time. I remembered thinking as a kid: the house was like something you might see in a magazine or in a store, like nobody actually lived there yet. My dad had just gotten married, his new wife Celeste had insisted they get all-new furniture, and obviously her favourite colour was blue.

Dad sat me down in the living room on the ottoman. He sat on the couch so we were facing each other. I remembered the conversation as if it were yesterday. Dad, with his Danish accent, held my hands in his as he stated:

"Celeste and I have some very exciting news, honey. You're going to be a big sister. What do you think of that?"

"A sister?"

"Yes, we're going to have a baby and that will make you a big sister."

"I always wanted a sister or a brother! Marie has a baby sister, and she's so cute!"

I remember dancing in the living room with Celeste, seeing the ultrasound picture, and touching Celeste's belly, wondering how the baby got inside her tummy but being afraid to ask.

It was at my seventh birthday, after my second party that Celeste went into labour. The first party had been with my friends from school and from my Suzuki violin group. It was one of my most memorable birthdays from the minute I woke up till I went to bed. There were balloons outside on the front gate and at the door and streamers all over the house. Instead of a cake, Mom baked chocolate cupcakes, and we all decorated our own with sprinkles, Smarties, whipped cream, icing, strawberries and blueberries and lastly, multi-coloured candles. Then Mom put them all in a circle and I blew out the candles after they sang to me. Everyone brought their Barbies, and Mom rolled out our portable Hoover washing machine and filled the wash tub with water for the swimming pool so the dolls could dive off the counter into the water. We played pin the tail on the donkey, and then ended the party with the gift opening and dancing to my new records played on the new record player Mom had bought me. They all left by five o'clock, I remember because I didn't want them to leave, but Mom said that the grown-up party was starting in an hour and that she had to clean up and get ready for that.

Dad and Celeste came over soon after, and we all had supper and a big chocolate birthday cake that Celeste had made and topped-off with strawberries and blueberries and fresh tiny purple violet flowers. Just after I blew out the candles, Celeste stood up from the table. There was a puddle of water on the floor. Dad explained it was time to go to the hospital because my brother or sister was about to be born. I tried to stay awake, but I was too tired and full from the cake and cupcakes. Mom made me go to bed, promising to wake me the minute she heard anything. I woke the next morning to her shaking me. "Wake up, wake up, honey. You have a sister."

I will never forget the feeling. It was like fireworks going off inside my head. When my mom retold the story, she would say that I was literally vibrating with excitement.

Brittany was born on the early morning of November 17, 1987, one day after my seventh birthday. Dad asked me what I thought about getting a sister for a birthday present. And that is how I saw little Brittany: my very own birthday present. It wasn't long until my Barbie dolls were put away, and replaced by my real life doll—Brittany.

I think about how everything changed when Celeste came into our lives. Before she came into Dad's life, he was miserable and sad and was always making excuses as to why he couldn't come and pick me up from Salt Spring Island and bring me to his place in Victoria. After Celeste, one of them picked me up at the ferry every Friday evening and returned me on Sunday afternoon. Dad actually looked different, and he smiled all the time and was fun to be around. He even dressed better, gone were the T-shirts and Levi jeans. He now wore buttoned up shirts and designer pants. There was a big change in him. Even at a young age, I could see that Dad and Celeste were crazy for each other. Even Mom would say: "They're a good match. I'm happy he found true love."

Celeste was not only pretty, she was also an amazing cook, a seamstress, and an artist. One of things I loved about her was that she always had activities planned for all of us to do together, but she also made sure we had things just for the two of us. She would start out by saying, "Let's you and me . . ." And it was usually something fun like finger painting, shopping, going to the petting zoo, painting our nails, or going to a movie. My own mom even liked Celeste, and as soon as she and Dad got married, she decided that we should move from Salt Spring Island to James Bay in Victoria to be near them. I had just started grade one. Dad and Celeste lived on Menzies Street in a nice, pale-green three-bedroom heritage home with a big backyard. Mom bought a small, white, single-storey house on Oswego Street, a half block from school and two blocks away from Celeste and Dad. I could walk to school and to the conservatory of music and easily go from one parents' house to the next after school or on weekends. I just had to make sure I reported where I was to Mom or Dad or Celeste so they knew where I was at all times. Which I didn't mind one bit. They called it co-parenting, and I loved it. Mom said it was a win-win situation. Knowing what I know now, I realize the sacrifice Mom made for me. She loved Salt Spring, it was her home, and she gave it up for me so that I didn't have to go back and forth on ferries, and I could spend more time with Dad and Celeste.

The arrangement worked well, and everything was great till I hit my teenage years and started hanging around with the gothic crowd at school, which got me into more trouble than I care to admit. For a couple of years, I was a real pain in the ass when I look back. After I came back from Saskatchewan when my mémé told me stories about my mom and her while we weeded the garden, the seed was planted that I needed to change my ways. I think my parents thought the talk with Mémé was going to be the catalyst for change, but I wasn't quite there yet. The seed was planted, but it hadn't taken root. I wasn't home a week when I was grounded for a week for staying out after curfew and lying to Mom.

Dad sat me down at the dining room table and looked into my eyes. The expression on his face scared me. His face was red, and there were blotches on his neck, a sure sign that I was going to get a real blast.

"We need to get something straight, young lady. First of all, your mother and I have rules that you must follow. And do not roll your eyes at me or you'll have another week of grounding. Listen, and listen good. Do not try and play your mother and I against each other because it won't work. We may not be married, but we talk every day, and we're very close. You're our top priority. We may not agree on everything, but we agree about how you're to be raised. You must treat your mother and me and Celeste with respect. End of story. No lies and trying to get away with things. When you're out late, do not say you are at your mom's or my place. We know! Got it?"

I recall feeling scared. He wasn't one to raise his voice often, but when he did, I knew I was in big trouble. I nodded and looked him in the eye.

"Your mother sacrificed a lot for you so that we could co-parent. It was really hard for her to move away from Salt Spring. She loved it there. But one thing about your mother, her family comes first. That family is you, young lady. She deserves respect, and she does not deserve to be lied to. Do you understand? She is feeling really betrayed right now by your behaviour, and I am too. She thought you had smartened up after your trip to Saskatchewan, but I can see you are up to your old tricks. Before this day is through, I want you to apologize to her for lying. And change that attitude because we're all really sick of it. We want our old Stormy back, not this ridiculous version you invented. It's not you. Quit trying to fit in with people who are a bunch of losers."

It was after that conversation that I decided to give up the gothic look and quell my rebellious nature. It wasn't really my thing anyways, and to be honest, it was a relief. My best friend was into it, and I just followed. I never got the impression my friend knew what the gothic culture was even about. I certainly didn't. I just went blindly along with her. I was glad when Dad put his foot down because I realized I was tired of acting like that anyhow. I was starting to feel uncomfortable and bored with hanging out downtown, hitchhiking around, and with taking drugs that made me feel out of control. I went to my room and chucked my black goth clothes into a garbage bag along with the black makeup. I really just wanted to get back into my music and spend time with Brittany and help at Celeste's restaurant again to make some extra money for a new, custom-made five-string violin that I wanted.

It was after I stopped hanging around with my druggy friends that Mom started taking more and more assignments writing for travel magazines and books. That meant that she went away for weeks at a time. And it was fine. We were all happy when she started back. She had an extra spring in her step, and at times you could almost see the melancholy lift from her face.

Despite those couple of rough years, I had a pretty incredible life. We had an unconventional family, but it was an amazing family and the older I became, I appreciated more and more how lucky I was.

Just thinking about my parents made me wonder how I was going to break the news to them: first that I had cancer, and second that they may need to get tested to see if they were possible bone-marrow donors. I decided to tell my parents separately about the cancer and let that sink in, and then Cody suggested having everyone over for supper and speaking to them as a group about the transplant and testing. For that we could wait till after the last chemotherapy session. Dr. Lafontaine made it clear that there were many routes I could take and that a transplant using a family member as a donor was only one. Reluctantly, I agreed, although it was hard to hold it back. I wanted to get everyone on board and ready to go. But Cody was right. They didn't need to be stressed out any more than necessary, and he reiterated that it was a long way off yet. "One step at a time," he would say. "Get through the chemotherapy first." That was Cody: take things slow, first things first. Patience was not in my DNA. I was like my mother in that respect. My mémé said we were alike: *no moss growing under you or your mother's feet.* Which is a good trait to have in some circumstances, and bad in others. Like anything. Sometimes our best trait is also our worst. In this case, I wanted to get on with dealing with the whole situation, getting prepared for both my death and for getting cured. Being patient for me, and probably my mother as well, equated to procrastination in our minds. There was nothing I hated more than someone who continuously put off things till the last possible moment. It drove me crazy.

The chemotherapy took place in a room in the hospital that held ten nice cushy recliners lined up in a semi-circle. There was always soft relaxing acoustic music playing in the background, or recordings with nature sounds, cut out cartoons on the walls, and soft throw blankets in every colour. The walls were painted an aqua blue which gave it a supposed cheerful feel. It made me smile at the irony. A cheerful welcoming place with a concoction of poison hanging in bags hooked up to your arm that kill your cells, make you sick to your stomach, lose weight, and make your hair fall out. In time though, the oxymoron did seem to disappear mostly because of the amazing staff who worked there. They were a special breed to be able to work in an environment where patients were in deep despair and fighting for their lives. They listened to you, cried with you, laughed, told jokes, comforted you. They had a strength of character that I had never witnessed in my life.

Brittany sat with me and held my hand as the first chemo drugs began to pulse through my veins. She asked me, "Can you tell me stories about when I was a baby?"

I laughed a little, thinking that it was a silly idea. But then I realized it was a great way to make the time go by and get my mind off the poison that was coursing through my veins. And it was easy to recite because I had told the story to Brittany many times when she was small.

"Good idea, Brit. Keep my mind off the chemo. Well, let's see . . . The first time I held you, your mom unwrapped you from the baby blanket so that I could see your little toes and your long fingers. You had such a perfect little round head with loads of blonde hair. You were tiny, and so beautiful, and I just couldn't believe a person could be so small. Your eyes were open and they were dark blue, and I swear you looked at me. I sang you a little song, I don't remember what song it was, but I sang it very softly, and you fell asleep in my arms. I was so hooked. From that day on, I swore I would love and protect you forever, no matter what."

Brittany sobbed. Tears filled her eyes.

I handed her a tissue. "You can't cry after every sentence." I said, smiling. I continued. "You were a good baby, that's what everyone said. You never fussed much. I'll never forget the first time you laughed. We were at the park, and I was wearing the snuggly with you inside it. Dad put us in a swing with one of those closed-in seats so we wouldn't fall out, and then he started to push us, and you giggled. You were only two months old. It was the sweetest sound I ever heard. Dad and Celeste and my mom all said that it was very unusual that a baby that young would laugh."

"You are such a good sister, Omy." She lay her head on my shoulder. "How does it feel? The chemo?"

"Hot, and I am feeling so frickin tired."

"It's okay to close your eyes. You probably didn't sleep very much last night, knowing you. I am staying right here. I won't leave you." She grabbed the blanket on my lap and pulled it up to cover me to just below my neck, then adjusted the chair so I could lay back. "Just picture the chemo as being little guys running around inside you like construction workers like Dad, fixing your blood, repairing your cells. Can you see them?" Brittany asked.

I closed my eyes and grinned. "Yes, they have hard hats on, and they are really good-looking guys. They are shirtless, their muscles are bulging and, oh, wow, they have the cutest little asses."

We both started laughing.

The nurse came by. "Okay, didn't I tell you no laughing allowed in here?" She chimed with a smile while she stroked my hair lightly. We told her about the construction workers, and then we all started to giggle.

On my second appointment, I told Brit stories about when she first called me Omy.

"You were only nine months old, and you kept saying Omy. We didn't know what you meant. But you kept saying it. And then finally, Celeste exclaimed. 'I know what it means! She says it whenever Stormy comes over.

She is saying "Stormy!' We tested you over and over and sure enough, your first word was my name. Of course, I was over the moon. I even wrote a story about it and read it at a show-and-tell at school."

The next session, I told Brit about how I tried so hard to turn her into a clone of myself.

"I remember," Brittany said, "you were trying to teach me violin, then flute, and then piano, but I hated them all, and I was so bad at music."

"I know. Then your mom gave me the talk and explained that it was our job to figure out what you liked and were good at and not force you into things that we liked and were good at."

"Oh, I remember the lecture. I got it too. How her parents wanted her to be a lawyer like them and her two brothers, how she went to university and hated it, and then how she finally got the nerve to tell them she wanted to quit and go to culinary school and become a chef."

"Yes, that famous lecture."

"I got that speech when I went to high school and had to pick electives, and then again when I went to university," Brittany recounted.

"Yes, the find-your-passion speech. She even gave it to me when I was first going through my gothic phase and then, yes, come to think about it, I got it again when I went to university too! Gotta love Celeste. She's the best."

"Yeah, she's a pretty good mom."

"Yeah, but really you were not a difficult kid to raise. Your parents had it easy with you. A lot easier than with me. You were goody-two shoes, never getting into trouble. As long as you got to play sports you were happy."

"Oh, you weren't that bad. Okay, maybe when you were a teenager you were a little wilder than most," Brittany reassured.

"Mom and Dad both confessed that, when I was twelve and thirteen, they were ready to give me away to the next person who came along. I laugh at it now. But I was terrible. When I think back. Don't you remember me coming to your games and cheering you on dressed in my striped mini skirt and bra-like thing, black lipstick and nail polish, torn tights, and army boots? Oh, my

God. Your coach wanted to kick me out, but you ran up to him and told him I was your sister, and so he let me stay."

"I forgot about that! I remember him saying 'she's your sister?' And laughing like a hyena."

"What a pair! You miss squeaky-clean and me with my rebellious attitude. Mad at my parents, teachers, and the world basically. For the life of me, I have no idea what that whole anger thing was about. I think I was just trying to fit in with my friends at school, or stick out! I'm not sure. Thank God it didn't last too long."

"I know we laugh now, but you know what, no matter what crazy phase you were in, you rarely missed one of my games."

"Nope. I don't think I missed very many. Miss artsy-fartsy, who couldn't catch a ball or kick one if I tried, and made up every excuse in the book to skip Phys-ed class was your cheerleader and biggest fan. Well, I certainly learned all about sports when you came along!"

"You were my own personal cheerleader."

"Yes, I was, and I still am, kiddo. Even now."

"I know you are. You're the best. I love you so much," Brittany said as tears welled up in her eyes.

"But, hey, you cheered me on too! When I finally smartened up and got into the youth orchestra you came to my performances and all my recitals over the years."

"Yes, but I have to confess, I slept through most of the performances! When I woke up, I clapped really hard though," she laughed.

"Yes, you did. I was watching, believe me."

"I only fell asleep a few times!"

We both laughed and chatted and before we knew it, the chemotherapy treatment was finished.

The following session we talked about when Jonas was born and how good old Cody was sweet enough to ask Brittany to be in the delivery room. We agreed that he was the best husband.

"I hope I find someone like Cody," Brittany sighed. "I seem to be kissing a lot of frogs these days while I wait for my prince to show up. I'm not even sure I like men in the romantic sense."

"First off, I'm not sure Cody is a prince. We've had our ups and downs like any married couple. But yes, I did luck out. He is a sweetheart. And you will find your person too, most likely when you least expect it."

And it was true when I thought about it. When Cody and I began to date, he used to ask me: "What is it tonight? Game or a gig?" None of my family was much into television or going to the movies. We did eat out a lot, usually because we were headed to something. When I started dating Cody in university, I wondered how long he would last. I really liked him right away. He was so easy-going and calm, and I felt so relaxed around him. And he was the best listener and kisser I had ever met. But I did not hold on to the hope that he would stick around for long. Every boyfriend I ever had complained about my family and my busy lifestyle. "Do we have to take your sister on every date?" I remember Pat, my first real boyfriend complaining and finally saying enough was enough. I had given up hope of ever finding someone and was beginning to accept that I might be alone for the rest of my life, like my mom. But Cody never complained about my family, and he seemed to really understand me.

In fact, Cody later confessed that the close bond I had with my family was part of why he loved me. Cody's upbringing was not the greatest. He often told me that I had no idea of how fortunate I was. His parents were devout Catholics and had insisted he become an altar boy. He begged to quit. He really did not like the priest and for good reason. Father Greer was a pedophile, and he molested Cody and many other boys over the years. Despite the fear Father Greer had instilled in him if he told anyone about the molestations, Cody finally got up the nerve to tell his parents. But they refused to believe him. They said he must have been imagining it. They would not let him quit being an altar boy. The experience scarred him for life. Indeed, the main reason he became a child psychologist was to help other children through similar trauma. It was when he was in high school and severely depressed that he finally found a child psychologist who worked at the school and who helped him heal from the abuse. He became a staunch atheist, and though he was so kind and generous to most people, he had little time for anyone who was even the least bit religious. Being that I wasn't brought up with religion, it didn't really bother me. When he graduated and got his first job as a child psychologist at a high school, that's when he proposed.

"You'll find someone, so don't worry, Brit. After every break-up Mom was adamant that there were many more fish in the ocean, and it was better to wait for the right one. She'd say, 'You'll know the real thing when it comes along. Just promise me that you'll never ever settle for anything less than true love.' Of course, I didn't believe Mom then. But as usual, she was right. Cody came along when I wasn't even looking, and I knew almost instantly that he was the one for me. And thankfully, he felt the same way."

On my week off from chemo I was allowed to leave the hospital and go home for a day. I was folding laundry and watching Jonas, his science project sprawled across the living room floor. My sweet little Jonas. I never thought I'd ever marry, let alone have children. And here was this beautiful, perfect little human being who I loved more than life itself. I was so lucky to have such a beautiful family.

It's funny but when I was diagnosed, I seemed to be always reminiscing about the past. I guess it was a way to cope with an uncertain future. As I watched Jonas that day, I looked over at the blue irises Cody bought me when I came home. Typically, Cody bought bouquets of cut flowers but the potted irises seemed to give me hope somehow. Cut flowers die, potted ones grow. I didn't know if it was a conscious choice on his part, but it seemed that every gesture or comment those days had a deeper meaning, a metaphor to help cope with the ambiguous nature of not knowing if I was going to live or die.

Cody was romantic from day one. He bought flowers and chocolates and frequently gave me handwritten cards. When he proposed, he asked if I wanted to go to a gallery opening with him. His friend was a photographer, and I had met him a few times. He knew full well that I would say yes because I was always trying to get him to go with me to galleries. We arrived at a small building on Fort Street. His friend met us at the door. We were the only ones there. I thought we were just really early. Then I looked at the photographs hanging on the walls. They were all of me and Cody and my family. One photo was of Brittany holding up a sign that read, *Say, yes*. Another was of Dad and Celeste looking at writing in the sand that said, *We Love Cody*. And one photo was of Mom with a gigantic grin, holding a balloon that had a heart drawn on it with the words, *Cody loves Stormy*.

I let out a squeaky laugh. "What is this? Are you asking me to marry you?"

"Yes, I am, and I asked your family first for permission, and they all agreed. I figured if I'm going to be married to you, I'm basically going to be married to your whole family. I know how close you all are, and I wouldn't have it any other way." With that, he got down on one knee and proposed. His friend, on cue, brought out the champagne and politely left us alone.

That was my Cody. I never doubted his love for me even as the cancer took hold of me and the chemotherapy turned me into a very sick pathetic looking shell of who I once was. I was probably going to die. But, in some strange way, because of Cody and my family, there was a part of me that felt okay about it, as I knew my entire family would share in the raising of my precious son. And Jonas was my main concern—not being there for him, not seeing him grow up. The thought of my little boy without a mother or at least without me mothering him, brought tears to my eyes. I was certain Cody would remarry quickly once I was gone. He was made to be a husband. He was good at it. He loved the role, he told me so, many times throughout our marriage. He loved being my husband and being a dad. The thought of Jonas having a step-mother was strangely comforting. Even though he was surrounded by such a loving family: Brittany, Celeste, Dad and, of course, Mom, who had turned into the most amazing grandmother, I didn't want Jonas to be motherless. The thought made me wonder about Mom and Dad and Celeste, and how hard it would be when I died. Children weren't supposed to die before their parents. It just wasn't right. I wondered how they would cope.

As if reading my mind, Jonas got up from the floor and came over and gave me a hug. "I love you, Mom." I almost crumbled to the floor. The thought of him losing me was hard to fathom. Jonas and I were a pair. We even looked the same. We had the same light-red hair and freckles and green, almond-shaped eyes. Cody was dark skinned. His mother was from Mexico, and his dad was from Quebec. They had met when his mom was an exchange student in high school in Montreal. I had never met them, as he refused to have anything to do with them the day after he graduated and left home for good. From what I could surmise, the only thing he got from them that was any good, were his looks. He was tall, gorgeous, with light-brown skin, dark, curly hair and large hazel eyes. So handsome! When I found out I was pregnant, I had secretly hoped our child would resemble Cody. He was much better looking than I was. But it was not meant to be. Somehow, Jonas turned into a clone of me, except for his height. He was already in the 99th percentile for height for his age. I was a measly five-foot-two like my mother.

I always found it funny how genetics worked. Brittany was nothing like me despite having the same father. We were totally different. She was the perfect blend of Celeste and Dad: tall, blonde, with a very athletic body and Celeste's eyes and square jaw. She could have easily gone into modeling and had been approached several times, but fashion was never something she was into. Brit's idea of fashion was sweatpants and T-shirts. To think of her in fashionable clothes made me smile. Me, on the other hand, I loved to dress up, especially when I was performing. I had a ridiculous number of expensive sparkly dresses, and Dad built me a special rack for my funky shoe and boot collection because Cody complained there was no room in any closets anymore for his footwear. I always had manicures and pedicures and the latest hairstyles. I never went anywhere without makeup. We were so different, not only in appearance but in personality too. I was a people pleaser, which often meant people took me for granted, especially when I was young. I was serious and analyzed everything to death, worrying about what people thought. But at the same time, ambitious as hell, as Mom would say. I knew from an early age that I wanted to be a performer and teach, and there was never any doubt in my mind I would succeed at both. Brittany was so much more confident than me. She was stubborn and competitive and always the star on every team she played in. It wasn't just her athletic abilities that made people adore her, it was her wicked, dry sense of humour. Any chance she got to play a practical joke, she would. Even when she was playing a serious game it was nothing for her to do a crazy, victory dance for the fans that would get the fans chanting her name. The only thing we did have in common was teaching. We both chose teaching as a profession. I had a PhD in music performance and taught at the university, while Brittany became a high-school Phys-ed teacher. We also both chose to do more than just teach though. Brittany played on the provincial volleyball team, whereas I played first violin with the Victoria Philharmonic Orchestra and sang in a jazz quartet called the Omy Hera Trio. I mostly only performed with the jazz quartet at festivals in the summer months when I wasn't teaching. When I thought about it, I credited our parents for agreeing not to have a television in either house. It was probably what contributed to us both having successful careers.

When I was halfway through chemotherapy, I decided it was time to give up on my music performances all together. The late nights and rehearsals just took too much out of me. I didn't have the energy. I also told the dean I would need a break from teaching too, until I felt better. She was more than accommodating. My colleagues all got together and paid for a house cleaner to come once a week. I was always a busy person, but now folding a tiny bit of laundry felt like I was climbing a mountain. I knew the treatments would be hard on me, but I didn't realize how hard.

I was in the kitchen watching Cody make supper. "Are you okay, honey? You look like you're deep in thought," Cody said as he handed me a spoonful of the soup he was making.

"Mmm. Very tasty . . . Yeah, I'm fine. Just thinking about how supportive everyone has been, especially Brit, you know. She has been so great, taking time off her busy schedule to sit with me. I always find it so strange how we are so different yet so close."

"Well, you're different, that's for sure. Brittany is the spitting image of your dad: tall and blonde, with Celeste's smile though, and more of her disposition I'd say. Whereas you look a lot like your mom. Except for the red hair and freckles. Where did that ever come from?"

"No idea, but Dad was adopted in Denmark, don't forget, so we figure it must have come from his birth parents' side."

"But, otherwise, you look a lot like your mom, that cute little cupid mouth, your green eyes that I love so much, her inquisitive nature . . ."

"Except," I interrupted, "for the boobs! I'm so glad I didn't inherit those! I like my 34B just fine."

"Me, too," he said as he came over and kissed me. "They are so perky and perfect."

I slapped him lightly on his arm, "What did I ever do to deserve you? You have been so amazing through all of this."

As he held me, I could feel his tears wet on my shoulder. "Don't get me started. I never cry, and I have been crying like a baby ever since . . ."

I placed my finger to his lips to stop him. "Not tonight. Tonight, we are taking a break from the C word." We held onto each in the kitchen with the carrot soup simmering on the stove, rocking back and forth like it was our last goodbye.

When I finished the last chemo treatment, we invited everyone over for Sunday dinner to celebrate and to explain to them about getting tested to see if their bone marrow would be a match, in case I needed the transplant. Mom came over early to help prepare supper.

"Mom, nice dress! Were you out shopping?"

My mother always had a unique look about her. We teased her that she dressed like a rich hippy. Lately, though, I noticed she wore more free-flowing linen clothes, wore mascara and eye-liner, her white hair, which was usually in her signature bun with pencils sticking out of it, was now in a beautiful side braid. She wore only one ring and one necklace at a time, and her earrings were gorgeous copper and gemstone designs from the Suzannah Hahrt collection, an island jeweler who was just featured in the *Times Colonist* newspaper. The more sophisticated look really suited her. She seemed to have finally given up on designer jeans and tie-dyed tops and wearing stacked gemstone bracelets, three or four necklaces, and heavy silver rings and earrings. Thank goodness.

"Thanks. Darlene told me I needed a makeover, so she took me shopping. I still feel like an old woman though. I have a hump on my neck. I got measured when I went for my physical the other day, and I've shrunk a whole inch! And my feet are growing, and I noticed my nose and ears have grown. Have you noticed? God, I remember seeing my grandfather as he aged. His ears and nose got enormous! I think I'm starting to look like him. This getting old is depressing." She raised her hand to her mouth, and her eyes grew big. "Oh, God, I can't believe I just said that. I'm so sorry. After all you have been through."

"Mom, please. You don't have to censor yourself around me. Really. And you look amazing. I love this new look."

I could see Mom was putting on the pounds again. I felt sorry for her. She had sizes eight to twelve in her closet, and she was forever dieting. I felt such relief that I never inherited her weight problems. I could eat anything and not put on an ounce. Like Dad. It was the only thing we seemed to have in common. I couldn't figure out how she put on the pounds so easily with all the walking she did. You'd think she would walk it off since she walked at least twenty kilometres a day, if not more.

There was a little knock on the door, and Celeste and Dad said hello as they walked into the house.

"Come in. Brittany should be here in about fifteen minutes. Get yourself a glass of wine," Cody said.

After the fourth chemo treatment, my hair started falling out. I knew it sounded so shallow, but I didn't want to lose my hair. "I love my hair. I'm afraid once I shave my head everyone will know I have cancer. I just don't want to see pity in people's eyes," I told Cody. Mom took me to look at wigs, but they seemed so hot and looked so unnatural. So, we went hat shopping instead. When Brittany came to the door, bald as a bowling ball with the biggest grin on her face, I screamed with laughter.

"You didn't! Brittany, you're crazy! Your long beautiful hair!"

Brittany howled. "I love it. It's so freeing! I might just stay bald."

"I can't believe you shaved your head! You're nuts!" I laughed, hugging her.

"A toast to the end of chemo!" Mom said, raising her glass.

"To our Stormy!' They all shouted and clinked their glasses.

I was tired by the time supper was served. I could feel my spine and my sitz bone on the chair. It felt like there were no muscles left on my bottom. When I looked in the mirror, I saw a skeleton of myself. Eyes with black circles under them, sunken cheeks, my clavicle bones sticking up, and my complexion a sickly yellow. But Linda assured me I would begin to get my appetite back soon, my hair would grow again, and I would get more energy. "You are in remission: think of it as the honeymoon stage," she said. "Do what you want, enjoy every moment till the next stage of treatments."

I wasn't sure about the honeymoon part. But I was looking forward to not feeling like a ninety-year-old woman who had just ran a marathon.

After supper, Cody gathered everyone in the living room. Jonas was in bed listening to a progressive relaxation CD for kids that Cody had picked up. He thought it might help him sleep. He had not been sleeping well since I got sick, and we were concerned.

"I know you are all wondering what the next move is, and Cody and I wanted to tell you in person all at once. The chemotherapy did a great job. The doctors said I am free for a bit till we start on the next set of treatments, which could be getting ready for a bone-marrow transplant. It's time to ask you all to get tested for a bone-marrow match just in case. That is, of course, if you want to." They were all staring at me. Finally, Dad broke the silence.

"Of course, we'll get it done right away."

"You should be aware that the best match is a sibling, with a 50 percent chance, whereas a parent is only 1 percent. So not great odds that a parent will match." I looked at Brittany.

"Half-sister's chance?" asked Brittany.

"You're my best hope, kiddo." I smiled weakly. "And Mom, Dad, if you have any other children, you haven't told me about, give them a call. Hah. Sorry, that was a sick joke from a desperate woman."

"We will all get tested, even me. I'm not related by blood, but you never know," added Celeste.

Mom was looking down at her lap. She had a tissue in her hand and kept dabbing her eyes. She never said a word.

It was a week later when Brittany came over with the news. "Stormy, I got the results back," Brittany said as she sat down on the couch beside me. I was still pretty weak, but my appetite was coming back slowly. She held both my hands and looked into my eyes. "It's not good. I'm not a match, at all."

"What? Not even a small percentage?"

"No, the doctor actually said I couldn't be a match. I didn't understand what he meant."

"Well, that doesn't make any sense. You're a half-sister. I'll ask him when I see him tomorrow. I know Mom and Dad were not matches either, nor Celeste or Cody."

"I'm so sorry. I was so sure I would be a match. What does this mean for you?" She had a haunted worried look as she spoke.

"I don't know. They may not even do a transplant, and so I'm not going to get worked up about it. Dr. Lafontaine said there are clinical trials and other ideas." I was trying to sound like I was optimistic so Brittany didn't feel bad, but inside I felt like the earth had just crumbled beneath my feet, and I was sinking into an abyss.

"Stormy Hera, come this way," said the receptionist at the cancer clinic.

Dr. Lafontaine asked me to take a seat.

'Mrs. Hera, sorry, I mean, Stormy, as you probably heard your tests came back, and I'm sorry to say, no one in your family is a match for a transplant."

"I know. They all told me. I don't get it. I understand about my parents, but why is my half-sister not a match?"

"There's something else you ought to know." He shuffled the papers on his desk and looked down at his desk.

"What is it?" I asked, my heart pounding in my ears.

"You are no match whatsoever to Brittany. I mean, she cannot be your half-sister."

"What? You must be mistaken. We have the same dad."

"I have your father's blood work here because we tested him as well and, I am so sorry, it is genetically impossible that he is your dad," he said finally, looking at me with concern.

I could feel the colour drain from my face. My head felt light.

"I don't understand. How is that possible? There must be a mistake."

"I have struggled myself over this. I wasn't sure if it was my place to tell you. I talked to some colleagues without mentioning your name, of course, and we all agreed that you should be told. I would suggest you get a paternity test. We can arrange it right away, just to be sure."

"Yes, let's do that. I'm sure it's a mistake."

"Do you want to call your father, or should I?"

"I, I don't know. I just . . ."

"How about I call him into the office tomorrow and we sit down and tell him together."

"Okay, I guess. Yes. Okay."

As I stood up to leave, the room spun, and I dropped to the floor. When I came to, the doctor was looking at me. "You're going to be okay. Sit up, drink this water. The receptionist called your husband to come get you."

The next day, Cody and I were holding hands in the doctor's office when Dad walked in.

"Stormy, Cody, what are you two doing here? I had a call to come in to talk to Dr. Lafontaine."

The doctor entered, sat down, and looked at Dad, then at me. Dr. Lafontaine had a gentle manner about him despite his directness. He never made small talk, yet he was kind. I wondered how he could be so sweet when he was dealing with so much death all the time. I thought that he would have built up a hard shell to protect himself. But I never saw that. He was genuinely empathetic. And it showed as he explained to my dad what was happening. Then he asked Dad if he would be willing to have a paternity test.

Without skipping a beat, he said, "Of course. I'm sure there's a mix up." He looked over at me, "Don't worry, honey, it'll all be okay."

CHAPTER THIRTEEN

FEBRUARY 2015

It was eight in the morning when I burst into my mother's house, screaming uncontrollably. I had hardly slept the night before. I was so angry at her, so hurt that she had lied to me. Cody tried to help me make sense of the whole revelation, and by morning I felt much more calm and ready to confront her. But the minute I reached my mother's front door, I felt the blood rushing to my head. I thought I was about to explode; I had no control over it. I pounded on the door like I was some kind of lunatic.

"Mother! Let me in!"

She opened the door and stood there; eyes wide.

"What is it? Oh, my God, what happened? Is it Jonas?" Her voice trembled, but I didn't care if I was scaring her. I was out of control with anger.

"How could you!? How could you have lied to me all these years and to Dad, to everyone? Who do you think you are? You're a liar! Who is my father? I want to know now. Do you understand? I want to know NOW. Or do you even know? Oh, my God. I hate you! You should have seen Dad's face when he found out. He was devastated! How could you do this? And Brittany! She's not my sister?"

Mom stood there in her purple flannel nightgown. Her mouth hung open. Her face was getting paler by the second. "Well, say something! Who is he? I have a right to know!"

Mom plunked herself down on the sofa, put her face in her hands, and bawled. The sound was almost inhuman. Her piercing wail was so loud that I thought the neighbours would surely come running over any minute.

It took what seemed like forever for me to hear any actual words in between the wails. Finally, she said something that was coherent enough to understand.

"I never knew for sure. I just never knew. I tried to figure it out, and it seemed that Karl must have been your father. I calculated it a million times. How did you find out?" She rocked back and forth, her long white hair falling over her face as she cried.

I finally sat down at the coffee table and looked at her. It was like I was seeing her in a different light. In front of me was a sixty-one-year-old woman who had been living with a lie for over thirty-five years. I could see it so clearly. The melancholy that plagued her for as long as I could remember, never dating, her failed marriage. She had suffered. I saw it. It made sense.

Softly and gently, I said, "Mom, it's okay, I'm sorry, I yelled. Let's just get a hold of our emotions and work this out. I'm going to get us a cup of tea, and we're going to talk like sane grown-ups."

I could hear Cody's advice in my head: *Take it easy on her, and wait to hear her story*. He was right, screaming wasn't going to get me anywhere. I could see that now. As I handed my mother the mug of tea and a box of tissues, I looked at my watch and realized it had been at least a half an hour of yelling and crying. It was enough.

"Mom, look at me. Let's start at the beginning. Look at me. Mom. Who is my father?"

Her face got all screwed up, and I could tell she was about to cry again.

"He was the only man I ever truly loved. His name is Valentino Lombardo. He was from Australia. I met him in Greece."

"Okay. Good. Next question. Is he alive?"

"I don't know."

"Come on, Mom, the only man you ever loved, and you never Googled him?"

She shook her head.

"You never tried to find him?"

"No. You don't understand. I promised him I would wait for him to come back, but I got scared and left. I . . . it's so complicated."

"Why were you scared, Mom?" The thought that my mom was raped crossed my mind. "What did he do to scare you?"

"No, you don't understand. It wasn't like that. I was married for less than a year. I . . . we fell in love and I never told him I was married, and he never asked or even guessed."

"Why didn't you tell him?"

"Well, I did, eventually."

"Okay, let's back up a bit, Mom. Let's start at the beginning. Why were you in Greece?"

"I was writing for a magazine about traveling in Athens on five dollars a day. I left all my jewelry at home, including my wedding ring. I wanted to blend in. Like a young backpacker . . . I just couldn't. We were in love. It was the real thing, and I knew it, but I was married. How could I do that to your father? To Karl. I loved him too, and he trusted me when I went on my travel assignments. I just couldn't give up on a marriage that was just getting started. We never fought. We got along. My mother said I married too quickly; I didn't want her to be right. And besides, I just couldn't think of a reason to leave him for someone I just met and spent a mere week with."

"But you said you loved him, my father, this Valentino guy."

"I did. I still do. There's not a day I haven't thought of him in over thirty-five years."

"Jesus, Mom. You thought about him for thirty-five years? But you said you told him eventually. So why haven't I heard about him till now?"

"Yes, well, like I said, it's a little more complicated than that. He had to go back to Athens and change his ticket. It was not like it is today. There were no cell phones. He had to go in person. Olympia, where we were, was just a small little village. I promised him I would stay and wait for him, and we would spend another week together. I promised him. But I couldn't do it."

The tears began again, so I handed her a tissue. I sighed. I was trying to be empathetic, as Cody had suggested, but it was hard. The rage was bubbling up with each breath I took.

"The minute the train left and was out of sight, guilt overtook me. I went to the hotel and packed my bags and checked out. I left him a note saying I was married and, yes, I did love him more than life itself, but I couldn't leave my husband."

"So, you left him a note and took off back to Canada like the next day?"

"Yes, the next day."

"So, oh, boy, this is an awkward question, but Mom, were you having an affair and not using protection?"

"Only once. The first time. A week before. That's why, you see, I thought it was your dad. I calculated it to the exact day from when you were born, and it came out it had to be Karl."

"So did it ever cross your mind that Dad, that Karl was not my father?"

"I don't know," she whispered, looking down at her trembling hands.

"Mom, I'm going to ask you again, all these years, did you ever think that this Valentino guy was my father?" I knew I sounded too stern, but I couldn't help myself.

She looked up at the ceiling. "I . . . yes, I wondered. I don't know. I thought about it a lot. I . . . I . . . secretly even hoped he was your father. I know none of this makes sense."

"You wished he was my father, but you never tried to know for sure? Are you fucking kidding me?"

"I knew you wouldn't understand. I was married! I loved Karl. I had to try and make it work. I was ashamed."

I took a long deep breath, hearing Cody's words in my head. *If she kept this secret for all these years, there must have been a lot of pain around her decision. Be gentle.*

"I get it, Mom. It's okay. You loved the guy. You betrayed your husband and felt ashamed. You're not the first woman who has gone through something like this."

"When your dad finally left me, telling me I was too hard to love, I knew it was because I could never love him like I loved Valentino. I tried, oh, God, how I tried. But I just couldn't. And I thought about it then—I mean going to find Valentino and seeing if he was your father and seeing if we could try again. But by then you were four years old. And when Karl left the marriage, you were so devastated. You adored him, and he adored you. We were all hurting so much. I just couldn't add to the hurt. Then Celeste came along, and she loved you instantly, and you were part of a family. I couldn't take that away from you. You had a family, a real family, a normal, happy family. She was a better mother to you than I was. I saw it right away. She was so happy and loving, and then Brittany was born. I couldn't do it then either. You were so happy. You were a family. And I tried my best to allow you to have a normal life."

"So, you knew, Mom. You knew Dad was not my dad? I mean Karl was not my dad."

"Well, at first, I was always searching for clues. Even when you were born, your hair, your facial features, your mannerisms. You know, anything that could be an indication. But I didn't know for sure. The hair colour maybe, but Karl was adopted and never knew anything about his birth parents and had no wish to find out, so there was always that factor. I even tried to encourage him to go back to Denmark and dig for information on them, but he refused. Said he didn't need to know who they were or why they gave him up. He was quite comfortable in his skin, he would say. His adopted parents were good people, and he wasn't about to do anything to upset them. Well, you know your dad, he's not one to delve deep into anything—especially emotions. He is so damn stubborn. And you know his motto, 'never look back, only look forward.' That says it all."

"Yes, I know it well, Mom. I get it."

"But then we discovered your love of music. To me, that was when I began to have my doubts. It was like music was somehow in your blood."

"What has music got to do with it? Was he a musician?"

"He was an opera singer."

"An opera singer? Are you kidding me?" My eyes must have become enormous.

"Yes. He had the most beautiful tenor voice I've ever heard. He sang to me many times."

I laughed sarcastically. "Sorry, Mom, but you and an opera singer? It just sounds like an odd combination."

"Why? Love is love. There are no rules."

"Touché! Sorry. Let's move on. How old was he?"

"He was three years older than me. Born February twenty-eighth. We celebrated his twenty-ninth birthday, and we had so much fun."

"So, that means he was born in 1951. That would make him sixty-four, or sixty-five in a few weeks."

"Yes."

"Mom, where is your computer?"

"In the kitchen. Why?"

I sat at the kitchen table and Googled 'Valentino Lombardo, opera singer.' It took less than two minutes to find him. He was a professor at the University of Melbourne and was head of the training program that offered elite-level training for opera singers.

"Mom, come here. Is this him?"

"I can't look, I just can't see his face."

"Mom, come here. Look at this picture. I need to know if this is the right guy." I pointed to a picture of a middle-aged man with snow-white hair and a short beard that had a hint of red showing through.

Mom looked at the picture.

"Oh, my God, that's him. He looks the same." She touched the screen of the computer, her eyes misting up again.

I studied the screen and zoomed in on his face. "I have his eyes. I always thought I had your eyes, but I have his eyes," I said dreamily.

"Yes, you have his beautiful, laughing eyes. I know."

"Jesus Christ, Mom! You know I have his eyes?" I sighed, and my eyes rolled back into my head. "So, you knew, you knew it all along. I can't believe this. I just can't fucking believe any of this. I need some paper and a pen."

Crying, she handed me some from the desk drawer. "What are you going to do?"

"I'm writing down his office number. I'm going to see him."

I searched for flights to Melbourne. There was one that went direct in two days. I went on Skype and called his office.

"Yes, I'm wanting to make an appointment with Professor Lombardo on Friday, February thirteenth, preferably the last appointment of the day. Yes, Stormy Hera. I am wanting to enroll in his program. Yes. Thank you."

I called the airline and booked the flight.

"Mom, I need your credit card. I didn't bring my purse."

"What are you doing?"

"I'm going to meet my father."

"But you can't just go meet him. Shouldn't you call him first? It's been just over a month since you finished your treatments. You're still recovering from chemo. Don't you need to talk to your doctor to see if it's okay?"

"No, I don't need permission from anyone. And I want to do this in person. Card please, Mom."

"But isn't this a little rash? You're moving too fast."

I stared into her eyes. I gritted my teeth in anger and in a stern tone I had never used with my mother before, I said, "No, Mom, you," and I pointed my finger near her face, "moved too slow. I'm not wasting another minute in this madness. I want to meet my father. And, by the way, didn't it cross your mind that maybe he has a child? A sibling for me? Geez, Mom, didn't you think of this when we found out that none of you here were matches for a bone-marrow transplant? This might be my chance at finding a donor, never mind finding out before I die that I have a father I have never met, and maybe siblings?" My face grew hot. My forehead felt sweaty. Anger rose up again. This time I couldn't control it even if I tried. "How fucking selfish of you not to at least tell me when you knew I needed a donor!" I screamed.

"I didn't mean not to tell you. I was waiting till . . . I was waiting to see if you really needed a transplant. We still don't know if you need one. Unless you're hiding that from me."

"I'm not hiding anything from you. Unlike you! I don't know if I need a transplant or not but for fuck sakes, Mom." I raised my arms in the air. "I give up. This is just unreal. Un-fucking real. I don't even know what to say to you anymore." I knew I shouldn't be yelling and swearing, but it was like I was not in my body, like my emotions were out of my control. I couldn't harness them even if I tried. "I gotta go. I can't look at you right now," I screamed at the top of my lungs as I slammed the front door.

CHAPTER FOURTEEN
SUNNYDALE FORENSIC HOSPITAL

One of the things I miss most about living in this hospital prison is good food, in fact I'd even be happy if it was half-decent. I've always prided myself on being a food connoisseur thanks to Celeste and my mother. Good tasting, healthy food is important to me. Organic whenever I can get it, fresh rather than frozen, and never anything from a can. The food in this *state-of-the-art facility,* in most cases, is barely edible, and there is no variety. The menu every frickin week is: Mondays - hamburgers, Tuesday - liver and onions, Wednesday - spaghetti and meat sauce, Thursday - ham and scalloped potatoes from a box – (yes, I actually saw the box), Friday - the worst bland tilapia fish in the world, Saturday - hotdogs, which I didn't even realize people still ate, Sunday - chicken thighs – never breasts, never roasted, only ever baked in a tomato paste thing with absolutely no spices. There is dessert every day, though—cake, apple crisp, and ice cream. I often see people eating only the sweets, and I have to admit I have been tempted to follow suit. The odd time there are apples and bananas. Popcorn without salt but plenty of tasty trans-fat filled margarine to clog your arteries on Friday nights, if you are lucky enough to be allowed to go to the gym and watch a movie. Lunch is always sandwiches—bologna, egg salad, tuna, or ham—paired with canned soup—chicken noodle, tomato, and the favourite of most everyone, and I am ashamed to say, even me, Campbell's mushroom with tiny specs of mushroom pieces that I savour in my mouth like they were caviar. Breakfast is always porridge, which I usually skip because it just looks so gross, or a couple slices of white Bimbo bread— again, I saw the package. Sunday is the exception, and we are treated to cold scrambled eggs and two slices of bacon so thin you can spit through them. I am pretty sure the eggs are not real, but I don't know for sure. Those are the big choices.

With fake money (tokens that are made to look like money, why I don't know) that I make helping out in the library (my job for two hours a day, Monday to Friday), I buy myself KitKat bars and bags of salt and vinegar chips, and each Saturday I get a can of ginger ale and pretend it is champagne, and I toast myself for surviving another week. You do what you have to do.

I eat only to survive. The worst thing is that I dream about food all the time, which makes it worse. Celeste's sushi rolls, her Crepes Suzette, and steamed Prince Edward Island mussels in her scrumptious garlic and white wine broth. Mother's garlic and lemon baby back ribs that fall off the bone like butter, her roasted potatoes smothered in fresh rosemary and her eggplant pizza baked with fresh tomatoes and Thai basil leaves and sprinkled with fresh parmesan cheese. Linguini vongole from Pagliacci's with New York cheesecake for dessert is another favourite dream—I am usually with Brittany, and we are listening to a gypsy swing band as we eat. I dream a lot about Jonas and I snuggled up on the couch munching on popcorn with just the right amount of Himalayan salt, churned butter, and nutritional yeast, licking the butter off our fingers and smiling at each other. He always says "you're the best," and I say, "No, you're the best," and then we giggle. The dreams are torture.

Back to the story…

CHAPTER FIFTEEN
MELBOURNE, AUSTRALIA

FEBRUARY 2015

On my way to Melbourne, I sat in the 747 airplane, thankful there was no one seated next to me. I couldn't imagine trying to carry on a conversation. There were so many thoughts swirling in my head, questions I wanted to ask my father. The first of which was: did I have siblings? I knew it was selfish to think about it. But now that I had found my birth father, I wanted desperately to live to see Jonas grow up. I knew my chances were slim, but for the first time since finding out I had cancer, I felt there was real hope. The thoughts were like fireworks in my head, firing off in different directions: from excitement at meeting my father; to incredible anger at my mother for denying me a relationship with him all these years; to fear that I would have no match for a transplant; to an overwhelming feeling of sadness that Jonas would grow up without me. But I knew I had to shut off my mind somehow. With the time change, I didn't want to be fighting jet lag for the whole week. I wanted to be rested and coherent when I met my father. I was feeling so much better though. I was gaining weight, getting stronger by the day. My hair had grown back enough that I was able to get a cute pixie cut, which didn't even look that bad. I was still needing a lot of rest though, and Linda had warned me not to push myself too hard.

"I wish you would have waited. But I know there is no stopping you once you make up your mind. Please promise me that you will listen to your body,

Stormy. Rest. Don't miss meals. You are going to be running on adrenaline, and you will crash if you aren't careful." She hugged me and told me she loved me.

I knew that I needed to get my rest and to try and stay calm. I could feel my fragility.

Within half an hour of being on the flight, I decided that the universe was shining down on me. The flight attendants on Japan Airlines were more than attentive and, luckily, I had two empty seats beside me so I could lay down and sleep. I wondered how first class could be any better than how I was being treated. They served warm tea and gave me a warm, mint-scented towel before we even lifted off. The smell reminded me that I should dig out my essential oils from my carry-on bag before taking off. It was a trick that Mom taught me whenever we traveled. She swore that her essential oils made traveling so much easier. Lavender oil to help sleep; peppermint to wake-up; and bergamot for the stress. I decided I would add alcohol to the regime, just to make sure I would sleep and to help me relax. They had an assortment of sake, and I chose the most expensive one on the menu. I felt I deserved it after all I had gone through—and was about to go through. Lavender on my temples, a half bottle of the rice wine, a nice soft pillow and blanket, and another warm cloth all did the trick. I woke to a flight attendant gently touching my hand and giving me a card with options for breakfast.

I remembered the vivid dream I had just before being woken up. I was with an older woman who looked like me. She was holding my hand, and we were walking in what seemed like an orchard or a big backyard that was filled with lemon trees. I could smell the lemons. I asked her if she was me, and she laughed and said, "In a way, yes." It was at that moment that the flight attendant touched my arm and woke me up. It was one of those dreams that seemed so real that it made me wonder if it actually was a dream or if someone was trying to connect to me somehow. I brushed the thought from my head, thinking I was beginning to sound like my mother. She was into all that new age stuff.

I chose the Japanese breakfast out of respect for Celeste, and it was surprisingly good considering it was airplane food: steamed rice, miso soup, grilled fish, Japanese pickles, fermented soybeans, steamed broccoli, and a green salad. Celeste, and my mother to some extent, raised me to try different kinds of foods, and I always appreciated that. There were never dull meals growing up. They were always discovering and trying new things. The latest trend that Celeste was experimenting with was Asian Fusion. Her tiny cafe in downtown Victoria always got a five-star rating. She was open from eleven to five, and if you didn't have a reservation a month in advance, forget it.

Mother loved eating out and trying different restaurants, but when I was growing up, I did prefer Mom's cooking to the restaurant food. I didn't let on, though, because she was always so excited to try new establishments and dishes. Before Mom started back to travel writing, restaurants seemed her way of escaping the mundane life of staying put in one place. She never came out and said it, but it wasn't hard to figure out. Mom's photo albums were dog-eared from being looked at so much. We would often sit down together, and she would tell me stories of all the places she'd been. And many times, I would come home to find her looking through her albums with blood-shot eyes, a box of tissues beside her, and a pile of used ones on the end table.

Mom was a good cook, not as adventurous as Celeste, but she cooked more wholesome dishes like meat and potatoes, and French dishes like tourtiere. There was only one peculiar thing about her cooking—she was addicted to Greek salad. By the time I left home, I swore that if I ever ate another Greek salad in my life, it would be too soon. And as the memory crossed my mind. I said to myself, *aha, Greek salads, that makes sense.* I knew she frequently traveled to Greece, but now knowing that Greece was where she fell in love with my father, it dawned on me that many things about my mom were going to make sense now that the secret was out; like her somewhat sad and lonely life, her choices, her behaviour and, yes, even what she loved to eat.

I looked at my watch to see what time it was in Victoria, and what time it was in Melbourne. Then I remembered my mother saying to me: "When you travel across time zones, always get into the new time zone as soon as possible, and avoid looking at your watch," so I changed mine to Melbourne time. I had been so exhausted from all the stress that I never slept at home, so in a convoluted way, it helped me slip into Melbourne time zone much easier.

As I looked out the window waiting to see land, my stomach did somersaults. It was nerves. I knew the feeling well. It was the exact same feeling I had when I had to defend my PhD thesis: Jazz in Higher Education: Toward A Pedagogy of Creativity. I had been so nervous I thought I would actually throw up just before entering the examination, but I took ten deep breaths as Cody had taught me. The minute I opened my mouth to speak, I felt my stomach relax. If I could survive having six professors dissecting my work and drilling me with questions, then I could get through meeting my father for the first time.

The only question that kept popping into my head was: had I made the right decision not calling him first? Even Cody told me I should have called and given him a head's up. But I decided to go with my gut. I wanted to see his reaction in real time and to be able to talk to him about it and not have him wait for days. It seemed everyone did everything either on the phone or in emails these days. So impersonal. I thought it was sad that our world had come to this. Nobody did anything in person anymore—I was sure that it was the right way to go, despite what Cody and my mother said.

I had downloaded a few pictures I had found of my father on the internet. Some were of him singing when he was much younger. One was of him laughing when he was in his forties, I guessed. And a picture of him with a woman holding onto his arm at some kind of award ceremony. I opened up my laptop computer and looked at the photos again. I could see the resemblance. I had his chin, not my mom's. And, funny, but I definitely had the same expression as his eyes when he laughed. When I smiled, my narrow eyes opened wide, my forehead wrinkled, and my eyebrows scrunched way up. It was like a look of surprise but at the same there was a softness within the expression. I knew the look on my father's face well, not just because I had the same reflection, but because Jonas had the identical one too. And the freckles, yes, I could see them in the picture. They were faint, but definitely there, and the reddish-blonde hair colour in the younger one was just like my natural colour.

And, of course, the music. It all made perfect sense. I had music in my head all the time for as long as I could remember. My mother often told people that I sang before I talked, and the only way I would go to sleep was if she sang to me. When I was two, Mom bought me a Fisher Price tape recorder so I could listen to music to go to sleep, and I continued to listen to music to go to sleep my whole life. Cody had to get used to it when we got together and, though it took some time, he confessed he found it quite soothing after a while. My love of music was why Mom put me into Suzuki violin, flute, and piano. She knew she had to nurture my obsession, but all the programs for kids were way too elementary. She finally found the answer after reading an article about the Suzuki method of music where children learn to play violin or flute or piano much like a language; by imitation. She found a teacher, and I began playing the violin at three-and- a-half, flute a year later, and eventually piano when we moved to Victoria, all the same way. Sitting there on the plane it hit me that I really had to thank my mother. It was one area of my life that she unquestionably did not screw up. Music was a language. My violin, flute, and piano or really any instrument I played, were an extension of me, a part of me. I was never told to practice my instruments. I just played, just as one speaks. "Music is just another way to express yourself," my mom would say. And she was right. It was a language to me, and my fingers instinctively knew how to speak the language. It was hard to be angry at her, thinking about how she really understood me and made sure my gift for music was nurtured and explored throughout my life—from three years old to the present. Except for my rebellious teen years, I never talked back to her. We were close. And since Jonas's birth, we grew closer than ever. I teared up, thinking about Mom. I felt sorry for her. She did sacrifice so much for me, but I still felt the anger. There was also a deep love that couldn't be denied though. It was all so confusing. I was beginning to really regret how I had yelled at her.

CHAPTER SIXTEEN

FEBRUARY 2015

I knocked lightly on the wooden door. "Professor Lombardo?"

"Come in, and have a seat. What can I do for you?" He looked at the note on his desk that his receptionist had handed to him earlier. "Stormy Hera?"

I studied him. His hair was white with soft waves. There was a beautiful gentleness about him. He was handsome in a distinguished professor kind of way. Jeans and a white T-shirt with a tweed blazer. I looked at his green eyes; it was like looking at Jonas's eyes. His hands had long, slender fingers, like mine. There was no wedding ring.

"Ms. Hera. Are you alright? Can I get you a glass of water? Tea? I'm guessing you had a long flight coming from America?"

"Sorry, I, it's just that . . . No, I'm from Canada."

"Canada. Well, your name is very unusual, Hera, the Greek Goddess, wife of Zeus. Very intriguing."

"Yes, well, my mother changed her name when she got divorced from my father when I was four. She didn't want to keep his name or use her maiden name, which was Boisseau."

"Boisseau? I knew someone with that name who came from Cana . . ." His face went white, and his mouth hung open.

"I'm Evangeline's daughter," I said, staring right into his eyes.

He looked at me as if searching for something. Then, very slowly, he said: "You look like my mother. I . . . I . . . ah, I mean your mother."

My eyes filled up with tears, and I struggled to speak. "I need to tell you a story. I have rehearsed this hundreds of times, so please let me tell it, and then we can talk." I blurted out my opening statement that I had prepared in my head all morning.

He nodded, not taking his eyes off me.

I cleared my throat and took a deep breath. "I recently found out that I have cancer and may need a bone marrow transplant. My best chance at having a compatible donor is from a sibling. When my family got tested, the doctor told me my half-sister was not a candidate, and I was not even related to her at all. He said it was impossible. To make a long story short, my father did a paternity test, and we found out that he was not my father. I confronted my mother, who told me that she was never 100 percent sure, but that if he wasn't my father, you were. So that is why I'm here. I believe you are my father." I swallowed hard, and my shoulders dropped. My hands were sweating, so I rubbed them on my jeans.

Valentino took off his glasses and grabbed a tissue from his desk. He dabbed his eyes and his face screwed up, a facial expression I somehow recognized. He held his head in his hands and sobbed.

I didn't know what to do. I had rehearsed my speech so many times, but I hadn't thought about what to say after I had told him. I didn't even have a plan for whatever his reaction would be. I felt stupid for not thinking it all through first and being better prepared. I walked over behind his desk and handed him another tissue, then knelt down and put my arms around him and gently rubbed his back, like I would do for Jonas. Thankfully, he didn't resist my embrace.

Softly, I said, "I'm so sorry for just springing all this on you like that. I have a tendency to act first, then think later. I'm so sorry. Please, forgive me, Dr. Lombardo. If you want me to leave, I will."

"No. No. Please. I, I, it just took me by surprise. Please stay. Don't leave." He raised his head and looked into my eyes.

"I'll stay," I said as I handed him another tissue.

He blew his nose. I'd never seen a man cry so hard. It was as if the tears just couldn't stop. They kept coming and coming. I stayed beside him for what seemed like fifteen minutes, rubbing his back, repeating "It will be okay," until finally, he gained some composure.

"I'm okay now." I took a step away, grabbed a chair, and sat close enough to him that our knees were almost touching. He looked at me with so much compassion. "I'm so sorry you have cancer. So terribly sorry. But at the same time, I'm happy, really. I am so happy. I wondered when I saw you if we were related. I could see it. You look like my mother's side of the family. It's uncanny."

He looked down at his desk. "Oh, God, your name. He looked at the receptionist's note again, "Stormy. Your name is Stormy Hera?"

I wasn't quite sure why he was so shocked at my name.

"Yes. I'm married, but I kept my mother's name. I have a son, Jonas. You have a grandson. He's ten years old. He looks like you, like you and me." I handed over my phone and showed him a picture.

"He is precious. He is so beautiful. He looks like you." And the tears began to flow again as he smiled.

"I'm so sorry for springing this on you, but I wanted to tell you in person. I hope you understand. I know it must be a shock."

"Oh, it is a shock," he said with a light chuckle. "But it's the best shock I've ever had in my life."

I smiled weakly. My jaw relaxed. I hadn't realized I was so tense until I felt my temples throb from clenching.

"How about we get out of here and go to my house? There's so much we need to talk about. Where are your things?"

"I came in a taxi cab. My suitcase is in the reception area. But are you sure? I don't want to impose."

"You're not imposing. I'll call Margaret and let her know we're having company for tea."

∞

It was a short drive from the university. We arrived at 215 Lansell Road in Toorak. The electric gates opened into an estate on at least two acres of land. A woman in her fifties greeted us at the door.

"Hello, I'm Margaret. Welcome." She bowed her head slightly and smiled at me. "Let me show you your room. Valentino said you're staying for a bit?" She grabbed my luggage and, without another word, carried my suitcase up the stairs. I followed her.

Valentino yelled at us as we walked up the stairs, "Why not freshen up a bit, then we can meet on the back deck and chat and have a drink before dinner."

"Okay. I won't be long."

Margaret showed me the room and the attached bathroom. "If there's anything you need Mrs. Hera, just ask. You've had a long flight, I understand, so feel free to freshen up. There should be everything you need in the restroom." She smiled and did a half-bow, then left.

"His wife?" I wondered. I decided I'd better call Cody before I went downstairs. "Cody, it's me. I guess you're not there. I just wanted to tell you that he is wonderful. My father is so sweet. Oh, my God. And he invited me to his house, I mean his mansion. I'll call you later. I love you. Oh, can you call Mom and Dad and Brit, and tell them all I'm fine? I'll call you back later."

The brick house was large. Outdated, for sure, but clean and well cared for. It was like stepping back in time to the 1940s, I guessed, based on the Art Deco feel throughout: geometrical designs everywhere; a pink vanity and bathtub and toilet. But there was something else—columns everywhere and statues, as if I were in an Italian villa. It was a strange combination. Although, from my art history class, I remembered that Art Deco was highly influenced by Italy and Greece. Out on the back deck, the trees and shrubs and flowers seemed to make up for the gaudiness of the columns. Somehow, the house just didn't reflect the man I had just met.

I stepped off the back deck and made my way to the shaded area where a white, wicker bistro dining set sat on the manicured lawn that overlooked the large pool. He stood up as I approached. It was hot, maybe in the high thirties; the shade looked inviting.

"Please, have a seat. What can I get you to drink? Alcohol? Tea? Whatever you want."

"A glass of red wine would be nice," I said as I sat down on the chair that was shaded by a huge lemon tree. As Margaret approached us, I noticed a man pruning shrubs at the back of the property. He looked to be in his fifties, and he had light-brown skin like Margaret.

"Margaret, can you please get us a bottle of Wolf Blass Brown label and some ice lemon water?"

"Of course. May I bring some appetizers? I'm sure your daughter is hungry from her journey," she said as she smiled at me.

"Great idea. Thank you."

"I hope it's okay that I told her you were my daughter. I tell Margaret everything. I couldn't hold back my excitement. She's like part of my family. She has spent the last thirty years with me and has tried everything in her power to get me married off and to start a family. To say she was excited when I told her, is an understatement."

"No, I don't mind a bit. I'm so relieved that you're happy."

Valentino leaned forward in his chair. "I feel I need to clear the air about something so you are not confused," Valentino said with a serious look. I realized that Jonas, when he was explaining something to me, had a similar look. It was comforting.

"Please, Professor Lombardo, say whatever you want. I was hoping we could speak freely. I want all the secrecy to be done within this family."

Margaret silently poured us two glasses of wine, placed the water jug and glasses on the table, and left.

"My feelings exactly." He hesitated for a moment before he spoke. "When your mother left me with just a note saying she was married, I was heartbroken. I thought about her every day and relived our time together over and over in my mind. No matter how I looked at it, I knew it was real love or else we both deserved an Oscar for our acting performances. I was hopelessly in love. When I got the note, I was devastated. I mean I was totally crushed. My mother was very concerned about me. She told me to get on a plane to Canada and talk face-to-face with her otherwise, I was going to be depressed forever. She said I needed closure at least. After a year and a half of being utterly miserable, I finally agreed with her, and I flew to Victoria, rented a car, and drove to Salt Spring Island. I knew she lived there, and I had conjured up a ridiculous, hopeful scenario in my head that when she saw me, she would run into my arms and immediately change her mind and leave her husband and come to Australia with me. I was convinced that she loved me like I loved her. A once-in-lifetime love. You understand?"

"Yes, I do."

"But I couldn't find her. The last name she gave me was Boisseau, and there was no such person with that name on the island. So, I had to find out where she worked, which proved to be quite easy. I remembered she told me she worked on Pender Island but lived on Salt Spring. There was only one publishing house on Pender Island. I phoned them and got her last name, then drove to the address I found in the Salt Spring phone book. Just as I drove up, I saw your mother and father come out of their house. The man, your father, had you in a front-pack carrying thing. He kissed your head several times. Evangeline and your dad held hands as they walked. They were laughing. I followed them in my car to the Salt Spring Fall Fair. I parked my car and watched them from a distance. I could see that she was so happy. She sat down on a picnic bench and nursed you, and your dad came over and brought her a drink, and they kissed. That is when I turned around and left. I took the next plane back to Melbourne."

"Oh, my goodness. You came to Canada? Did it cross your mind that the baby could be yours?"

"I don't remember but if it did, it was a fleeting thought. You could have been one month old or one year old, I wouldn't have known the difference. I had never been around babies ever. All I saw that day was that my darling Evangeline was happy, she had a husband who obviously loved her, she loved him, and she had a baby. I couldn't take that away from her. It wasn't fair. I loved her enough to let her go, if that makes any sense." He sat back in his chair. A look of sadness came over him.

"I understand. I really do. And thank you for telling me that. From the little bit Mom told me, I gathered you two had something very special. You never married or had children of your own?" I asked, feeling relieved to fit the question into the conversation.

"No, I came close once, but I couldn't go through with it in the end. Her name was Anna. She was a lovely, sweet, quiet woman with a gentle soul. We were set up by a mutual friend. We dated for two years. She finally told me she wasn't going to wait forever. Either I made a commitment, or she was leaving. We got engaged but a month before the wedding, I called it off. I didn't love her like I loved your mother, and I decided it wouldn't be fair to me or to her. I wanted the real thing. I wanted your mother. I never dated after that. I didn't see the point."

My heart sank. He had no children and, because he loved Mom so much, he had never married or opened his heart again.

"I'm so sorry. Really. Do you mind if I ask if you fathered any other children? Is there a possibility that I may have a half sibling somewhere? It's just that, well, in case I need a donor."

"Oh, God, I'm so sorry, Stormy, I'm going on and on, but, of course, this is important information. I'm sure I never had any other children, although I wish for your sake I would have."

I sighed, maybe a little louder than I intended. "It's okay, it was a long shot. There are lots of other options, my doctor says." I felt utterly devastated, but I didn't want to show it. I didn't want to spoil what was turning out to be a wonderful discovery: that my father was an amazing, kind, gentle person.

"Please, is there anything I can do? I can get tested, no?"

"Yes, of course, the percentages are low with a parent for some reason I don't quite understand, but it's worth a try. Thank you," I said, forcing a slight smile.

I looked at him and felt his sadness, and I felt bad that the dynamic had changed between us so quickly. I didn't want to dwell on the disappointment. I needed to change the subject. I took a sip of wine and said, "I'm going to tell you something that might be interesting."

He leaned forward. "What is that?"

"My mother said almost the exact same thing to me not a week ago."

"Said what?"

"She said that she only ever loved you, and that's why she never dated, and why her marriage fell apart."

Valentino teared up.

I realized that my father was a very sensitive man. I was not used to seeing men cry. My dad certainly never cried, and I had only seen Cody cry three times: once when Jonas was born and he held him for the first time, and two times when I got the news that I had cancer.

Margaret brought a plate of fresh vegetables and tzatziki dip and an assortment of cheeses and pates and set it down. She took one look at Valentino and gently patted his back.

"It's okay, Mr. Lombardo. You're allowed to cry. You have your beautiful daughter here with you now. You're so lucky to have found each other."

He placed his hand on hers. "Thank you, Margaret. Yes, I'm a very lucky man. Yes, indeed," he said as he wiped the tears from his eyes with a napkin.

Margaret smiled at me, touching her hand to her heart, and walked back inside the house.

I looked at my father. I saw the same grief in his eyes that I had witnessed in my mother's when she revealed how she had lost the love of her life. It was just days before, but it felt like years.

"I'm sorry, I really am. Both you and my mother have suffered for so long. I hope that somehow the suffering can end now that we all know the truth."

"I'll be okay. I just . . . I mean, there's so much to digest. You understand? To know your mother feels the same way as I do . . . you have no idea what that means to me. No idea. It's a pain I've carried with me for so long, and now to know Evangeline felt the same way all these years? It seems such a waste. Such a waste. But at the same time, I'm so touched to know that, even though it has been a secret, I was loved all these years. It's so much to take in, I don't know what to think." And he began to sob again.

I just watched him. My heart was aching for him, for my mother, and for myself. It was all such a shame.

It took a few minutes for him to gain his composure. "Okay, I'm better now," he said as he took a deep breath. "Understand me when I say, I'm not just concerned about what your mother thinks: I want to get to know you and hear what you think. And I know you must have so many questions. Is there anything you want to ask me? Anything at all?"

I took a moment to digest his question, then I said, "It dawned on me when we were driving here that you said Hera is a Greek goddess. Mom changed our name to Hera when she and dad divorced. I mean I knew who Hera was, of course, but now I see there was a reason behind it. You were in Greece together."

"Yes, your mother and I went to the temple of Hera in Olympia the day after we met on the train. I told her I had a soft spot for Hera, as she is the goddess of marriage and family. She represents the ideal woman, who would do anything to protect her family. Even practice deception." He chuckled. "So fitting when you think about it. Evangeline kept me a secret to protect her family. To protect you."

"Protect me? I never thought of it that way. But, hmmm, when I think about my mom, it fits. She gave up so much for me. I'm beginning to see it the more we talk. I mean, I realized it more when I became a mother myself, how she sacrificed so much for me. But now I see that she gave up the only man she ever loved for me—in a way. I still wish she hadn't lied to me though. I think it's going to take a long time to forgive her."

"I have a feeling you'll forgive her sooner than you think, and I will too."

He dipped a carrot in the tzatziki. "You gotta try this. Margaret is from the Philippines, but my, oh, my, she learned overnight how to make Italian and Greek dishes better than any Greek or Italian."

I tried the dip. "Oh, yes, that's quite good. My stepmother, Celeste, is a chef and has an incredible restaurant in Victoria. So, I've been raised to be a bit of a food snob. So, when I say it's good, I really mean it."

"Well, wait for tonight. She made roast lamb that has been marinating for forty-eight hours in mint sauce that she made from scratch and the best Greek salad and rosemary roast potatoes this side of Greece."

"Greek salad? You like Greek salad?"

"No, I love Greek salad. I have the olive oil from the Peloponnese shipped in by the case."

"And don't tell me, you marinate your salad in lemon first?"

"Yes, how did you know?" His smile lit up his face.

"I grew up on Greek salad and, to this day, I swear Mom eats it at least two or three times a week. She always tells me about the lemon marinade."

"She learned that from me."

"Oh, this is strange in a funny way. I'm sorry but you and Mom . . . I'm beginning to see a pattern here."

"True love. Love for eternity. I knew I felt it, but to know she felt the same way all these years, it really . . . it really means everything to me," he said as he looked off into the distance.

I took another sip of wine. I was a bit tipsy, but relaxed.

I waited till his attention was back to the here and now before asking, "Speaking of names, do you know why I was called Stormy? I always wondered about that, but when I asked my mom, she just said she liked it. It's such an unusual name. I even checked to see if I was born on a stormy day but no, it was a sunny one. No storm. Is there more to it?"

He closed his eyes for a moment, then opened them with a slight grin on his face. "You were conceived during a horrific rainstorm that flooded the streets and shut down the power for hours. It was the first time we made love. It was not planned, and it was the one and only time we didn't use any protection. Yes, it was a horrific storm. It blew down trees, rained buckets in a very short time, I recall." He paused, then looked me in the eyes. "If it is any consolation, you were conceived in pure love. On a stormy day." Joy lit his face.

"Oh, wow. This is like finding jigsaw puzzle pieces that have been lost for over thirty years!" I was excited at the revelation but like a ton of bricks, it hit me that my mother knew all along that Karl was not my father. Or, perhaps as she had said, she secretly hoped Valentino was my father. It was confusing. I didn't know what to believe. And I could feel the anger come alive again in my chest as I thought about my mother. But I didn't want to let on to Valentino what thoughts were going through my head and spoil the moment.

"I was in love with your mother even before the train reached Olympia, to be honest. We met on a train. I don't know if you knew that."

"No, tell me about it."

"First, I'll tell you something about why I knew I was in love. I need to go back to my childhood." He took a sip of his wine. "When I was a small boy, I had a terrible stutter. When I was six and starting school, I was teased so badly that I became very withdrawn. My parents were academics. My Papa, your grandfather, was a mathematical genius who taught at the university. He was not the greatest at social interactions. He was more comfortable with numbers than with people. My mother, on the other hand, was a linguistics professor and a social butterfly. They met at the university where they both taught. They fell in love and married in their late thirties and had me when they were in their forties. It was not planned. They didn't know what to do with a child, as my mother often told me when I was growing up. She would laugh when she told me they were as well equipped to raise a child as a carpenter was to raise a barn with no hammer." He laughed quietly. "Her favourite saying was, where there's a will, there's a way. That's how they raised me, with this belief that somehow it would all work out, even though they had no clue about raising a child. Neither of them had siblings growing up, which didn't help matters. When I was a little boy, my mother would always tell me not to worry so much because the answer would come, but perhaps not always in the way I imagined it would. She confessed that she and my papa didn't know what to do with a child who stuttered. But she reassured me that the answer would come, and she was right. She came across an article in an academic journal that proved how people who stuttered didn't stutter when they sang. So that was her solution. She took me to a music teacher at the conservatory. However, by this time I was eight years old and very shy and withdrawn. The music instructor said it would be an upward hill and not to expect too much. The surprise for parents and my teacher was that I was good. I excelled at music and when I was on stage, I turned into a different boy. The stuttering completely disappeared when I sang. I gained so much confidence by knowing that whenever I sang, I would be free of my stutter. I was still terribly shy, and I was teased constantly, but underneath I had gained incredible confidence. It was like a seed that had been dormant inside me got watered and began to grow, little by little."

"I'm so sorry you had to go through that. I know children can be so cruel. My husband Cody is an educational psychologist in a school. He tells me stories about the cruelty of children. It breaks my heart every time."

"Yes, they were cruel. It was like I had two personas. This confident boy when singing, then this shy, introverted boy the rest of the time. And this continued all the way through school until I graduated. At university it was a little better. My classmates were much more forgiving of my stuttering, though by that time I was so shy and introverted, it was hard to make friends or, God forbid, date. I tell you this not because I want sympathy but because, when I met your mother on the train, within an hour of talking to her, my stutter disappeared. Completely stopped." He hit the table with his hand. "Just like that. It was quite astonishing really. Never, in my entire life, had that ever happened. Not even with my own parents. But with your mom, I guess I felt so comfortable that the stuttering vanished like magic." He flung his hands in the air.

"Wow. That's an amazing story. But I don't hear a stutter now. How come?"

"You're right. It rarely shows up anymore. It's a funny thing, but the older you get the less you stutter, in most cases anyway. And I've learned a few little tricks along the way to help too."

Margaret walked in and told us 'Tea' was ready. "Lamb roasted in mint sauce and a nice Greek salad and roast potatoes," she said. "Your favourite, Mr. Lombardo," which made us laugh, to which Margaret said, "What? Did I miss something?"

The evening was short. I was exhausted from my trip and went to bed early. I was so glad I stayed at the house. I felt comfortable in its oddities and extravagances and with Valentino's oddities and extravagances too. When I asked him about the house, he explained that it was his parent's and that he had never lived anywhere else. When he was twenty years old, they built the guest house, which he lived in until his mother died at the age of seventy from lung cancer. His father lived to seventy-five and died peacefully in his sleep from a stroke. Valentino, however, told me he believed his father died from a broken heart. He told me they were an odd pair but totally devoted to each other. When his mom got sick, he and his father realized quickly that they could not handle the house. His father hired Margaret through some program that found work for immigrants. Margaret looked after his mom and, when she died, she stayed on and looked after the two of them.

"Papa was a mess when mother died. We had a big house and a big yard. As you probably guessed, he was Italian. He loved Italian architecture, hence the columns everywhere."

"I was going to ask about the Italian influences," I giggled.

"I know," he said with a grin. "I haven't had the heart to get rid of them, or of anything, for that matter. Or maybe it's just I'm too lazy. I can't make up my mind. Regardless, there they stand in all their glory."

"So, you moved out of the guest house, and Margaret and her husband moved in?"

"Yup, and their eight-year-old son, Hector. I moved back into my old room. I'm still there in that same room," he said with a little laugh that was edged with what I thought was regret.

I learned that Joseph was the gardener I had seen pruning the trees, and he was Margaret's husband. Hector, their son, was now a cardiac surgeon and lived in Melbourne. He was married with a baby on the way.

As I lay down on the bed, my last thought was not the usual worry about my transplant and my cancer, or even about Jonas being motherless, it was how happy I was to have found my father. I felt at home with him somehow. Comfortable in a way that I had never felt with anyone else. I felt I could tell him or ask him anything without feeling judged.

The next morning, I decided to call Cody and try to catch him before he fell asleep.

"How's my little boy? God, I miss him so much and you too. But it's been amazing here."

"I'm so happy for you, honey. Jonas misses you, but he's fine. Brittany and your mom and Celeste and your dad have been over a lot, which helps distract him."

"Good to hear. He's one lucky boy."

"How is it going there? How are you holding up? Any siblings?"

"I'm holding up really well actually. My energy increases every day, and my appetite is great. As for siblings, Valentino has no other children, so the hope of finding a donor that's related is gone. But somehow, I feel okay about it. Strange, I know."

"Oh, honey, I'm so sorry," he said quietly.

"But the good news is, I'm so glad I came and met my father. He is so wonderful. Meeting him means so much more to me than I could have imagined. He is intelligent, sensitive, and genuinely a good person. I can see how Mom fell in love with him. They would have made a great pair. It's so sad to hear their story. I'll have to tell you all about it when I get home."

"What's his house like? You said it was a mansion?"

"The house is huge. There are at least six bedrooms and an actual library stacked with books from the floor to the ceiling. The house is dated from the forties, but it's grand in a way. He inherited the house when his parents died. Margaret, his housekeeper, and her husband Joseph, who takes care of the grounds, live in his guest house. He's wealthy, but you would never know it. He is so down to earth, just wears jeans and a T-shirt and a blazer. Nothing fancy about him at all. If you saw him on the street, you'd never think he was famous. He is so easy to talk to. In a way I feel I have known him all my life. It's so strange. He wants to take me to the opera in Sydney. Guess I can check that off my bucket list, eh? We have already talked about him coming to Canada too."

"Oh, Stormy, I'm so happy for you. You were so right about meeting him in person. I was totally wrong on that call."

"Listen to your gut. Isn't that what you always tell me? Well, in a way you were right. I did. I'm feeling bad about my last conversation with Mom though. I was swearing at her and screaming when I left. Have you talked to her about it?"

"Yes, we've had some long talks. She's suffering, there's no doubt about it. But you need to know: she did it all because she loves you and wanted what was best for you. She gave up the love of her life, really. Perhaps she didn't do it the best way, but you have to see that her intentions were good."

"I know, I know. I'm beginning to understand it the more I talk with Valentino. I do know one thing, I have to try and put it behind me, but it's hard, especially now that I have cancer. My life is going to be cut short, and I still feel angry that I'm going to miss out on spending time with my father. And I feel so bad for Dad. He invested so much love and care toward raising me, and I wasn't even his child. He must be going through a lot of anger at Mom. I know it sounds strange, but I feel guilty about it. Him raising me, and all that I put him through. It's all so confusing." I wept into the phone, shocked at how fast the tears came.

"Oh, Stormy, I wish I was there to give you a hug. Karl genuinely loves you. I know that much is true. He is worried about you. And don't be so sure you're going to die soon. You don't know that."

"It's okay. I know you don't like talking about it, but Cody, we have to start accepting it. The transplant was the best hope, and now that's gone. They can try and find an unrelated donor, but the chances are pretty slim there too."

"Honey, there are other options. Don't discount them. The most important thing right now is just trying to live each moment. Enjoy your time with Valentino. Soak up every single moment. Promise me."

"I promise. I miss you. Talk in a couple of days?"

"Yes, call anytime, I'll pick up the phone even in the middle of the night."

At breakfast on Saturday, my father told me we were going to the opera on Sunday, and so we should leave in a few hours. He wanted to take me shopping for something really spectacular for my first opera. He had already arranged for the penthouse suite at the Park Hyatt overlooking the Sydney Opera House, and Sunday afternoon we had pedicures and manicures and hair appointments.

"You arranged all that already? And hair appointments? I have so little hair. It is just starting to grow back again since the chemo treatments. I'm not sure what they can do with it," I said, laughing.

"I don't know, maybe a little colour to brighten your mood?" Valentino said. "Purple highlights? And just so you know, I made one phone call to the concierge at the hotel, they know me there, and they made the arrangements. I just made the call."

"Well, thank you never-the-less. And as for the hair—I love the idea of purple hair. It's my favourite colour!"

"I can't wait to introduce my daughter to everyone. We'll go backstage and then, after the show, we'll go to a cocktail reception. I have arranged for the conductor, Maestro Greta Hauns, and Phillip, the first violinist, to join us for a late dinner before the reception. So, if you need to sleep off any time-change you can do it on the drive to Sydney."

"I don't know what to say. I hope you don't feel like you must go out of your way for me. This week so far has been way beyond what I ever expected. Any time I can spend with you is going to be great. You don't have to do anything over the top. But, to be honest, I've dreamt of going to the Sydney Opera House ever since I was a little girl. Mom bought me a book about orchestras and there was a picture of the Sydney Opera House in it, along with a story about a girl who grew up to become a violinist and played there. It was one of my favourite books. Mom kept it, and I read it to Jonas over and over." I stood up and walked over to my father and put my arms around him. "Thank you so much. I'm so happy." We hung on to each other and cried.

The conversation came easy as we drove to Sydney. We found out we had so much in common. Music, of course, but silly things too, like putting peach jam on everything: cereal, yogurt, and even meat. We both hated ketchup. We both rubbed the edge of our fingers together when we were thinking about something, and we both had a habit of tilting our heads to the side. Margaret pointed the latter one out as she served us breakfast.

My father brought photo albums to go through in the car. "I thought you might want to see these. When I first saw you, I had this strange feeling that I had seen you before. And then this morning, it came to me. I won't say another word. See if you see it."

As we drove, I looked through the family photographs; they were mostly of his parents and his grandparents, some of whom he had never met. Then I saw it, the writing under the picture indicated it was my maternal great grandmother. It was quite remarkable. I felt like I was looking at a picture of myself.

"Oh, my God. Is this the one?"

"Yes!" he said as he glanced over. "I never knew her, but as a kid, I loved to go through old photos and ask my parents to tell me all about them. I think it was the start of my obsession with history. Her name was Irene. I don't know much about her except that she lived in Ireland and was terribly poor growing up and that she died when she was only forty years old. She had twelve children, apparently, and only three survived into adulthood. So, I can imagine she had a very difficult life."

I touched the black-and-white photo of my great grandmother from 1845. It looked like she was walking down a street when someone took her picture. She was thin, but she looked so vibrant. It was hard to believe she died so young. But perhaps that was my fate too. To die at forty. I hoped Irene was looking down on me. The second the thought crossed my mind, it dawned on me that Irene was the woman I met in the dream I had on the plane. I was sure of it. I didn't mention it to my father though. What if he didn't believe me? I couldn't take the chance of looking crazy or unhinged.

As we sat in the library after dinner—or 'tea,' as they called it—having a glass of wine on our last evening together, my father asked me, "It's our last night. What do you want to do? I feel I tried to fit thirty-five years of father-daughter things into one week—the opera, the zoo, swimming in the ocean, shopping, taking you to my two most favourite restaurants, and all our talks and looking at photos. It's been a whirlwind."

"It has been. And it's been one of the best weeks of my entire life. How about we steal some of Margaret's chocolate cake from the fridge and just drink wine and eat the rest of the cake while we sit outside and talk?"

"Perfect, I'll get the cake."

There was a slight breeze in the backyard, which helped with the humidity. The sun was just beginning to set. The scent of lemons filled the air. The lights were on in the guest house, and we heard distant laughter. As I poured the wine, I said, "I had a chat with Margaret today. She told me how much you've done for her family like paying for their son's university, paying for their groceries, and even sending money to their family back home for years after they first came to Australia."

"Margaret is a tattletale. Well, I'll tell you something about her. When my mother got sick, my papa was a disaster. I mean he became so depressed I thought he might try and take his own life. I had to coax him out of bed and almost force feed him. Mom was so sick and needed a lot of care. I was at the height of my career, traveling a lot, to Europe mostly, so I wasn't much help to either of them. It was funny, but when mother got sick, Papa and I quickly realized how much we relied on her for everything. She was our confidant, our chef. She organized everything. We were both feeling like lost souls. She was the glue that held our little family together. My papa heard about a program bringing Filipinos over to Australia and applied to get a housekeeper. Margaret came and within days she turned our lives around. She cared for all of us. She had the house running like clockwork and had us all laughing and living again. She was like a human generator. We all plugged into her energy, and we survived and actually thrived. When Mother died, my father decided he wanted Margaret to stay on and live with us. I gave up the guest house, happily. It was the perfect solution. By then we were so attached to Margaret that neither one of us could imagine her ever leaving.

So, she and Joseph and their son Hector moved into the guest house, and I moved back into my room. I helped as best I could, but it was Margaret who cared for my father and believe me, he was not the easiest man to care for. He was so helpless and depressed for the first few years, and then he just started to really age. He may have had some brain damage from mini-strokes at the end because he was not himself at all. He would get angry and shout and swear which was not his way. I never heard him shout or curse in my life. But Margaret knew how to handle him, and she was better than any professional caregiver we could have hired. She's a remarkable woman. She cared for him till the day he died. I can't imagine how our lives would have been without her. So never mind a word she says. It was the other way around. You can't put a price on all that she and Joseph have done for us."

"It sounds like you all need each other. A union made in heaven."

"Yes. Well said. So lucky, so lucky . . ." As he sipped his wine, his face suddenly turned grave. "Can I ask you a question? You don't have to answer if you don't want to."

"Anything. No secrets anymore, remember?" I leaned forward, placing my hands on the table and making eye contact with him to let him know I was serious.

"You haven't talked much about your mom. I get it, you're still angry with her, but how is she? What has her life been like?"

I knew the question was coming. And I wanted to be as honest as I could be and try to put my anger aside. I took a long breath.

"Mom, well, she has a small house in Victoria with a sweet garden. She doesn't own a car. She walks everywhere."

"I remember her walking. Is she still so fast?" he asked, smiling.

"Oh, she's fast, and she walks every day on the beach, rain or shine. She walks to get groceries. Rarely does she take a taxi or ask for a ride. She's quite healthy, which she attributes mainly to Dr. Pan, a doctor of traditional Chinese medicine, who lives in Victoria. She rarely goes to her Western doctor except for a yearly physical, which she always passes with flying colours. She prefers her smelly, herbal concoctions from Dr. Pan and gets acupuncture on a regular basis to deal with any health issues. Humm, she has written several travel books and guide books and one novel. She has even won a few awards for her writing. She still travels but slowed down quite a bit once Jonas was born. She takes her role as a grandmother very seriously. She is terrific with Jonas and a real help to Cody and I. She insisted from early on that Jonas have a sleepover there at least once a week so that we should have a date night, even if it means just sitting on the couch watching a movie. So, we agreed. Of course, Jonas adores her. She is probably a better grandmother than she was a mother, but I'm sure that is not an uncommon phenomenon. She has so much patience with him. Not something I remember her having when I was growing up."

"Is she happy?"

"I guess you'd have to ask her that yourself. She seems happy enough. She's always had a melancholiness about her though. I was only four when her and Dad divorced, so I don't remember much about it. She told me once that Dad said she was too hard to love. I think that still really hurts her because she brings it up now and then. I'm ashamed to say it, but when I found out that she lied to me, I told her that Dad was right all along. It was a terrible thing to say and, since meeting you, I regret saying it. I've been thinking about it a lot, and I'm going to apologize to her when I get back. It was really a cruel thing to say."

"Ouch, that is harsh. I agree it'd be good to clear that up."

"Yeah, I know. She was a good mom, really, overall. But there has always been a part of her that she kept hidden. It's like she didn't want anyone to get too close. As if she was always holding back. I don't know how to describe it. I never saw her go on a date. She does have lots of female friends, though, and they do crazy things like go to Hollyhock, which is a retreat place on Quadra Island north of Salt Spring Island. People go there for all kinds of self-help workshops. The last one was on "Breathwork and Your True Nature," whatever that means. She loves all that spiritual, new age stuff. And she loves to go hiking. She usually goes to Sedona, Arizona a couple of times a year to hike and experience the energy vortexes, as they call them. Again, I don't know much about that hokey new age stuff. Every year she goes to Europe around this time, but not this year because of—well, you know—the cancer. I don't know what she does there, but she's never missed that trip as long as I can remember. Let me see, oh, yeah, she hikes the bluffs on Hornby Island, a quaint island north of Salt Spring, and I think she goes to the nudist beach there, but she would never tell me that. But I noticed once that, after two weeks there, she had no tan marks when she got back. Cody and I think she is a closet nudist." I laughed as I remembered when Cody and I figured it out.

"A nudist. Somehow that seems to fit the Evangeline I remember." He grinned. "Do you think she would like to see me?" The eagerness in his voice made me giggle. He sounded like a teenage boy.

"Ahh, that would be a 'yes.' She told me she has thought about you every day for over thirty-five years. I somehow get the feeling that she saved her love for you. So, my guess is, yes." I felt my eyebrows raise as I grinned.

"I was thinking last night that I want to retire, sell my house, and move to Canada. I don't want to miss out on another minute of your life, and I want to meet my grandson and Cody."

"And Mom?"

"Yes, if she will have me. That would be the ultimate bonus."

We stood at the security gate at the airport. I was feeling excited to go home and tell everyone about my father, and to make amends with Mom, but at the same time, I didn't want to leave Melbourne. Even though I knew he would come to Canada, I had the sense that my time on earth was numbered, and I wanted my father in my life till the very end. I was beginning to feel a huge loss, and I hadn't even left the airport yet.

My father pulled out an envelope from his pocket and gave it to me. "Can you deliver this for me when you get home?"

I took it, and smiled. "Yes, of course. And I'll text you the minute I arrive."

"I love you, Stormy. You have no idea the joy you have brought me. I'm forever grateful that you had the guts to just get on a plane and find me."

"I love you too, Dad, or wait . . . gee, what am I going to call you?"

"How about Papa. That's what I called my father. That is what we say in Italian anyway."

It felt right. "It fits like a glove. I like it. Papa it is. I love you, Papa."

CHAPTER SEVENTEEN
VICTORIA, BC

MARCH 2015

I handed over the letter that Papa gave me to my dad when he and Celeste came over the day after I arrived home. He read it out loud.

> *Dear Karl, I want to thank you from the bottom of my heart for raising the most amazing person—our daughter. Though I wish I could have been there to see her grow up, it was not written in the stars, and I have already come to terms with that. You will always be her dad and that will never change. My hope is that we can, from this day forward, co-parent and co-grandparent. I look forward to meeting you and shaking your hand in person, sooner than later.*
>
> *With my deepest gratitude, Valentino*

Karl began to cry. It was the first time in my life I had seen my dad cry outright. Celeste hugged him, and soon we were all crying.

"I gotta say, he must be one hell of a guy to write this letter," Dad said as he wiped the tears from his eyes.

"Dad, he was wonderful. I know you will all love him. He is a gentle man, very humble, and I'm not sure you want to know this part but, Dad, he was so in love with Mom. He never married. Said there was only one woman for him, and he knew he could never love anyone like that again. It was so sweet."

"I have no problem with it, Stormy. Not now anyway. Thirty-five years ago, I doubt I would have been okay with it. But I know what he's talking about. When I met Celeste, I knew right away she was my match, my true love, and that we were meant to be together."

"Oh, sweetheart! You never told me that before," Celeste said as she grabbed his hand and looked at him with dreamy eyes.

He looked at Celeste, "Well, I'm telling you now. This year has been an eye-opener for me. A time to really examine my life and be grateful for what I have. I've come to realize how lucky I am. All the love I have in my life, you, my girls, Cody, Jonas, and Evangeline. We have an amazing family. And now we have a new member, Valentino."

I was shocked when Karl began to tear up again. Celeste grabbed a tissue from her purse and held him. I had never in my life seen him break down emotionally. It was as if the cancer had become a wake-up call not just for me, but for everyone around me. It was having a snowball effect that no one could have predicted. I couldn't help but think that my dad could have chosen to become more distant when he found out I was not his biological daughter, but it did the opposite. His response made me realize that family is more than just blood. We cultivate a family. We work at it. It is not always about blood relatives. I decided at that moment that no matter what the outcome was, if I died or if I lived, I was so grateful for all of them in my life—my mother included.

I sat in the doctor's office waiting for Dr. Lafontaine to arrive. There was no doubt that I was nervous. My finger was almost raw from rubbing it, and my stomach was in knots.

"Stormy, I'm happy to tell you that you are in complete remission," Dr. Lafontaine said with a smile. "Now, our next step is to gather some of your stem cells while you are healthy."

"Oh, thank God! I figured I was in remission. I feel really good. I have energy. I feel like my old self. And I Googled what remission was like," I joked.

"You and your Googling." He grinned. "Well, I've set up an appointment to do the extraction. It's just like giving blood. Not to worry. We'll store the stem cells and then, if we need them, we will use them for a transplant."

"No donor needed then?"

"Well, yes, that is our hope. We will harvest the stem cells from your own body. It's the best way. Coming from your own body, there's no rejection issues since it's your own cells we are transplanting."

"Why are you saying hope? Is there a chance they won't be good enough?"

"Let's take one day at a time. You are well, so go live your life. We will keep checking on you and if you need a transplant or some other drug treatment, we will deal with it then."

"Go live your life," I whispered to myself as I walked out of his office. I felt like I was walking on air. They were the words I had hoped for. I decided right then and there that I was going to live my life as if I were cured. As if the cancer was gone for good.

CHAPTER EIGHTEEN
VALENTINO

FEBRUARY 2015

Valentino got out of the limousine near the entrance to the ruins at Olympia and walked to the statue of Zeus. With a pair of tiny gold scissors he had purchased at a market in Melbourne, he snipped a small branch from the wild olive tree that stood near the statue, gently wrapped it in tissue paper, and placed it into his leather satchel. He walked back to the limo that was waiting for him and told the driver to take him back to the airport in Athens.

CHAPTER NINETEEN
EVANGELINE

MARCH 1, 2015

My mother answered the door. It was a FedEx driver with a small package. "Evangeline Hera?"

"Yes?"

"Please sign here."

My mom opened the parcel. She untied the gold cord from the gold box and opened the lid. An olive branch rested on a nest of white tissue paper. A handwritten note lay underneath.

My Dearest Evangeline,

I am requesting that you join me in Olympia. I have enclosed a first-class ticket to Athens for March third. A limousine will pick you up at the airport and drive you to Olympia and to our pension, where I have reserved our room for five days. I have reserved first-class airline seats to Rome on the sixth day, where we will attend the opera. You will then fly back to Canada.

With Oceans of Love, Valentino

CHAPTER TWENTY
EVANGELINE

MARCH 2015

The second after my mother read the letter from Valentino, she called me and said she was going straight to bed. She was determined to get her body used to the time change so that when she arrived, she was not going to experience jet lag. I came over the next evening and helped her choose out her clothes and offered to give her a pedicure just to calm her down. She was terrified that once Valentino saw her, he would be disappointed.

"I'm so old, what will he think? I have a hump from these big breasts. I should have gotten breast-reduction surgery like everyone told me to get, but I didn't want to have cosmetic surgery. Tell me again, what does Valentino look like now? What did he say about me? I feel like I'm a teenager or something. What's wrong with me? What if he doesn't like me? You know people have expectations and then . . . well, you know. I'm sure he has some kind expectation of what I will look like and how I will act. I'm not young anymore."

I really had to hold back from laughing as I listened to her fretting. I knew in my heart the minute they saw each other; it would be better than what they both anticipated. I was sure they were perfect for each other.

"Mom, Valentino's probably going through the same scenario you are right now. For heaven's sake, he flew to Athens, got into a limo, and drove to Olympia just so he could cut a branch from a tree and mail it to you, then flew back to Melbourne. Think about it. Only a man hopelessly in love would do that. Quit worrying."

CHAPTER TWENTY-ONE
VALENTINO

MARCH 2015

As I recall the story that Papa told me so many times, I smile. I can picture it perfectly, him getting ready to meet his long-lost love.

Valentino looked in the mirror. "God, did I shave too much off the left side?" He said under his breath. He looked back and forth. If he hadn't had a tan, he might have shaved his whole beard off. But then he realized that would look silly—the top of his face tanned dark and the lower, much lighter. He was clean-shaven when he met Evangeline, no beard, but he remembered she liked the five o'clock shadow. But it was not going to happen. Darn tan! He combed his hair. Oh, God, the bald spot. He didn't have a bald spot back then. He'd only realized how much hair he'd lost when he saw a picture that someone had taken at the faculty's annual Christmas party from the open balcony above where he was standing. His first thought had been, "Who's the bald guy?" Then he realized it was him, and he was horrified. He knew his hair had been thinning badly the last few years, but clearly it was much worse than he had realized. Hopefully, she wouldn't notice. Evangeline was much shorter than him, so that was good. "These glasses don't look right," he muttered, looking into the mirror. Margaret had gone with him to pick them, and he had liked them then, but now he thought maybe they looked too professor-like. Black, rectangle frames. He always gravitated to round, wire rims. Thankfully, he didn't really need to wear them all the time; just to read and drive at night. He would take them off when Evangeline came into the room.

Valentino sat on the balcony of the pension waiting for the limousine to arrive. Everything was perfect. He had the bottle of Peloponnese Moschofilero opened and it was breathing with two wine glasses ready. The octopus ceviche was on ice, and two small plates with forks and napkins were set on the table. On the dresser was a plate of cheese and crackers. He had some fruit ready if she wanted. He wanted it to be perfect, like when they first met. His Evangeline could have whatever she wanted.

He had texted the driver and, if all went well with the traffic, she was scheduled to arrive within the next fifteen minutes.

He could feel his stomach churning and his heart pounding. Over thirty-five years had passed. He was not the same man, and he expected neither was she the same woman he fell in love with. But he knew that he had to go through with his plan. He hadn't had any word from her to say she accepted his invitation, but he knew from talking to me that my mother, his Evangeline, was on her way and even more nervous than he was.

I wished I could have been a fly on the wall when they saw each other again after so long.

When Papa first met me, he had confessed to me that, for a brief moment, he was not sure what he felt toward my mom. Evangeline had robbed him of being a father. That was a fact. And he was angry about that, especially since I had cancer with a poor prognosis. But as Valentino got to know me and heard about my upbringing, he realized I had a wonderful life. I had grown up with a dad who loved me, and I had a half-sister and a stepmother who adored me and, yes, a mother who had clearly done an amazing job of raising me—even nurturing my talents. In a strange way, Valentino felt my musical upbringing honoured him just as much as my name did. And when I told him how Mom had suffered over the years, never finding love again, he knew he had to forgive her. It was true that Mom emulated the goddess Hera to the core. Family was everything, and she sacrificed her own happiness for her family. Like Hera she had not always acted with honesty, but she did always act with good intentions, that was, to protect her family—me.

Papa said it was Margaret who stayed up for hours talking to him, helping him to deal with the anger and see his way through it. He remembered Margaret's words, "You cannot live in the past, what could have been, is a useless endeavour. You must only ever live in the present. Only fools live in the past. If I would have asked you last night: 'Who is the love of your life?' You would have told me about this young woman you met in Greece. And, in fact, Valentino, you told me that story not too long ago. Remember? Your love for this woman is embedded in your heart. If I asked you today, at this moment, who is the love of your life? How can it change? Love is love. It is eternal."

Papa knew Margaret was right, as usual. True love was eternal. It never died, and he knew he and Evangeline were bound together at such a deep level that time was irrelevant. And that was when he decided to go to Olympia and get the olive branch and send it to her as a peace offering, along with a plane ticket.

An hour passed, and Papa still had no word from the limo driver. He was not answering his texts. He finally decided to go to the hotel office and ask the young woman who now ran the pension if she had received any messages.

"Have you heard from an Evangeline Hera or a limousine service?"

"Evangeline? No, she is not coming this year. A family emergency, she said. That is why you got her room."

"I don't understand, you know Evangeline?"

"Well, yes, she has been coming here for thirty years at the same time every year, in the same room. You know her?"

"For thirty years?" He felt light headed and could feel his knees begin to shake. He sat down on a stool.

"Yes, sir, thirty years. When I took over the pension from my parents, I had strict instructions to make sure I kept the same standing reservation for Miss Evangeline. Are you okay, Mr. Lombardo? Can I get you a glass of water?"

He pulled out his phone and called the limousine service he had hired.

"Mr. Lombardo, we've been trying to reach you, but there was no answer."

"I had my phone on." He looked at the button for the ringer. It was off.

"Oh, dear, sorry. I see my ringer was off. Can you tell me where the driver is that I hired?"

"Sir, there was an accident. Just a few kilometres from Olympia. Please go to the hospital in Pyrgos immediately."

Valentino called a taxi and arrived at the hospital to find my mother in a bed. The top of her head was bandaged, and her face was covered with tiny cuts. Her eyes were closed, but he could see from the monitors that her vital signs were stable, just as the doctor had told him. He studied her. She had the same beautiful face he remembered, only her hair was white, and she had tiny lines around her eyes and on her forehead. She was more magnificent than he remembered, even with the cuts and bandages. He held her hand, an older hand, yes, but her nails were perfectly shaped with tiny moons on each finger. She wore no polish on her fingernails, but her toes, which were sticking out from the blankets, were freshly manicured in bright purple. Valentino smiled.

The doctor told him my mother had a mild head injury and would fully recover. The driver was not so lucky. He was in intensive care with internal injuries. The car had been hit on the driver's side by a man who had come from a side road and never saw them because they were coming around a switchback. Valentino knew that the road was very windy. He imagined he was driving too fast. The driver who hit them had not been injured except for a few scrapes.

It was five in the evening when my mother finally opened her eyes. Papa was in the chair next to her, still holding her hand. He had not left her side for over two hours. He didn't want her to wake up in a hospital and not know where she was. He wanted the first pair of eyes she saw to be his. My mother looked at him and squeezed his hand and smiled, her eyes looking into his soul, just like he remembered.

"Hey, there, you woke up. How are you feeling?" He put his other hand on her head and stroked her hair.

"Valentino. Oh, Valentino. You're here," she whispered.

"Yes, I'm here. I'm never going anywhere anymore without you," he said as tears rolled down his face.

Mom sold her little house and she and Papa were married on the beach in James Bay, steps away from their new home on Dallas Road in Victoria. Their two-storey house was across the street from Ogden Point overlooking the Juan De Fuca Strait, only a few blocks from their extended family. Cody and I stood up for them, and little Jonas sang in his beautiful, tenor voice that was beginning to resemble Valentino's famous tone. Those in attendance were: Mémé Lil, all six of Mom's brothers with their wives; Margaret and Joseph from Australia, along with their son and his wife and their new grandson; Mom's best friend Darlene and her husband Jack from Salt Spring; and, of course, Karl, Celeste, and Brittany.

They rented out Santorini's Greek restaurant in Victoria. Olive branches donned each table. My parents wore crowns of olive branches. They served octopus ceviche with ouzo for an appetizer, followed by Greek salad with olive oil imported from the Peloponnese (that Papa had insisted on gifting to the restaurant to use for the meal), souvlaki, roast chicken, roasted potatoes with rosemary and lemon, spanakopita, dolmades, and baklava for dessert. Each table had an imported bottle of Gaia Wild Ferment Moschofilero wine.

They spent their honeymoon on Hornby Island in a waterfront cottage, steps away from the nudist beach.

CHAPTER TWENTY-TWO

APRIL 22, 2016

It was the last day of classes at the university, and Cody and I had planned to go out for the evening to celebrate. Jonas was already at Mom and Papa's house. They had informed us that they were taking him for the weekend so that we could just relax and enjoy ourselves. My parents were experts on coming up with reasons to keep Jonas overnight or for the weekend. Jonas had as many toys, games, and books at their house as he did at ours. He wasn't spoiled, they told us, he was just loved to pieces. Between Dad and Celeste and Brittany, Jonas was never starved for love or attention. I hoped Brittany would have a baby soon to take some of the pressure off trying to share Jonas. She had finally found her true love, but it wasn't a prince. Brittany met Sarah at Pagliacci's restaurant. It was packed as usual, and the band that was performing was one of Brittany's favourites. As she stood in line waiting to get in, she eyed a woman sitting alone at her usual table. She asked the hostess if she would ask the woman if she minded if she joined her. Sarah, who had just moved to Victoria, was a curator for the Royal British Columbia Museum. It was love at first sight. They were married within three months.

As I was getting dressed to go out, I couldn't help but smile as I thought about my parents. When Papa came to Canada, our lives were enriched. He was a natural at being a parent, grandparent, and for Mom he unleashed the cocoon she had wrapped herself in over the years. It was like she was transformed into a happy, fun-loving woman, the person that Mémé Lil had told me stories about. She became the Evangeline from before life's choices stripped her of optimism and joy. The melancholy that had plagued her for so many years, and the holding back, faded away. She was a new, vibrant person, who had the world at her feet. There were no more secrets. She was finally free to share her story of the love she lost for so many years and finally found. She literally glowed. They both did.

It was Papa Valentino who encouraged Mom to reconnect with her family and small town back in Saskatchewan. Mémé Lil at ninety-one, fell in love with her son-in-law. He would sing to her, dance with her, and send her cards and flowers on a regular basis. They made many trips to Saskatchewan—at Papa's insistence—and Mémé Lil came to Victoria regularly. He would send her first-class tickets and dote on her the entire time she was there.

Papa loved going to visit Saskatchewan and was like a kid in a candy shop; driving tractors and quads, herding cattle, and even helping butcher chickens and, to my mother's dismay—snowmobiling. None of which I would have believed if I hadn't seen the pictures posted on Facebook by my cousins. It wasn't just my uncles either that he hung out with, my aunts taught him how to make jelly and pickles, and he taught them to make his mother's famous risotto, all the while singing to them and twirling them around in the kitchen. It was nothing for him to be singing and cooking in the kitchen in the morning, and then be out on the tractor picking rocks in the afternoon.

Paris by this time had transformed into the most amazing small town. The change had been spear-headed by a woman named Dominique, who was the younger sister of Guy, the man that my mémé had wanted my mom to marry and settle down with. Dominique was a successful entrepreneur and, like my mother, had left Paris right after graduation to pursue her dreams. She had returned home after her parents died and decided to stay. Filled with ideas and hard work, she put Paris on the map. The town had a replica of the Eiffel Tower and became a tourist destination dubbed *The Paris of the Prairies*. She opened up a clothing boutique and a bistro. Artists came and painted murals on the walls around town; other townspeople came on board and began to open small businesses and worked on beautifying the community. The town expanded the park, added a golf course, an RV park, and a swimming pool, and even started a music festival. It was Dominique who, within minutes of meeting Valentino, invited him to perform on the Friday evening of the annual music event.

"It's such a pleasure, Valentino, to finally meet you. Congratulations on your marriage to our Evangeline. We always knew she would be successful at whatever she put her mind to. She was my idol growing up, a year ahead of me in school. She's famous in our little town."

"Thank you, yes. She is a remarkable woman in more ways than one. I am a very lucky man."

"I understand you are an opera singer?"

"Well, I am retired now, but I was teaching at the university in Melbourne for the last ten years. I haven't performed much in that time."

"Well, how would you feel about coming out of retirement for a short while? I had an idea and talked to our committee and well, we would be honoured, no, thrilled really, if you would perform a few numbers on the Friday evening of the music festival. It is a small fair, usually only about five hundred people. And perhaps Stormy could back you up with some of her colleagues?"

"Well, that sounds delightful. But I will have to get back to you on that. See if Stormy is interested. But it sounds like a wonderful idea." He smiled and shook Dominique's hand, holding her palm in both of his. Dominique blushed. She, like so many of the townspeople and our family, were captured by his charm.

Of course, I was overjoyed at the thought of being on stage with Papa and needed no time to think it through. I invited some of my colleagues from the orchestra to come to Paris for the weekend—Papa kindly paid their expenses. On Thursday evening, we rehearsed three numbers. It was a sold-out show and probably the most fun I ever had performing in my life. The icing on the cake was the surprise performance by Jonas. Unbeknownst to me or Mom, Jonas came on stage and sang the same aria that Papa had first sung to her in Olympia. He and Papa had rehearsed it without any of us knowing. We had rehearsed it with Papa, so when he walked off the stage when he was supposed to start the song, we were all stunned. But then, out came Jonas, who took to centre stage and nodded at us to begin with the biggest grin on his face. It took everything for me not to cry as I played my violin that evening, hearing my son sing opera.

It was one of those moments in my life that I remember every single detail and relive it over and over in my mind. This was our papa. His charm was infectious to all of us, but especially to Mom. She became connected to her family in a way she never had before. Even the tone of her journals as I read them after they reunited in Olympia, was so different. Her perspective on life changed. She saw the world through rose coloured glasses. I once overheard my mom consoling Jonas; he was talking about how he felt like an outsider at school because he liked opera music and yoga. My advice earlier that day had been something to the effect of 'tell them to go to hell and mind their own business,' which apparently was not the advice he was looking for. In true Jonas's fashion, he went to his grandma Angie to see what she had to say. In her sweet gentle way, she explained:

"Being weird is wonderful! Don't ever forget that. It doesn't mean you don't belong; it means you're living the life you are meant to live and when you are living authentically, people will accept you. It may take them a while but, remember, it takes all types of people to make the world go round. It sounds to me that what you need to work on is accepting you, just as you are. Celebrate that. We are all unique and wouldn't it be a boring world if we all acted the same? Or liked the same things?"

They were wise words. Words I never heard growing up, probably because she hadn't learned those lessons yet. What I saw in those later years was that Mom had come around full circle. Her enthusiasm for life, her fearlessness, her passion for life, and her childhood optimism returned. She was living authentically.

As we drove to the restaurant, Cody said, "You seem quiet. Everything alright?"

"Yah, just still feeling overly tired today. I've been so busy."

"Well, now that classes are over, you can wind down. And maybe rethink your performing schedule. Like I already told you, you are going too fast.

You're trying to get back to where you were before you were diagnosed. You are pushing yourself, and you don't need to. We don't need the money."

"I know. I know. It's not about the money. It's just that I want to live my life to the fullest. Do the things I love to do. I love my work, you know that. I'm worried. I know it sounds stupid, but everything just seems so wonderful right now. Brittany found love, Mom and Papa are like teenagers in love, even Jonas is doing so well. Tonight, he was so excited to go to my parent's place because Papa promised him a vocal lesson. So funny, what eleven-year-old kid would get excited about that? And Mom was going to get him to help her make his favourite linguine vongole. He is such a great kid."

"So, everything is wonderful, and that worries you? I'm sorry, am I missing something?" He laughed.

"I'm just worried that it's the calm before the storm." I gazed out the window.

"Don't be so superstitious. Just enjoy the moment."

At the restaurant, I was trying to enjoy myself, but the tiredness I was feeling all day was rapidly turning into a feeling of exhaustion. I felt drained, as if the blood was draining from my body. Before the main course arrived, I told Cody I wasn't feeling well.

"I am so sorry, but we need to go home. I am afraid I might pass out. Something is wrong."

"Of course. You look so pale all of a sudden. Stay put, I will get the car and bring it to the front, and then I'll come back in to get you. Just stay put."

It had been over a year since I had my stem cell extraction, and I had a feeling at that moment that my honeymoon, as Linda called it, was over. I noticed that in the last few weeks, I had been feeling more and more tired. But with rest, I seemed to be able to bounce back enough to make it through the day, and so I never mentioned it to anyone. It was that time of year—correcting exams, getting marks ready for students for the end of the semester—it wasn't uncommon to feel tired; there were a lot of late nights. But this feeling was different. It was more than just tired. I felt completely exhausted. So much so, that by the time we got home, just opening my mouth to talk was too difficult, and Cody had to help me walk into the house. My muscles felt so weak; even holding up my head was too much work. Cody laid me down on the couch, as there was no way I could walk up the stairs to our bedroom. He then called Linda, who came over right away. I don't remember her being there, or what happened next. I must have passed out. When I finally came around, I was in a hospital room with Dr. Lafontaine peering down at me and an IV bottle hooked up into my arm. I didn't know if it was day or night.

Dr. Lafontaine confirmed what I had suspected. The honeymoon remission was over. He said the next course of action was to do another round of intensive chemotherapy, and then they would do the transplant with my own stem cells that they had safely stored.

This time, he warned me, the chemotherapy would be stronger, and I was not allowed visitors. I had to be in complete isolation in my hospital room. To be honest, I don't remember much during this period. I only remember thinking I was not doing well. It was nothing like the first time I had chemo. There was no Brittany to hold my hand; there was no laughing and joking around. I was alone, in my sterile room, listening to my shallow breathing and racing heart. I couldn't read, and I could hardly talk on the phone. Even thinking was too much work. No one could come visit, the staff that cared for me were in full protective gear to protect me from getting any infections and to protect them from the chemotherapy drugs, which were highly toxic.

Two weeks into the treatment, I woke up in the morning with no tubes or needles in my arm. Shortly after that, Dr. Lafontaine and Linda came into my room without any gowns or face coverings. I realized, even before they spoke, that it was over. They sat down. Linda—my best friend, my faithful doctor—held my hand.

"Stormy, I'm afraid your heart and kidneys have been affected by the intense chemotherapy. We're going to have to take a break," Dr. Lafontaine said as he looked down at my chart. "I'm sending you home. You need a rest from the therapy."

I was so weak at the time; I don't even remember how I responded. I just remember thinking I was going to die and that it was comforting to know it was over. I had no energy, and my will to live was gone. I'd had enough. There was no fight left in me.

"The stem cell transplant is on hold for now," Linda said, explaining how sometimes the organs just can't take the chemo drugs. "We have some other plans, some clinical trials we can start, but we need to get your heart and kidneys in better shape. For now, go home and rest. I am so sorry."

I went home, but my body was too weak to recover from the chemotherapy. My organs began to shut down slowly. Linda came to the house every two days and finally gave me the news that I already knew in my heart. There was no more hope. The end was near. I was hardly speaking anymore, and my appetite had dwindled to a few spoons of bone broth every now and then. And I was at peace with it. There was a point, I don't remember exactly when, where I felt the fight or the will to live, just release and a sense of calm acceptance come over me.

"I want to set up hospice care. I know you don't want to go back to the hospital. So, I have arranged for a nurse to come three times a day and, if you want, we can arrange to have 24-hour care." She held my hand and talked slowly and softly.

I shook my head. "I've already talked to my family, and they want to help by taking turns staying with me." My eyes closed. It took every ounce of energy to speak.

"Of course. I will arrange for a nurse to come and administer just enough drugs to keep you comfortable. I'm so sorry, Stormy. You gave it a good fight," she said. She gently leaned over the easy boy chair I was lying on and hugged my frail body.

I knew I was near the end, but I wasn't sure how long it would take to die. Mom was the only one I could talk to about dying. We had discussed death openly—about the possibility of having an assisted death instead of waiting for it to happen on its own—even before I began the last chemotherapy. I had a feeling that I wouldn't get through the next round of treatments.

"Stormy, whatever you decide, I will support you. Now that assisted death is a legal option, I want you to think about it. I hate to see you suffering. We are so lucky in Canada to have that choice. There are even death doulas now who could help you, help us all, to support you, should you choose to go that route." The look in her eyes was pure love. It was as if she understood what I was going through.

"Mom, I'm afraid to die. I don't know what to expect. I know you have your spiritual beliefs, a belief in an afterlife, but me, I . . . well, me and Cody, we don't really subscribe to that. I mean, it does cross my mind that there may be something after death, but I dare not talk about it with Cody. You know, as well I do, what he thinks about anything even remotely spiritual. But the closer I get to death, the more I'm unsure of what I believe. The fear is coming from not knowing what happens after."

"Oh, my sweet Stormy, I regret that I wasn't a better mother to you, and that I didn't share all I've learned about my spiritual quests over the years. I held back because of Cody. He was so judgemental about anything spiritual. And I do get it. Based on what he told me about his experiences growing up, it's not surprising. I wanted to respect his beliefs. I didn't want to impose. But this, Stormy, is not about Cody." She took both my hands in hers, sat on the side of my bed, and leaned in closer to me. "This is about you, honey. I want to assure you, there is an afterlife. And whether you die naturally, or with some assistance to avoid pain and suffering, makes no difference what-so-ever. You will go to another realm of existence. A place where only love exists, pure unconditional love."

I wanted to believe her. She seemed so confident. "I hope you're right. I really do, Mom. I hope Cody is wrong. But I think I'll try and just let my life unfold as it may. I know I'll be in even more pain than I am in now. Linda explained how things will progress from here. But I think I just want to just go naturally, painful as it will be. No euthanasia."

Living with cancer was brutal near the end. Even though I was adamant that I didn't want to be drugged up too much, I wound up pumped up with morphine, which was not the way I had envisioned the end. I had read stories about dying a good death, and I had decided I wanted to be present when the end came. Coherent. I wanted my death to be pure. Like when I gave birth to Jonas. No drugs, only natural. My argument was: I may not have had any control over the cancer, but I wanted at least to have some control over my death. But when the time came, the pain was unbearable; it overrode my desire to be present. So, I went out high on morphine, feeling confused and having strange visual hallucinations. Even though I was at peace with dying by that point, I still felt an underlying disappointment at not being able to die properly. But once I died, in an instant, those thoughts disappeared, along with the pain.

As I write this, the thought occurs to me that I must have had an unconscious knowledge that I was meant to die and to come back to life. If I would have had an assisted death, I don't think I would have had a near-death experience and returned and healed from the cancer. But, of course, I don't know that for sure.

I died on June 15, 2016, at the age of thirty-six.

It's funny when I look back now, all the fear about dying and not really knowing for sure where the heck I would go, if anywhere. All the intense sadness of leaving family and friends, even my house, my work, the earth. All the disappointment and, yes, anger at my body for failing me. All the pain that permeated every inch of me. All vanished the instant I died. But I, me, Stormy Hara, still existed somehow, only I was in another realm, just as Mom said I would be.

The first thing I noticed was that the pain was gone. In the blink of an eye, I felt light, healthy, whole, and more alive than ever. I found myself near the ceiling of the room, looking down at my body lying on the portable hospital bed in our living room that the hospice had thoughtfully delivered the week before when I could no longer walk up the stairs to our bedroom. Cody had tried to carry me up the stairs, but he was terrified of hurting me and causing more pain. I weighed sixty-nine pounds, and I was as fragile as a butterfly.

As I looked down from above, I saw Cody sound asleep on the couch, oblivious to the fact that I had died. No worry, I thought, it would do him good to get some sleep anyway, considering what he was going to have to deal with when he woke up. I floated up the stairs to where my eleven-year-old son was asleep in his bed, his hands still holding his favourite book that his grandpa had bought, *The Luciano Pavarotti Story*. I noticed that Cody hadn't turned off his night light, the one that lit up the ceiling with dancing stars. So, I kissed Jonas on the forehead, turned off the night light, and closed the door. It was strange, but I didn't need to touch anything. I just shut off the light and closed the door with my thoughts.

Then I was at my parents' house. I saw my mother sitting in her favourite, purple chair with a card resting on her notebook. She was writing something on the card. I looked closer.

> *Dear Stormy, I love you so much. The day you were born was the happiest day of my life. The second happiest day of my life was when I married your papa, and you were there by my side. I am so sorry to have deceived you all those years and of robbing you of your dear papa's love. I thought I was doing the right thing. Please forgive me. I love you so much. If I could, I would trade places with you in an instant so that you could live.*

My mother looked up from her writing. Tears and mascara smearing together ran down her cheeks. A pile of tissues was beside her. Even with the cloak of sadness, she looked the best she had in years. She had lost weight. Her complexion and skin glowed. Even her clothes were different, more vibrant. I touched her arm to comfort her. She had made a decision with the best intentions. I understood that, and I had already forgiven her the moment I set foot back on Canadian soil after meeting my papa. Perhaps she hadn't forgiven herself, though, and held on to those hurtful words I had uttered so long ago.

She looked up again and felt her arm where I had touched her. *She felt it? She could feel me?*

I went to the stove and turned on the timer for two seconds. It beeped when it was done. She jumped up, dropping the notebook and the card. *I could do things just with my thoughts?*

"Who's there?" she asked.

Mom, it's me, I'm here, I said to her but without words. It was like I was communicating with my thoughts. There was no need for words. I'm so sorry that I said you were a hard person to love all those years before. Let it go. You're anything but hard to love. I was angry at you, and I was wrong. Let go of the guilt, Mom. It's not necessary. And, please, don't worry about me. I'm free, and I feel amazing right now. You were right. You were so right. There was no need to fear death.

I felt a tug, an urge to rise up. It's hard to explain because there is no such feeling or sensation like it on earth. I could feel myself begin to rise as if being pulled gently upward and, as I did, I heard my mom calling me, "Stormy, Stormy is that you? Are you here? Have you passed? Oh, Stormy. Oh God, you're gone."

I am here. But I need to go now, but I'm here for you always. I could sense I was leaving, that I was being pulled, and that I was becoming fainter to her.

As I rose, I felt like I was flying. Not like when I flew in my dreams, which was something I often did: lifting off the ground and flying over the earth. This was more like floating in a sunbeam. And I hate to be so metaphorical, but it is hard to put into words when there are no known words to describe your experience. The sunbeam was a particular color I had never seen on earth. It was like an iridescent yellow but not yellow. It was a hue that doesn't exist to the naked eye.

Then, I began to have a sensation of an enormous love. Unconditional love. It wrapped around me like an envelope. It felt like my mother's embrace but even more than that. I knew love. I was in love. I felt an understanding of everything. The best way I can describe it is to say that life on earth is like walking in a room with a flashlight and only being able to see what the flashlight is shining on, whereas the afterlife is like walking into a room and the whole room is lit up, and you see absolutely everything. Not only that, I understood how every soul is connected. It was so clear, this understanding of interconnectedness; like threads of a tapestry. I understood that all the worrying, fear, sadness, and anger were so unnecessary. There was, and is, only love. I realized that love was my only lesson to learn. It's what connects us.

My great grandmother Irene appeared, the one in the picture that Papa showed me, the one I dreamt about on the plane. She looked young and vivacious and iridescent, like a beam of energy. We spoke without words. Words were not necessary; we knew each other's thoughts. She held my hand as I saw my life unfold before me. I understood every single decision I had ever made. I understood my illness. My life's purpose. And I understood everyone close to me. I say 'understood,' again, because I have no words to explain it any better. I knew why and how. I saw previous lives and future lives all at once, but at the same time, there was no past or future. I have to apologize here because I know it doesn't make sense what I am describing, and it doesn't sound logical or linear either. And that is because it wasn't and isn't.

The entire experience, even though it sounds like a dream or hallucination from the morphine, was more real than anything I had ever experienced on earth. It was my life on earth that seemed to be the dream. I felt like I had awoken from a dream.

Suddenly angelic beings of light appeared. They explained what was happening. They said I was at a crossroad, and it was here where I had to make a choice.

You can go back. You have a choice. If you go back, you will be well. You will be free of cancer; your organs will heal. You will live a long life and become a grandmother. You will teach people about this experience, but it will be in an unexpected way. You will make decisions that people will not agree with but that you know in your wisdom to be right.

But there is so much love and beauty here. I don't want to leave. I said

You must make a choice. Neither one is wrong.

I felt my spirit being pulled down and entering my body. With a jolt, I opened my eyes. Cody, Mom, and Papa were standing over me, crying and holding each other. I don't know how long I was on the other side but when I woke, I felt clear headed.

"It's okay. I'm okay. I am going to live."

INTERLUDE

SUNNYDALE FORENSIC HOSPITAL

This is where I basically ended my story before Mrs. Brown gave me the lecture on writing it up until my crime. The following is the hard part, the part that I didn't want to delve into because of the pain.

I know, as I look at the photos on the wall of my room, that I have to finish the writing assignment, no matter how painful it is, if not for my sake, then for Jonas's. I have to give it a try. Maybe my writing will somehow help him, or even Cody, understand why I did what I did, and we can go back to being a family again.

The dinner announcement over the speaker startles me. I'll have to try and start writing tomorrow. After dinner, its yoga, and I am not missing the yoga class, not for anything. It's one of the activities that make me feel normal. I've taken yoga classes for the last ten years, and it just makes me feel good. Brittany and Linda and I have gone religiously. Yoga has been the only physical activity I've ever liked besides walking or hiking. But here in Sunnydale, walking around in circles with a bunch of mentally ill criminals is not the most enjoyable exercise, I assure you. When I first got here, I tried to imagine I was walking on the beach in Beacon Hill Park in Victoria, but I realized quickly that my imagination is the shits. So, yoga is my main exercise, and it grounds me mentally as well as keeping me in shape physically. Believe me, when you are in a place like this, regardless if it is a state-of-the-art rehabilitation facility, your mental health can deteriorate quickly. Yoga helps, and so does music. Thankfully, there is a music room and a half-decent piano to play, but I missed my violin. I've played it since I was three and half, and it's an extension of me. After pleading with them relentlessly for a month, they finally allowed me to have my violin brought to me. But I was only allowed to play it in the music room at scheduled times.

After the yoga class, I lay in bed, Mrs. Brown's words playing over and over in my mind. I finally conclude that what she is trying to get at, is that writing is a way for me to accept what is. Embrace the pain. Learn from it. Understand it. I conclude that I need to be more present, in the moment. I know in my heart I need to trigger the memories hidden deep in my subconscious from that fateful night. Perhaps as I continue the writing, they will resurface.

I have so much anger and confusion over my feelings toward Cody, and even my son. I've heard nothing from either of them. Not a letter or a call. I need to find out what is really true. Is it true that Cody and Jonas don't love me anymore? Is it really true that I've lost them forever? Just saying it out loud I know I need to do some journaling on those questions. Perhaps I need to read the book Brittany gave me too. She keeps telling me that it will really help, but I don't pick it up. I know I have no control over what Cody or Jonas think or how they act. I know the jargon well, having been married to a psychologist. *I only have control over my own thoughts and actions.* I'm guessing the book is basically saying that, and so what? Information doesn't change things, experiences do. I've convinced myself that reading a book isn't going to change anything. But maybe, as Mrs. Brown alluded, the writing will help me. I do know one thing for sure, and that is, I have to do whatever it takes, or I might actually go crazy and then they will never let me out. I need to continue with the story not so that Cody or Jonas understand me, but for me to understand me.

So, I continue . . .

CHAPTER TWENTY-THREE

VALENTINO

SEPTEMBER 2021

In the summer of 2021, Papa found out he had a rare type of aggressive prostate cancer. After many consultations and no definite answers, he finally got in to see Dr. Patten, an oncologist in Vancouver who specialized in the type of prostate cancer they thought he had.

"Valentino, I've looked at all your test results and, along with my own exams, I have a diagnosis. Let's go into my office and go over a few things," Dr. Patten said.

Papa held my mother's hand. She was gripping it so tightly he felt her nails digging into his skin. *I need to cut her nails.*

"Come on, Evangeline, we're going to another room," he said as he led her down the hall. She stared at him the whole time and did not look where she was walking. "Hon, the doctor wants to discuss what she found," Valentino said, a slight tremble in his voice.

"Okay."

Earlier, when Mom had been lucid for about half an hour, they had discussed the possibility that he may be diagnosed with an aggressive type of cancer. "The worst-case scenario is what?" she had asked. Papa had been so surprised by the question that he almost didn't answer. Having a normal conversation was so rare these days.

Dr. Patten sat behind her desk and turned the computer screen toward them, then pointed at an image on the screen, explaining what they were looking at. She took her glasses off and clasped her hands, holding Valentino's gaze before speaking.

"I'm sorry, but your diagnosis is neuroendocrine prostate cancer. It is a cancer of the large cells, and it is quite aggressive. It is, I'm afraid, in the later stages, and so I am recommending surgery."

"Removing the prostate?" he asked.

"Yes. But we'll have to do further tests to see if it's metastasized before proceeding. I have set up a test for this afternoon. The surgery will be done in two days, providing the results show there has been no spread."

"Cancer? He has cancer!" Evangeline said, her eyes growing large.

"Yes, I'm sorry, Mrs. Lombardo."

"Cancer. He has cancer?" she repeated.

Valentino put his hand on top of hers. "It is okay, cheri. It'll be okay."

As they drove to the hotel, she looked out the window of the taxi. "Where are we?"

"We're in Vancouver. We're going to the hotel now."

Valentino felt his heart pounding. Calm down, he told himself. But the tears began to stream down his cheeks. Cody had taught him how to deal with the stress. "Breathe, Valentino. Inhale deeply, and then let the breath out completely. Watch your breath as it goes in and out. That is all you need to do. Inhale and exhale. Inhale and exhale. Do those deep breaths ten times, then notice how your body relaxes?" He closed his eyes. Inhale. Exhale. Inhale. Exhale. He felt his body beginning to let go.

"Where are we?" Evangeline asked again.

He opened his eyes. "We're in Vancouver. We're going to the hotel now," he repeated.

"What in the devil are we doing in Vancouver?"

"I had to go to the doctor for an appointment," he said, looking at her to see if his words were registering in her brain. It was getting easier to figure out when she was in the present or in the past or somewhere else.

In retrospect, he told me later, I had been right. He probably shouldn't have brought her along for the trip. But he was insistent that he take her with him. He explained how she loved their trips to Vancouver. They would spend hours and hours in Chinatown, go to their favourite restaurant Aki for sushi, and then to the theatre. "Maybe if I take her to our favourite places the old Evangeline will return," he said, sounding so hopeful.

Papa was an eternal optimist when it came to Mom's illness. Any time he could have her back in the present, even if for a short while, it was worth it to him. But it was becoming less and less frequent that his old Evangeline would appear and be in the present.

Papa looked over at Mom lovingly, and just then she burst out, "Fucking asshole driver!" The cab driver jumped.

"Please, sorry for the outburst." He said to the driver. She continued to swear as he tried to calm her down.

When they arrived at the hotel suite, he got her settled in the bedroom with some travel magazines and their collection of photo albums that he now always kept within reach. Her type of dementia meant that she always struggled to remember who people were and where they fit. Papa and I made a photo album of the important people in her life. We had a picture of her mother with the words *your mom* written on it and one of Jonas with *your grandson Jonas*. She seemed to like looking at it. We had all of us, including her brothers, her friend Darlene, Brittany, Dad, and Celeste. Her world was getting smaller and smaller by the month. She also seemed to like looking at pictures of places she had traveled to over the years, as well as the magazines she had written for on a regular basis, so we kept those handy too.

Papa went into the sitting area of the hotel room and sat down at the little kitchen table and facetimed me on his phone. He told me later that as soon as my face appeared on the screen, he realized he should have just phoned, as seeing my face made him cry instantly.

"Stormy, how are you?" There were tears streaming down his face as he tried to sound normal and upbeat.

"Papa, fine. How did the appointment go? What did the specialist say? Why are you crying? Oh, God, what happened?"

"It's as the other specialists suspected. Unfortunately, it is prostate cancer and quite an aggressive type. I'm tentatively scheduled for surgery the day after tomorrow. That is, if all is clear and the cancer hasn't metastasized. So tomorrow I have a bunch of tests."

Cody popped his head into the frame. "Hi, Valentino, how are things going?"

"Cody. Not so great, I'm afraid. It's cancer—neuroendocrine prostate cancer—not the best to have apparently." He blew his nose and dabbed his eyes. He suddenly looked old and worn out.

I knew he could hear me crying softly as I looked away from the screen. I had so hoped that it was just an easily treatable type.

Finally, I looked at him, trying to keep my composure. "Papa, I'm so sorry! I was hoping the other specialists were all wrong."

"Yes, me too." His voice was cracking and all I could think of was how I should have been more insistent that I go with him and leave Mom back home with Cody.

"I hate to ask, but how is Mom?" knowing full well it wouldn't be good. It never was these days.

"Not great. You were right. I should have listened to you. I think I need someone to come over and take her back home to Victoria. She doesn't realize what's happening half the time, and she's starting to swear and act out in public more and more. And with this darn Covid pandemic, I'm having a hell of a time getting her to keep a mask on. She keeps ripping it off. And my plans to go to our favourite places? . . . I must have been dreaming. There are so many restrictions now and rules. We basically have to stay in our room and order food."

"I know it's getting more and more hard to do anything or go anywhere with all the restrictions in place now."

"Her behaviour reminds me so much of your uncle John's at your grandpa's funeral. The outbursts and odd demeanour." He paused, and I just kept silent as he tried to get some composure. "I need help. I really need help." His voice quivered, and he began to weep.

My heart was breaking. Mom's moments of sanity made him cling to hope. It was so clear that he cared for her with so much love and patience. The type of dementia she had was not an easy one. Not that any are. But this type—frontotemporal dementia—was the same type her brother John had, and it was really trying. The anti-social behaviour made it difficult to go out in public. She could be so mean and say such inappropriate things, which was so unlike Mom. It wasn't easy for any of us, especially Papa. I could tell he was wearing out—not that he ever complained.

I was so mad at myself for not being more insistent that I go with them to Vancouver. But he had been so sure that everything would be okay. I knew he didn't want to burden us. That was his way. He wanted to give and give—love, attention, money, gifts, emotional support—but he didn't know how to receive it. "Papa, Cody and I will be over on the next ferry. I'll stay with you, and Cody can bring Mom back." I tried to hold back my tears, but I couldn't. I looked over at Cody with a pleading look.

"Yes, absolutely," Cody interjected. "We'll get packed and be over as soon as we can. We'll try and get on the six o'clock ferry. If we can't make the last one back to Victoria, we'll just stay overnight. You have a two bedroom?" asked Cody.

"Yes, I got a two-bedroom suite at the Fairmont Pacific Rim, your mom's favourite hotel. But what about Jonas?"

"We dropped him off at music camp in Nelson on Sunday, remember? He's there for four days."

"Oh, yes, I forgot. But they didn't cancel it because of Covid?"

"No. They have very strict protocols in place though. He had to get a test before going, and they will test them again before the camp is over."

"I hate to impose on you and Cody."

"Please, none of that talk. This is what families do. Now I'm going to hang up and get ready. Don't worry, Papa, we're on our way. We love you," I said as I blew him a kiss, tears falling like rivers down my face.

Cody forced a smile and said: "Don't worry, Valentino, we're here for you and Evangeline. We'll get through this together."

Papa sat on the couch and looked out the window to the busy street below. His mind floated back to three years earlier on his sixty-ninth birthday. They had decided to go to Hawaii with their friends, Darlene and Jack, who had won a free vacation for six at the Four Seasons Resort on the small island of Lanai. Darlene was one of Mom's oldest friends from Salt Spring Island. The other couple were Darlene's sister and her husband, whom they had met many times. He and Evangeline had even met up with them when they walked the Camino de Santiago Trail in Spain.

Valentino remembered they were looking forward to the trip. They traveled a lot since getting married; mostly across Europe, but neither of them had ever been to Hawaii. On the second evening, when they were on a catamaran sailboat on a sunset cruise celebrating his birthday, Evangeline exhibited the first signs of frontotemporal dementia. The symptom was the same one her brother John had exhibited: inappropriate social behaviour. He recognized it immediately. He had read up on the symptoms to understand his brother-in-law's behaviour when they had gone to visit the family in Saskatchewan a few years before.

"Can I pour you another glass of wine, Evangeline?" The deck hand asked. It was a private tour, just the six of them. There was a slight breeze as the sailboat glided across the water. The women were sitting on the netting in the front of the boat and seemed to be having a great time. Valentino had just slipped down to use the washroom when he heard the commotion.

"You bitch, you slept with my husband!" Evangeline was shouting over and over.

"Evangeline, what are you talking about? I just said your husband is a real gem, but I'd never sleep with him."

"You're a fucking liar. And all of you! You all knew and didn't tell me." She screamed, and then threw red wine in Darlene's face.

Jack grabbed Darlene and helped her up. He looked over at Valentino with rage and bewilderment and said, "What's going on, Valentino? Is there something I need to know about?"

"Oh, God, heaven's no. I don't know what's going on or why she would say that!" He crouched down and touched her arm, and then sat down beside her. She was staring into the water.

"Cheri, are you okay?" he asked gently, afraid to arouse her.

"Oh, hi, honey. Yes, isn't it beautiful here? I can't believe we didn't come to Hawaii sooner. I love it here. Oh look, spinner dolphins!" she shouted as she pointed to a pod jumping and twirling in the air not far from the boat. "Look everyone, dolphins, do you see them?" she asked, turning to look at everyone. They stood on the deck, gob-smacked.

The others just stared at my parents in shock and confusion. Darlene finally came over, her white bathing suit and hat covered in red wine, and sat down beside Evangeline and held her hand.

"They're amazing," Darlene said.

Evangeline smiled at Darlene then her eyes opened wide. "What happened to you? Did you spill red wine on yourself? Oh my. You know, I brought another bathing suit if you want to change. I brought an extra in case I got wet. I don't like sitting in a wet bathing suit. We can rinse that out in the sink with cold water. It'll take the stain out if we do it right away."

Later, when they arrived at the hotel, Darlene took Valentino aside and told him she had witnessed another outburst when they went for a walk the week before. "We were having a nice chat when a man passed us with a small, black poodle, and she started screaming at him that he had stolen her little FooFoo. I remember her telling me about her little poodle when she was growing up on the farm. So, I knew what she was talking about. But he died when she was in grade twelve, she told me. Valentino, I'm so sorry, I should've told you. As fast as the outburst happened, it was over, and she was her old self as if nothing had happened just like today."

The rest of the Hawaii trip went without incident. But once they got home, the outbursts happened more and more frequently. She would be rude to their friends and say terrible things, often times accusing them of stealing from her or telling them to fuck off, and then the next minute being sweet as pie.

He had seen the exact behaviour before in her brother John when they traveled to Saskatchewan for her father's funeral. The family explained that his dementia was possibly genetic, and Evangeline should get tested. But Evangeline refused, saying she was fine. He wished he had been more insistent back then, and perhaps they could have been more prepared. Now, when they were in the thick of it, it was a huge deal just trying to get her to see a doctor and get a diagnosis.

He called his sister-in-law Diana in Saskatchewan and asked for help. She had been going through it with John for a few years.

"It's tough, Valentino. But at least you have a good idea of what you're dealing with. I don't know how many doctors and specialists we saw before we got the diagnosis. They first said he had a bladder or kidney infection, then it was thyroid, then schizophrenia and finally, they got it right. As far as anyone knew, there were no family members with it from the past—that were diagnosed anyway. But they did discover that he had the type that was genetic. All his brothers were tested and came back negative. Evangeline was the only one not tested. Such a pity, Valentino, I know how long it took to get the two of you together, and you two are truly the sweetest couple. Everyone here agrees. Evangeline was the happiest anyone had ever seen her when you came back into her life. I'm really truly sorry."

It was with Diana's help that he finally found a way to get her to the doctor to get a proper diagnosis. It was not easy. By this time, Evangeline had decided that her doctor, whom she had been with for over twenty-five years, was evil. He had to trick her into going. He made up a story that they had to get immunization shots for their next trip, and it worked. The doctor confirmed the diagnosis of frontotemporal dementia and explained it was a rare type that usually, but not always, showed up in people when they were under sixty years old. The fact that her brother had it, meant she had a 30 percent chance of getting it.

Mom wasn't only convinced that her doctor was evil; there were others as time went on. Poor Cody got the brunt of her wrath. She was convinced for the longest time that he was a thief. She believed he stole all her paintings. Much of the artwork in their house and our own were pieces that Mom had bought over the years on her many travels. But for some reason, she decided that the paintings in our house were her paintings and that Cody had stolen them from her. It was part of the hallucinations. She would tell anyone who would listen that Cody was a thief and shouldn't be trusted. He stayed on her 'shit list,' as I called it, for months and months. And even though Cody knew it was part of the disease process, I could see it hurt his feelings. Luckily, she had not yet turned her wrath on Papa, me, or Jonas. Auntie Diana was not as lucky. Uncle John called her awful names and even hit her on several occasions. It was a difficult stage of the disease to get through, Diana told us. But she said it would pass.

As Papa sat there in the hotel, seeped in memories, he realized they had been living with this terrible disease for over two years already. Their lives had changed so much since then. The worse she got, the clingier she became. It got to the point where she didn't even want him to go into another room without her. She held his hand constantly. It was a struggle just to go to the bathroom by himself. She would scream if she couldn't see him.

Then he recalled the conversation he had with me about the incident at the mall two weeks earlier. "I don't want to burden you, Stormy, but I think you need to know about an incident at the mall so you don't make the same mistake as I did. In the last month, whenever we went to the mall, your mother fixated on small children, always referring to them as either Jonas or Stormy. When she saw a child, she would stop and bend down to their level. She would be so sweet, saying how cute they were, and asking if she could buy them a book. It was always a book. The parents would usually look on kindly in the beginning, but as she talked on and on, they'd grow more uncomfortable. Usually, I would just apologize and mouth to them that she had dementia and they would be on their way. But this particular time, she bent down to this little boy and asked him, "Hello, little Jonas, can I buy you a nice book?" But, instead of waiting for a response, she grabbed his hand and started running with him toward the bookstore. The mother, who had another child in a stroller, started screaming. It happened so fast. Within a second, a security guard came running and grabbed hold of Evangeline's arm. I didn't have time to explain to the mother or the guard that she had dementia. It was horrible. By the time the police arrived, I had convinced the security guard that she was sick and not a criminal."

"Papa, we have to have a family meeting and figure out how to deal with her behaviour. I know if Mom was in her right mind, she'd want us to stop her somehow. She'd be mortified to know she was acting like this."

But he was reluctant to do anything yet. He wanted to wait till he got his diagnosis about his prostate before he made any decisions. He had set up a meeting with a lawyer to discuss getting permission for medical assistance in dying. He wanted to know what his options were when the time came. His appointment was next week. He didn't want his beloved Evangeline to suffer should he die first. He was glad that he had the wherewithal to make the appointment next week with the lawyer given his prognosis.

He looked at Mom, sitting on the bed, her face blank, staring into nothingness. He recognized the look now. Her mind was off somewhere, who knew where or what, if anything she was thinking about? She could no longer read. The photo album and magazines were the only things that interested her, and then only for short time spans.

He wrote in his journal: *Who will protect her? Who will look after the love of my life when I am gone? The kids have their lives and with a diagnosis of an aggressive type of cancer, I'll die before her. I can feel it. I don't have long to live. What will happen to my Evangeline if I am not here to look after her?* Then his thoughts went to Jonas. The anxiety began to rise in his chest. Perhaps, he thought, his family carried a cancer gene or had a genetic predisposition of some type to cancer, and Jonas might have it too. His mother with lung cancer, him and Stormy. The thought made him feel nauseous. He held his chest and rocked back and forth, pleading, "God, please don't give this to my

Jonas. Please, please, I beg of you. Let it end." He sobbed quietly at the tiny kitchen table in the hotel suite.

After a time, he got up and went into the bedroom where his Evangeline sat on the bed still staring into nothing. He sat beside her and put his arm around her waist. She automatically leaned against him and closed her eyes and gave a sigh. Tears streamed down his face as he caressed her and sang a tender love song. Singing to her was always a good way to calm her down when she seemed agitated, but this time, he was singing for himself to ease his heartache.

I stayed with Papa in Vancouver while he got his tests to see if the cancer had progressed to other areas and thankfully, they found nothing to indicate that it had. He had the surgery and the doctor said it went well, and all they could do now was keep checking him. "Go live your life," she said.

After the appointment with the lawyer, Papa and I decided that we needed to get home care for Mom. The lawyer had informed him that Mom was not eligible for medically assisted dying because she was not mentally stable. He was so angry. I had never seen him angry before. If he had a mean streak, he kept it well hidden. But he certainly showed it when they told him that though the laws may change in the future, as it was now, anyone who was not mentally competent was not eligible to receive euthanasia. And so, my papa began writing angry letters to our member of parliament, the premier, and even wrote letters to the editor to several newspapers. All which made zero difference.

Eventually Mom's outbursts lessened, but the next stage of the disease was equally frustrating. Mom would not change her clothes. She insisted on wearing the same attire every day, and she even slept in them. It was a struggle, but we had to change her when she was sleeping and wash her outfit at night. I even went out and bought two other identical outfits to make it easier. She began to soil herself and refused to go to the bathroom. She would sit in her peed-up clothing; it was a fight to get her to change, and she refused to wear an adult diaper. It was so difficult to watch her and not be able to reach her to make her see what she was doing.

I remember once when Papa had left to run to the grocery store, and I stayed with Mom for an hour or so. We had put plastic covering over the chairs and sofas by this time. "Mom, you need to change, you had a little accident. Quick, let's go change your clothes." *It reminded me of when I was potty training Jonas.*

"No, I did not pee."

"Mom, yes, you did. Can't you smell it?"

"No, I did not pee. Get out of here."

"Mom, please you can't sit in your urine all day. Let's get you in the shower."

"No! Don't touch me!" She began to scream.

The scenario played out over and over every day for weeks. She then began her obsessions with eating only chocolate. She wouldn't eat anything else. She would spit out anything other than chocolate that we tried to feed her. It was awful.

Papa and I agreed we did not want to put her into a home like her brother John. Papa was adamant that he wanted to avoid a care home at all costs. He understood why his sister-in-law had to put John into care. Aunt Diana had explained that she couldn't handle John anymore. When he went through the phase of refusing to go to the bathroom and to sit in his urine and excrement for hours at a time, and then when his anger got out of control, she had no choice; she couldn't handle it mentally or physically. When he became violent, he began to hit her and that was the last straw, she said. She had to put him in a care facility. Unfortunately, the expense of the care home was too great for her, so she got a divorce so that John could get the care he needed. The care would cost over $4000 per month, which Diana couldn't afford without going bankrupt. This way, the health care system would pay, she explained.

Diana told Papa, "It's so hard to believe that Canada, the land of free health care, has such a poor system to help care for people with dementia. I realized quickly that treatment and care meant drugging them up, putting them in a wheelchair all day and changing their diaper once in a while. I felt so terribly guilty for putting him in the care home. That first facility," she told him, "Was a nightmare. I would go visit him and find him soiled, sitting in a TV room in a wheelchair with his head down, drugged beyond recognition. It was hard work getting him out of the facility, especially since I had divorced him but, finally, with the help of our children, we got him into the best place I could find: a small, long-term care facility in a town not far from Paris. People knew him and many of the staff grew up with both of us. And the kids could visit him often. He is still drugged up most of the time, but it's nothing like the first place he was in. The difference," Diana told Papa, "Is that they show respect. They don't see him just as a number but as a human being who has an illness. He is well cared for now."

Papa and I interviewed agencies and private nurses till we found the right fit for Mom— and for all of us. The first nurse we found was an older woman in her early sixties. Theresa had lots of experience working with people with dementia. She came four days a week. She was a large woman and tall, over six feet, and she was strong. She told us in the interview, her strength would come in handy when Mom got to be an invalid. Theresa didn't mince her words. She told us straight out what to expect, how the disease would progress, and then she gave us a plan of action. She was so full of knowledge and experience; her gruffness was strangely welcomed by all of us. We realized after speaking to her that we needed to get the facts and be practical, and Theresa fit the bill. She taught us how to respond to Mom's outbursts, little tricks to get her to change her clothes and, later, how to get her to use the toilet instead of always soiling herself. Papa thought about Diana a lot and how she had struggled and wished she had been fortunate enough to have a nurse like Theresa. He felt blessed and would tell Theresa many times a day how thankful he was to have her in his life. She would always respond in the same matter-of-fact way: "Just doing my job, Mr. Lombardo." He confessed to me how he always wanted to give her a hug but felt it would make her uncomfortable. I smiled, thinking that was the sweetest thing I ever heard, but I agreed that Theresa would probably feel pretty awkward if he hugged her.

The other nurse we hired was for three days a week and two nights and was very flexible with her time. Julie was a young nurse who was newly married and had just moved to Victoria. Her husband was in the navy and away quite often because he was a recruiter. They had planned on starting a family, so she didn't want to work in a hospital setting. Her mother was a home care nurse and she wanted to follow in her footsteps. She had no experience with caring for people with dementia at all, and they almost dismissed her immediately. But there was something about Julie's bubbly personality that I thought would work for Mom.

"Papa, do you mind if I try something?"

"Please, go ahead, sweetheart."

I brought Mom into the living room where we were doing the interviews. She had been in the kitchen watching Celeste and Jonas bake her favourite chocolate cookies.

"Mom, come with me." I held her hand and guided her to the living room and sat her down on the sofa.

As I suspected, Julie was the perfect fit. She got up off her chair and sat down beside Mom and introduced herself without missing a beat.

"Evangeline? How very nice to meet you. I'm Julie. Have you ever met someone called Julie before?"

"In school, Julie sat beside me."

"What grade were you in?"

"Five. She's nice. She has a poodle, just like I do."

"You have a poodle?"

"Yes, his name is FooFoo."

And the conversation went on for over fifteen minutes as Papa and I watched flabbergasted as Mom engaged in the conversation. She hadn't stayed in a conversation that long in months, albeit she was in the past one moment and in the present in another moment. But still. Before Julie left, Mom gave her a hug and a kiss on the cheek and asked her to come visit again soon. It was astonishing. Julie was an angel sent from above. She was a natural.

So, with Theresa and Julie, and with the help of Dr. Pan, her brilliant herbalist of Chinese medicine, a little CBD oil for the anxiety, and by keeping her as active as possible, we managed to give her a much better quality of life than her poor brother John had.

CHAPTER TWENTY-FOUR

2022 - ONE YEAR LATER . . .

Papa and I sat in Dr. Patten's office waiting for her to arrive. I was not going to let him go alone to see the specialist this time. We both knew the news wouldn't be good. It was evident that Papa's health was deteriorating by the day. He was so exhausted, and I found him sleeping in his chair more and more. He always had a book in his hand, but I wondered if he could even read much anymore. His face was gaunt, and his eyes were sunken and had black circles around them, and he was losing weight.

"I'm so sorry, Mr. Lombardo, the symptoms you are experiencing and with all the tests we did, I'm afraid your cancer has spread. The cancer has metastasized into your liver. And there is nothing more we can do."

"I see." Papa stared straight ahead. I touched his hand and gave it a squeeze.

"I'm afraid, it's time to get your affairs in order," Dr. Patten said.

"Yes, of course. How long do I have?"

"Not long I'm afraid. I am so sorry, Valentino."

Papa was not surprised. He was so tired and weak, and he had read enough to know that chances were slim that he would survive very long with the type of cancer he had. His thoughts went immediately to Mom. He wanted more than anything to outlive her. She was so attached to him. By this time, Mom didn't know me or Jonas anymore; she hardly spoke and when she did, it was always the same question over and over, sometimes hundreds of times a day. Her favourite was, "Where do you live?" It was exhausting. She never went through the wandering away stage like most people with dementia, and for that, we were grateful.

Eventually, walking became very difficult unless someone was holding her up. She was mostly in her wheelchair by the time Papa's cancer spread, and we had to get more help so there was someone at the house twenty-four hours a day. Papa couldn't lift Mom anymore, or even feed her.

One thing that was constant, which was a surprise to even Theresa who had been working with people with dementia for over thirty-five years, was that she always recognized Papa. Whenever they were together, she held his hand, even when she was being fed. She loved to smell his skin and when she did, she made a humming sound of contentment.

The photo albums were eventually put away and the magazines; they had served their purpose and were of no interest to her now. On the suggestion of Theresa, I found a plush toy poodle that looked like her old dog FooFoo. She dragged that stuffed toy around with her for months and would even play with it like a small child would. The odd time we would even hear her humming French children's songs to her little FooFoo, the same songs she used to sing to me when I was little; ones I was sure her mother sang to her when she was a little girl too.

It was a cruel disease; Papa would tell people. She had been robbed of the things she loved most in life: her insatiable appetite for knowledge, her passion for reading, writing, and traveling. The only thing she had was him, and now he was dying. "It isn't fair to her." He would repeat over and over. It was heartbreaking to watch their health decline and to see Papa struggling to cope with his and my mother's impending deaths.

Papa was so angry that the only solution he could think of for Mom was euthanasia, which was legal in Canada. But because she was not mentally competent, there was no way they could proceed with a request. The lawyer had made that clear. They would have had to arrange it before she got dementia. It just didn't make any sense to him or any of us. He didn't want to give up. He knew his days were numbered, so he begged the doctor again to see if there was a way, anyway, around the courts. His only wish, he would tell me, was that the universe would somehow arrange for them to die together. He just couldn't imagine how his wife would be once he was gone. She clung to him, and he was the only person that could calm her just by merely sitting beside her or holding her hand. He was her entire world.

Papa sat beside Mom, telling her the cancer had spread, not knowing if she understood him on some level or not. He stroked her hair and cried. Papa was not a religious man, but he was a spiritual man and believed in a higher power like Mom did. He wrote in his journal that the moment when he told her the end was near for him, he decided that he would start a daily meditation with the intention of them dying together. His own mother's words playing out in his head, *Where there's a will, there's a way, son. Always remember that.*

CHAPTER TWENTY-FIVE

SEPTEMBER 16, 2022

"Hello, Julie? Is everything all right?" I said groggily into the phone. I was a bit hungover. Cody and I, at the insistence of Papa, had gone up the island on the west side to Sooke—a quaint little town where the rainforest meets the sea—to celebrate our anniversary. It was a little less than an hour away, but it was like going to a different world. It was known for its natural beauty and walking trails and for having one of the best resorts on the island, the Sooke Harbour House. The Covid restrictions had just lifted, and we were so looking forward to getting out and actually going to a restaurant. But at the same time, I hated to leave Papa—he was near the end. He was a skeleton of himself and often too weak to even speak. Hospice was there to administer drugs but Julie, Theresa, Brittany, Dad, Celeste, and I took turns caring for him and my mother and sometimes just sitting vigil, waiting.

As sick as Papa was, he had insisted that I needed a break from all the stress and so, with help from Julie, he arranged an all-expense paid weekend at Sooke Harbour House, along with a whale-watching tour for Cody and I as an anniversary present. I was in his bedroom, sitting on a chair beside him, and reading *The Mount of Olives* by Michael Ivanov—an inspirational tale about faith, wisdom, and self-discovery—aloud to him. I knew I was reading it more for myself than Papa to try and lift the anguish that consumed me. He drifted in and out of sleep as I read. Then, he opened his eyes wide and turned his head to look at me, as if he suddenly realized I was there. "I can't bear to see you so sad and exhausted, Stormy. You have been through so much, and you do too much for us and everyone. I am worried for your health. You need a little break."

"It's okay Papa, there is no place I would rather be than here right now with you."

"No, I have made arrangements already. It's your anniversary. It's my present to you. I insist," he whispered, almost breathless.

"Absolutely not. I can't leave you now, Papa. It is not the time."

"Too late, my dear. You leave tomorrow at three o'clock. I have arranged it all, and Cody is on board with it. Please, do it for me. I want you to be well and happy. That is all I want." He closed his eyes, and I could see he was drifting off to sleep again.

It had been difficult the last year or so with the pandemic and teaching online classes part-time, all the while trying to help out my parents and look after Jonas and a house, and pay attention to my husband. It was overwhelming, and I was so exhausted; I didn't know which end was up half the time. I was doing stupid things like putting my lipstick in the fridge, losing my keys and phone, and crying at the drop of a hat. It seemed there was a heavy, black veil over me. To even smile at anyone was a chore.

Cody and I left for Sooke on Friday night. We drove in silence the whole way. I don't even remember the drive. Normally, the road to Sooke was one I enjoyed. Especially the picturesque countryside once you left the city limits and meandered along the winding roads along the coastline. My mind was too filled with thoughts of my parents, who years ago were vibrant and so alive and in love and who now we're mere shells of themselves. I didn't know how I could have any room in my heart for joy, or even laughter.

"We need to make a pact," Cody said as we put our suitcases in the room. "Sit down, Storm."

I sat on the bed and looked at him. He looked tired and worn out. I hadn't noticed till then. "What kind of pact?"

"That we do not talk about the Covid 19 pandemic, death, dying, near-death experiences, dementia, or cancer the entire time we are here."

I looked around at the beautiful room with its ocean view and wood burning fireplace, as well as the beautiful bouquet of flowers and fruit basket and bottle of champagne Papa had somehow arranged to be put there before we arrived.

"He wanted us to enjoy ourselves. Those were his instructions he gave to me," Cody said.

"Okay. I agree."

For the most part it worked. We played our favourite music in the evening and danced and drank champagne and actually laughed a few times. We got lost in nature—walking on Whiffin Spit Trail just steps away from the resort. We soaked in the outdoor hot tub and went on the whale-watching tour, where we saw not only whales but sea lions and bald eagles.

I forced myself to believe it was like old times, back when Mom would make us go on our dates and she would watch Jonas. But it wasn't. Not even close. There were only a few moments that seemed good; nothing substantial. We were too stressed out with everything going on in our lives to be able to let go and enjoy ourselves. Perhaps if our marriage would have been stronger, we could have coped better. But our marriage was in trouble, and we both knew it. A weekend away was not going to heal our relationship. The bitter reality was that there was a chasm that was wide and deep between us and neither of us had the energy to even build a bridge to reach each other.

Ever since I died and had my near-death experience, I had this overwhelming urge to tell people about it. I wrote about what happened to me and sought out other people who had a similar experience. Even though I healed completely from cancer within seventeen weeks after my NDE, with no medical intervention whatsoever, Cody refused to believe my story. His perennial response to any discussion about it, was that the drugs caused the hallucinations and in no way was there a place, or another realm, where you go when you die. He believed I had a spontaneous remission—end of the story.

"I've had enough, Stormy. You need to stop talking about all this nonsense and writing about it because it's hurting my career and making you look like a New Age wacko."

So, for a while, I did refrain from talking about my NDE—for him, for us. But I knew in my heart that it was the most real experience I had ever had. More real than the life I was living on earth. Finally, I couldn't honour his request. He'd insulted my integrity and I couldn't live with that. It was then that we really began to grow apart.

Thankfully, Papa, Mom and Brittany believed me. Mom knew I visited her while I was in the other realm. She had no doubt that I had a spiritual transformative experience, and she insisted I write about it which I did.

As my mom read my account, I could see tears rolling down her cheek. "Stormy, you need to share this. You went far, farther than many people who have had NDEs. It will give people hope, help with healing from grief, and help people who are afraid of dying."

"I know, I want to, but Cody is dead set against it. He will have a fit. He doesn't want me to mention any of it to anyone."

"I have an idea. It is just an idea. What about if you use a pen name, you turn it into a short story format, and we get it published. He never needs to know."

"I like the idea. But how do I explain if I make money from it?"

"Any money you make can go directly into a trust fund for Jonas."

I looked at her. My heart was full of love. She not only believed me, she understood the significance of the experience. It hadn't been easy. It wasn't just Cody who didn't believe me, it was a lot more people than I care to admit. Friends and colleagues in particular. I wanted to stand on the rooftops and shout it out; I wanted to tell the world about what I experienced and what I learned. But when I said anything about it, people either grew silent and changed the subject, or dismissed me with a laugh or some other explanation.

"Must have been some serious drugs they had you on."

"It is called an electrolyte imbalance that causes the hallucinations, dear."

"Morphine does that."

I never told Cody about writing the short story, my pen name, or sending it out to publishers and magazines that Mom found. It wasn't that I wanted to be famous, do the circuit talking to groups or any of that. I was happy with just being able to raise awareness about the fact that we are spiritual beings having a human experience, not the other way around. I was amazed when the story was picked up by several magazines and even found its place in an anthology. I had to refuse any invitations for talking engagements in fear that Cody would find out and our marriage would end. To this day, I have never breathed a word to him about it. It was the only secret I ever kept from him in all our years together.

I read that many people who have had spiritually transformative experiences lost their fear of death, and that was true for me as well. My fear of dying was completely and utterly gone. I had witnessed something so extraordinary, and I just couldn't imagine that people did not want to hear about it. The response from my husband, and from so many others, was so disheartening. At times, I felt depressed and even angry because of it, even after several years had passed. The strain over the years of not believing me, or in me, took its toll. I became resentful toward Cody. My near-death experience was a spiritual awakening and would have been much more transformative if I would have been able to talk about it openly in my everyday life, instead of burying my knowledge and emotions deep inside. Writing helped, as well as having my parents and Brittany to talk to about it before they both became so ill. But it was Cody's support and understanding that I so wanted. Unfortunately, he never wavered from his stance. I thought about leaving so many times, but I didn't want to disrupt our marriage for one reason and one reason only—Jonas. I didn't want him growing up with divorced parents. I wanted him to have a normal childhood.

It was three in the morning when Julie called my cell phone in Sooke. "I'm so sorry to bother you, Storm, but I have to go home. I have a migraine from hell. I've been throwing up and, well, my husband is coming to pick me up. Is there someone I can call to come over? I know you are in Sooke. I'm so sorry," she said, sobbing into the phone.

"Please, don't worry about it. Go. I'll get dressed and head out. Lock the door. I have a key. Are they sleeping?"

"Yes, I tried to get your mom to stay in the other room, as Valentino is not doing well at all. I gave him something that the hospice nurse said would help lessen the pain and help him to sleep. But she wouldn't stay away from him. She started to do that high-pitched scream. You know the one. So, I put her with Valentino. As soon as I put her into bed with him, she cuddled up to him and fell asleep. I just checked on them twenty minutes ago, and they were both sound asleep."

"Julie, thank you so much. You came and did overnight shifts this weekend, and Cody and I really appreciate it. We had a much-needed break, and it was really nice. Thanks for all that you do. And don't worry about them, I'll be there in an hour. I'm sure they'll be fine until I get there, especially as you said they are sleeping."

"Are you sure?"

"Yes, please don't worry."

"All right. I'll call you when my migraine subsides. Oh, I just saw my hubby drive up. Gotta go."

"Thanks, and don't worry."

I dressed and left Cody a note.

> *Julie got a migraine so had to leave to stay with Mom and Papa. I didn't want to wake you. You looked so peaceful. I'll send Brittany to pick you up later. Love, Stormy.*

As I drove back to Victoria, I couldn't stop thinking about my marriage. I really tried to be nice with Cody, but the anger I felt toward him was deep seated like a lead weight in the pit of my stomach. I gripped the steering wheel as I drove. The weekend was a wake-up call. I just didn't know if I could go on pretending our relationship was okay. It was good to be out in nature in particular and get some fresh air, but it felt like the whole thing was just a facade.

I knew Cody would never change and that was the hard part. Being a strong atheist, he had said my claim of having had a spiritual encounter was embarrassing for him and made a mockery of his beliefs. My belief that there was—call it God, or a higher power—got his blood boiling. Any discussion about it and his calm, sweet nature would flip into anger and would lead to a fight. And there were a lot of fights as I looked back over the last few years. I was beginning to see that my reasoning for staying in the marriage was not only hurting me and Cody, it really was not doing any good for Jonas either. My belief that parents should stay together for the sake of their children was some made up rule in my head that made no sense. By the time I hit the city limits, I decided that Jonas deserved to be in a family where people had genuine love for one another.

I wasn't quite ready to give up completely on our marriage, but I knew we either had to heal the rift between us or separate. I decided that I would approach him and give him an ultimatum—either we go for couples counseling, or we split up.

I already knew what his response would be regarding the counseling because I had brought it up a few times before. For some reason, when I mentioned couples' counseling a year after my NDE, he said there was no way he was doing that. "How do you think that would look if a psychologist went for counseling? But you should go. You need to learn to let go of your crazy notions." But, maybe this time, I thought, if I gave him a choice, maybe he would change his tune. He wasn't blind. He knew, as well as I did, that we were not in love like before.

CHAPTER TWENTY-SIX

SUNNYDALE FORENSIC HOSPITAL

MAY 20, 2023

I didn't recall the actual event of ending my mother's life until one day eight months into my incarceration. What triggered my memory was not the hundreds of hours of counseling and group sessions. It was a song. A song my mother sang to me when I was a little girl. I was in the music room alone. I usually got my violin out of the security area but that particular day, the attendant was on her break and there was no way to retrieve it for an hour. I decided to go anyway, as my music time was already scheduled. There was a piano in the room that was surprisingly in tune, and an old stand-up base that someone had donated that stayed there too. I liked to play the stand-up bass for fun, for me it was like playing one big giant violin. The odd time I would play it on stage when my jazz group performed. I placed the base in the middle of the room and played and sang for about a half hour. Then I decided to sit down at the piano. The first song that came to my head was Peter Paul and Mary's "*Day Is Done*," a song my mom sang to me when I was small and that I often sang to Jonas when he was young. And like my mom, I would dance with him as I sang it. As I sang and played the piano, images played in my mind of Mom and I dancing and singing and gently twirling around the living room. Tears filled my eyes when I got to the chorus.

And if you take my hand my, son
All will be well when the day is done
And if you take my hand, my son
All will be well when the day is done
Day is done, day is done, day is done, day is done

I hadn't reached the third verse when an intense wave of memories and smells flooded every pore of my body; a tormented kind of euphoria. I sat frozen on the piano bench, trembling as the scenario played out like a movie.

When I reached my parents' house it was around four am. I stepped lightly on the floor of the hallway as I made my way to the bedroom where they slept. As I opened the door, the smell of nail polish remover mixed with urine hit me like a brick wall. The two of them were in the matching flannel pajamas that I bought for them for Christmas. My mom curled up against my papa, spooning him with her arm around his waist over the white thin blanket that covered them. As I approached them, I noticed the now familiar faint smell of urine coming from mom's diaper. She was sound asleep snoring lightly. I walked to the other side of the bed and looked at Papa. His mouth was open. So were his eyes.

"Papa? Papa?" I said again and again. I touched his shoulder. He was cold and unresponsive. "Oh, Papa!" I could feel my pulse in my throat. I was trying desperately to hold back the low-pitched sound of grief building up inside me. But to no avail. My guttural moans filled the room as I fell to my knees laying my head on my papa's lifeless body.

Consumed with grief, I hadn't noticed my mom till I felt Papa being pulled away from me. I looked up and saw Mom kneeling on the bed, her eyes opened wide, tugging at Papa. When she saw his face, the sound that came out of her, was a sound that I could only equate with an injured animal. "No! No! No!" Her body was heaving with anguish, her eyes were enormous. The piercing blood curdling screams were nothing I had ever heard in my life.

Over and over, she yelled, "No, No No!" It was the most words I had heard my mother speak in weeks.

I got up and went to her side of the bed and grabbed her trying to hold her: to comfort her. But as soon as I touched her, she was like a wild animal.

She started hitting me and scratching me and biting me and screaming over and over and over. "No! No!" And then "Kill me! Kill me! Kill me!"

I tried so hard to keep her from hitting and biting me. I grabbed her hands and attempted to hold her down. "Mom. Mom. It's okay, It's okay. Everything is going to be okay." But it was futile. It was like she had super strength. The adrenaline must have been surging inside her. She pounded my arms and grabbed at my face, scratching at me. She tried to kick me, her arms and legs flailing in different directions all the while screaming: "Kill me! Kill me!" Her face was bright red. Tears streamed down her face.

Then, a clear vision of my near-death experience came back to me. I saw myself lifting above my bed and seeing everyone below, and then gliding up to the other realm, to the place where there was no pain, only unconditional love. The vision was as clear as the day it happened. I envisioned my parents lifting off the bed together, holding hands as they rose up to the white light, with no pain, no anguish, only love, only the most amazing unconditional love. I could see them, free at last to love each other, forever. An overwhelming feeling of love for my parents came over me as I reached for the pillow. Mom never fought it. Her body twitched a few times, and then . . . relaxed.

I sat at the piano bench, sweat pouring off my face, and my hands drenched. The epiphany was profound. My mom had a moment of sanity as she screamed those fateful words. I smothered my mother to save her from living the rest of her caged-up existence without her husband. I did the right thing; I did what she asked me to do; I did what Papa had prayed for; for them to die together.

I sat with my parents for a while longer, I don't know how long. I placed their bodies side by side on the bed and intertwined their hands, then called 911.

It was ten in the morning by the time I arrived at the police station. I was handcuffed and confused. I asked the officers repeatedly why I was in handcuffs. They wouldn't answer. It was like they didn't hear me or were ignoring me; I wasn't sure. I felt like I was in a twilight zone, or in a bad dream. I didn't understand what I was being accused of. They placed me in a room with a table and three chairs and a plastic bottle of water. The room stunk of sweat and it was ice cold, so I began to shiver. Two men walked into the room and sat down. They introduced themselves as detectives.

"Do you want to tell me what happened?"

"I tried to hold my mother down and call for help, but she was inconsolable. She was like a wounded animal, fighting and screaming, begging me to kill her."

"Is that when you put the pillow over her face, over your invalid mother's face?"

"Yes. I didn't know what else to do. I couldn't bear to see her in so much pain. It was the only thing I could do. These two people were soulmates. They loved each other for over forty years. You don't understand."

"Did you ever try and kill your mother before that night?"

"No, of course not. My papa and I worked tirelessly to get my mother approved for medical assistance in dying because we knew that when my papa died, she would be devastated. She had frontotemporal dementia, and her death was imminent. But the courts would not allow it because she was not mentally competent. They said next year, in 2023, the laws would change, but that for now she was not eligible."

"So, you did contemplate killing her before that night?" the detective asked me with a stone-cold face.

"Are you kidding? I would hardly say that a medically assisted death, which is legal in Canada, is killing. My parents just died. Have you no compassion, Detective?" The tears began to roll down my face.

"Save your tears. Did you or did you not suffocate your mother till she died?"

"Yes, I did," I said weakly.

He stood up and looked at the other detective in the room and said: "Read Dr. Hera her rights." He walked out the door.

I began to sob. I could feel my body convulsing and shivering uncontrollably. I realized at that moment that what I did was not seen as a mercy killing but as a murder.

Apparently, my lawyer explained to me, the minute the detective walked out the door, I blanked out. I did not speak, and I could not even walk. They got a wheelchair and wheeled me to a cell. A psychiatrist was called, and I was transported to a psychiatric facility under guard.

I returned to my room and sat on my cot, staring at the picture of my parents. I felt numb, yet at the same time, I felt light. I hadn't realized till then what a burden I was carrying inside of me. My subconscious mind while protecting me, was at the same time tormenting me. I always felt deep inside that I did the right thing, but I didn't know for sure until that moment when the memories returned that day.

CHAPTER TWENTY-SEVEN
PRISON HOLDING CELL

SEPTEMBER 17, 2022

I woke up the next morning and tried to move my arm, shocked to see that my wrist was handcuffed to a bed. I remember screaming for help and at the same time wondering if I was having a nightmare. I had no recollection of what happened or where I was or why.

"Please Mrs. Hera, calm down, calm down." A nurse with dark hair said as she stood above me. "It's ok, you are okay. You are safe." She began to ask me questions, like, what year it was, where I lived, who the prime minister was and making me add up numbers.

I don't recall what answers I gave in the hospital that day, or if they were correct or not. I was then transported from the hospital back to a jail cell. There was a cot, a toilet, and a sink. I sat on the tiny cot, still not sure what was happening, feeling groggy, as if I was drugged. I don't know how long I sat there till a guard came and said, "Your lawyer is here. Come with me."

The lawyer was a friend of Brittany's, she said. We sat in a sterile room with a table and four chairs. The walls were grey and blank; the air was stale.

"Stormy, my name is Wanda Murphy. Your sister Brittany called me and asked if I would come and meet with you. I am a criminal lawyer. Are you okay to talk with me?"

"Yes. I guess. I don't really know why I am here." The grogginess I had felt was turning into a throbbing pain in my head. I felt exhausted, like I hadn't slept in days.

She opened a beige file folder on the table. "You are being charged with manslaughter. You confessed to killing your mother. Do you remember any of that?"

I looked at her, not sure what she was saying. "I killed my mother?" I said in disbelief.

"Yes, you told the police," She looked down at a piece of paper and began reading it out loud. "*I had a near-death experience, and so I knew my mother was going to a better realm.*" She looked up at me. I was trying to understand what she was saying, but the words sounded muggy. She continued reading, *"My papa was dead, and I had to kill her. She begged me, and she needed to be with him. You don't understand. They were soulmates.*" She looked up at me. "Do you remember saying this, Stormy?"

I hesitated. Shocked at what she just read. "I said that? When? I don't understand what is happening."

"Stormy, It's okay. I am here to help you. Just answer the best you can." Her voice was calm, and I nodded my head. "Is it okay if your husband comes into the room?"

"Cody, yes, where is he?"

Wanda talked with the guard at the entrance, then Cody appeared.

He looked terrible. Unshaven, bags under his bloodshot eyes. He never looked at me, just sat down on the chair across from me. I was so groggy that I just sat there staring at the two of them as Wanda talked. I felt like I was invisible and deaf, watching her mouth move and not understanding what she was saying, and not caring either.

"Temporary insanity, that's probably going to be our plea. I think it's your best chance of staying out of jail," Wanda said.

I finally seemed to perk up when she said temporary insanity.

"So, I don't understand. What is happening? What does this mean? I go to a mental hospital then, instead of a prison? Or I get to go home? I'm so confused. I heard a guard say I was going to prison. Why? What did I do?"

"You have been charged with manslaughter, Stormy. The judge will have to decide where you go. Let's just take one day at a time here. I'm pushing for a hospital so you can get some help. You've been through a lot. You have no recollection of what happened. On top of that, your cancer, finding out your father was not your real father, your near-death experience, your papa's cancer, your mother's dementia. The last straw was your father's death. Personally, I believe you have had too much for one person to handle, and that is what led you to kill your mother. You need help to deal with all your loss. A hospital setting might be the best course of action to help you get your life back."

"A mental hospital? Will it be one for criminals?"

"I don't know that. But the judge who is presiding over this hearing is fair and demonstrates a lot of compassion and is big on rehabilitation. I'm not worried." She looked over at Cody. "Cody, what are your thoughts? You've been pretty quiet through this whole meeting."

I looked at Cody. He was deep in thought. He looked so tired, and his shirt was dirty. Usually, he was so clean cut and proper and always had words of wisdom or some beautiful quote to deliver that would make everything make sense. But he just sat there and made no eye contact with me at all.

"Cody, honey, are you okay?" I reached across the desk and tried to touch his hand. He pulled away

"I'm just trying to assimilate all this," he said to the lawyer. "There's just a lot to take in. But I . . . I know I can't do this. I just can't even get my head around the fact that my wife smothered her own mother. The story that she had a near-death experience and that what she experienced led her to kill her mother out of love and compassion, a mercy killing, is just so . . . so unbelievably ridiculous. I just can't be any part of this, this whole crazy story-line anymore. I can't be part of her life anymore," he said, looking at the lawyer. It was as if I wasn't in the room. "I'm sorry, I can't have anything to do with this or with her right now." Without looking at me, he stood up and knocked on the door. The guard came and opened it, and he walked out.

It was the last time I saw him.

The judge was in her sixties. I saw a kind face that expressed compassion as she heard testimonies from Theresa and Julie. My lawyer nodded her head several times during the proceedings and patted my hand to let me know it was going well.

There was no jury like you see on television, only a judge. As the judge was deliberating, I was in a room with Wanda. There was a sofa, a television, a coffee machine, and a vending machine. We split a ham sandwich and each had a coffee. It tasted terrible but I didn't say anything, which for me was unusual. The TV was on a news station.

"Looks like you've stirred up people to protest. Look." Wanda pointed at the television hanging on the wall.

The footage was from outside the courthouse. There were hundreds of both protesters and supporters. The supporters were chanting "Have mercy" and "Let her go." They were holding up signs that read, Legalize Assisted Death for the Terminally Ill and Mentally Incompetent, Yes to Euthanasia for the Mentally Incompetent, Have Mercy! while the protesters—some in wheelchairs—held up pictures of people with severe disabilities, pictures of Jesus and crosses, and shouting and chanting for me to be put away for life.

We were called back to the courtroom and took our seats.

"Please stand. Dr. Stormy Hara."

I stood with Wanda and could feel my knees shaking.

"You have been convicted of manslaughter in the death of Evangeline Lombardo. In light of the circumstances, and the recommendation from the psychiatric evaluations in this case, I am hereby sentencing you to Sunnydale Forensic Hospital where you will begin to get the support and counseling you need. You will have visitation rights only once per month for the first six months, and then we will re-evaluate your progress and proceed with the next steps with the goal of getting you back home with your family and getting on with your life. What you did, Dr. Hera, was wrong in the eyes of the law. I can only hope our justice system will get to a point where all people, regardless of their mental capacity, will be able to have access to medical assistance with dying, and we won't have people like you showing up in our courts."

My lawyer was pleased with the outcome. I wasn't. Even now, after a year of being in Sunnydale, I feel no remorse for ending my mother's life. Even though it was a spontaneous decision and I was in extreme duress, I know what I did was what my mother would have wanted. She believed wholeheartedly in an afterlife. As did my papa.

Since my parents first kiss, in the small pension in Olympia, my mother only ever wanted to be with Valentino, and Valentino only ever wanted to be with his Evangeline. Now, they were together for eternity in the most incredible place.

Writing the autobiographical story you have just read didn't change the way I feel about ending my mother's life. But what it did do, was make it much more clear of where I need to go from here.

Learning about my mother, her life from when she was a small girl living in a tiny prairie town to her eventual demise, helped understand why she made the choices in her life that she did. It was our relationship and how we both grew that made the end of her life feel sacred in a way. She was exactly where she needed to be and wanted to be—with her Valentino, my precious Papa. I knew it deep down in my soul. And me, well, I guess in the scheme of things, I am where I need to be too.

When I was in the other realm, I was shown that our purpose on earth is to grow and learn. The one important lesson I have learned is that I have to learn how to live each moment, practice being in the present and keep the hope that somewhere down the road I will be reunited again with my son, and we can build a new life. My paternal grandmother's words, 'it will all work out and not always in the way we expect' are always lurking in the back of my mind. I wish I could have met her, she seemed like a wise woman.

I am forever reminded of what the angelic beings of light explained to me.

"You are at a crossroad, and it is here that you must make a choice. You can go back to earth. If you make that choice, you will be well. You will be free of cancer; your organs will heal. You will live a long life and become a grandmother. You will teach people about this experience, but it will be in an unexpected way. You will make decisions that people will not agree with but that you know in your wisdom to be right. Or you stay here. Neither choice is wrong."

I chose to return and continue my journey of learning how to love. I know now that true love is what connects us.

It is so clear now that I need to let go of Cody. He is a wonderful man and was a good husband, but he doesn't understand unconditional love. There were conditions to his love, and I don't want to live like that. My parents had unconditional love, love that was eternal. That is the only kind of love I want.

On April sixteenth, 2024 I thought my story was over. I was about to hand the revised writing to Mrs. Brown that afternoon, when a guard came to my little suite. By this time, I had been transferred to a new wing. I lived with three other women, we shared a kitchen, cooked our own meals, and I was weeks away from being allowed my first day pass.

"A letter for you, Storm," she said as she handed me an envelope. The only letters I ever received, besides the people from the pro-euthanasia group, were from Brittany, Dad, Celeste and Linda. They had all recently visited. I recognized the handwriting immediately. My heart skipped a beat.

> *Dear Mom, I want to see you. I miss you so much. I wanted to visit you but Dad wouldn't let me come, or even contact you. Now that I am eighteen, I don't need his permission anymore.*
>
> *I just finished a nine-day intensive workshop with Byron Katie. I know aunty Brit gave you the book Loving What Is a while ago, and she gave me a copy too. After I read it, I decided to go to the first workshop I could find. I had to wait for my eighteenth birthday to be able to attend, so it took a little longer than I wanted.*
>
> *Mom, it was the best thing I've ever done. I've learned so much. I know Dad doesn't understand why you did what you did, and that is his business. I can't change the way he feels, as hard as I have tried. But I do*

understand you, and I love you, and I'm here for you, always! I miss you so very much.

I've organized a visit on Tuesday at three.

Love you to the moon and back.

P.S. I am enclosing a letter that I found in Grama Angie and Grandpapa's safe. As you know, the house was left to me in the will when I turned eighteen, so I moved into their house on my birthday. I am hoping that when you get out, you will move in here with me . . .

Inside the envelope was a beautiful picture of Jonas standing with Byron Katie, smiling that beautiful smile of his: his eyebrows raised and his bright, green eyes scrunched up in merriment. They were, I decided, the most beautiful laughing eyes I had ever seen.

I finally got around to reading *Loving What Is*, and it was one of the best self-help books I had ever read. It sat at my side table for a long while. I was reluctant at first to pick it up and read it. Ever since Brittany married Sarah, a Buddhist, she has been giving me these deep, philosophical books by Eckart Tolle and Pema Chodron way before my incarceration. Out of respect I did read them but, to be honest, I found them hard to understand. But when I finally picked up Byron Katie's book, I was relieved. It was a down-to-earth, how-to-deal-with-your-shit kind of book, with exercises to do. It helped me to be able to live, no, to thrive, in an institution surrounded by the criminally insane. For that, I was grateful and so happy that Jonas was able to experience an intensive workshop with her. There was no doubt in my mind that he had to deal with so many traumatic issues: my illness, his grandmother's dementia, being teased because he was different and, of course, the issue of trying to understand how I could have killed my own mother out of love and mercy.

I opened the brown envelope and read the faded document.

To be opened upon my death . . .

1995

Dear Stormy,

Today is your fifteenth birthday. I feel I need to write to you and explain something before it is too late. I have a sense I will not have a long life, and I don't want to take a chance that you will not know the truth about who you are.

If you're reading this, I have passed on. And I am okay with that. We are all souls having a human experience and when our time on earth ends, it does not mean we are gone forever. Souls do not die; our bodies do. Our souls just leave this earthly plane, and I believe they return again and again. I don't know for sure, of course, but it is what I have come to believe over the years.

I want you to know I had a good life in so many ways. My favourite part of being alive was being your mother. You have been the light of my life since you first opened your eyes and looked at me.

I have only one regret in life. This is difficult to admit to you, and I always had the intention to tell you the truth, but I never found the courage.

Your biological father is a man named Valentino Lombardo. I believe he lives in Melbourne, Australia, but I am not sure, as I have never tried to find out if he ever moved. I am so sorry that I lied to you all these years. I loved him so much and, yet, we could not be together. I was married when I met him and had a brief affair. And although it was brief, it was the most important, loving relationship I have ever had with a man. We were true soul mates, and I believe that we have had past lives together because I never felt so connected to another person in my whole life as I was to him. I see you in him in so many ways: your expressions, your talent for music, your need to please. All of which makes me so happy. He is a decent and caring human being.

I met him in Greece and, as you might now have guessed, my trips every year in February to Europe were actually to the same place—Olympia, Greece. It was the place where we fell in love and where you were conceived. My hope was that he felt the same way and would return there one year, and we could be reunited. Please don't judge me too harshly. I kept the secret from you out of my love for you. I hope someday you will understand.

I have only one request now that I am gone. Please find your father. And together, I want the two of you to take my ashes and scatter them at the temple of Hera in Olympia. Please tell him I never for one moment stopped loving him.

Stormy, you are my light, my joy. Stay true to yourself.

Love Mom

EPILOGUE

For all its faults, Sunnydale Forensic Hospital introduced me to Mrs. Brown, and for that I am thankful. During our time together, we both grew in ways we never expected. She eventually changed her belief in an afterlife, and I learned so much about myself and about why I chose to come back to this earthly plane.

I was released in January 2024. With help from Mrs. Brown, I found a literary agent and my story—this story—was published. It was an instant success and was on the best seller list for two months.

In 2024, after much deliberation, medically-assisted death became legal in Canada for people who were mentally incompetent.

I didn't move into my parents' house with Jonas. I needed a fresh start. I live in Australia in a beautiful flat overlooking the Sydney Opera House in Kings Cross. When I was in Sunnydale, I had sent a letter to Greta Hauns, the conductor (and Papa's friend) that I had met in Sydney when Papa took me to the opera. I asked her if there was any way that I could play with her symphony orchestra. She was delighted I contacted her and said she couldn't wait for me to come. She was familiar with my work, as Papa had sent her several videos of me playing over the years, which I never knew anything about. I moved to Sydney as soon as I was released, and I found my tribe amongst the free thinkers who inhabit Kings Cross community. I am a hospice volunteer and freely talk about my near-death experience with anyone who wants to learn more about it.

Jonas comes often. He has become a sought-after tenor in the world of opera and travels the world. Brittany and Dad and Celeste keep in touch, and we all promise to meet up in Europe one of these days for one of Jonas's performances.

February 22, 2026, Jonas and I walked to the temple of Hera in Olympia, forty-six years to the day I was conceived. We had mixed Papa and Mom's ashes together and sprinkled them, along the gravel, at the entrance of the temple, melding their remains into the historical membrane that held souls and thoughts, myths and dreams, of the people throughout the ages.

Jonas and I went to the little deli and had octopus ceviche and Greek salad and toasted our ouzo filled glasses to Valentino and Evangeline.

THE END

CPSIA information can be obtained
at www.ICGtesting.com
Printed in the USA
LVHW050203041022
729908LV00004B/109

9 781039 154940